Shadow Play

Shadow Play

Barbara Ismail

FELONY & MAYHEM PRESS • NEW YORK

All the characters and events portrayed in this work are fictitious.

SHADOW PLAY

A Felony & Mayhem mystery

PRINTING HISTORY
First edition (Monsoon Books, Singapore): 2012
Felony & Mayhem edition: 2017

ISBN: 978-1-63194-113-9

Manufactured in the United States of America

Printed on 100% recycled paper

Library of Congress Cataloging-in-Publication Data

Names: Ismail, Barbara, author.
Title: Shadow play / Barbara Ismail.
Description: Felony & Mayhem edition. | New York : Felony & Mayhem
Press,
   2017. | "A Felony & Mayhem mystery."
Identifiers: LCCN 2017010301| ISBN 9781631941139 (pbk.) | ISBN
9781631941146
   (ebook)
Subjects: LCSH: Murder--Fiction. | Women detectives--Fiction. | Kelantan
   (Malaysia)--History--20th century--Fiction. | GSAFD: Mystery fiction.
Classification: LCC PS3609.S583 S53 2017 | DDC 813/.6--dc23
LC record available at https://lccn.loc.gov/2017010301

For Jerushah and Arielle

The icon above says you're holding a copy of a book in the Felony & Mayhem "Foreign" category. These books may be offered in translation or may originally have been written in English, but always they will feature an intricately observed, richly atmospheric setting in a part of the world that is neither England nor the U.S.A. If you enjoy this book, you may well like other "Foreign" titles from Felony & Mayhem Press.

———❦———

For more about these books, and other Felony & Mayhem titles, or to place an order, please visit our website at:

www.FelonyAndMayhem.com

Other "Foreign" titles from

FELONY&MAYHEM

Foreword

For most Westerners, Malaysia is an unknown. When it's mentioned, it's famed for its lush tropical landscape and grimly puritan Islam. In the 1970s, when this story takes place, Malaysia was still an overwhelmingly rural society, before globalization ignited the economy and brought toll roads and fiber optic cable.

Then, Malaysia was remote to much of the world outside of Asia, and Kelantan was remote to most of Malaysia. The "Land of Lightning" in peninsular Malaysia's northeast corner, Kelantan was isolated from the West Coast by untouched mountains, served by an inconvenient train, an even more inconvenient two-lane coastal road, and an expensive weekly flight. During the northeast monsoon, it was entirely cut off by floods.

Kelantan's coast was a patchwork of fertile rice fields clustered around the sluggish Kelantan River winding from the central jungle to the South China Sea. Kelantan was hot, humid, poor and isolated, with a unique culture, dialect, cuisine and attitude.

Kelantan was, and remains, the most Malay area in Malaysia. Other areas of the country had far more mixed populations of Malays, Chinese and Indians, while Kelantan was a proud bastion of Malay culture and tradition. Arts, theater and tradition long lost on the West Coast still thrived there.

Historically, it was closer to Thailand than to the Malay States on the peninsula, and had a wholly different outlook than the cosmopolitan urban centers of Kuala Lumpur and Penang. Its people stubbornly supported minority Islamic parties, true to their vision as a Malay and Muslim stronghold.

Mak Chik, older women, dominated the economics of the area with assurance and pride. The main market, or *Pasar Besar*, was the hub of commercial activity in Kota Bharu, Kelantan's major city, and the domain of mercantile *Mak Chik*. Food vendors took the outside ring of the main market: fruit and vegetables on one side, fishmongers—primarily men—on the other. Inside the building cloth sellers were on the ground floor; food stalls, from coffee and tea with cakes to full takeout meals, were upstairs. Local specialties were on display at the market, and also sold on the street as dinnertime arrived, providing home-cooked takeout for working women.

Unlike more retiring Malay women in other states, *Mak Chik* often smoked hand-rolled cigarettes and talked to men as their equals, or maybe not quite; it was well known men didn't have the same head for business that women did. Kelantanese women were famous for their looks and their proclivity for magic, a reputation jealously stoked by those less spirited, less assertive, less active in business than Kelantan's daughters.

This story is about Kelantan's finest: market women with enormous sense, courage and confidence. Though it is completely fiction, and none of the characters are actual people, I have tried to give a sense of Kelantan and the Kelantanese throughout.

Malay Glossary
and Idioms

Abang: Older Brother, a term of respect for someone a bit older or, at times, roughly one's own age.

Ayah: Father.

Baju kurung: The traditional dress of a Malay woman, consisting of a round necked, long sleeved blouse ending between the hips and the knees, with a sarong underneath.

Batik: Wax print patterns on a cotton cloth. Also used as a generic term for a woman's sarong.

Bomoh: Healer, both with herbs and spells.

Che: Short for *Enché*, mister.

Chik: Miss.

Dalang: Puppeteer.

Ikan bilis: Dried anchovies.

Ikan keli: A species of catfish with a poisonous spine.

Imam: Muslim religious official.

Jampi: Magical spell.

Jodoh: The person you are fated to love.

Kain songket: The queen of Kelantan's textiles. It is made of silk, with gold or silver geometric patterns woven into it.

Kak: Short for *Kakak*, older sister, a form of address for someone a bit older or, at times, roughly one's own age.

Kampong: Village.

Kecubong: Datura, a poisonous jungle plant.

Khadi: Muslim religious official.

Kurang ajar: Insufficiently taught; rude and badly brought up.

Mak Chik: Auntie, a polite form of address for an older woman.

Merbok: Zebra doves, raised for their song and often shown in competitions.

Nasi kerabu: A dish of rice dyed blue, served with mint, basil, lemongrass, kaffir lime, torch ginger flower buds, raw vegetables, egg, grated coconut, chili paste, and black pepper. Often sold as hawker food, wrapped in a banana leaf, it is a popular school lunch.

Nenek: Grandmother.

Onde-onde: Small cakes made of rice flour, coated with coconut, with *gula melaka* (palm sugar) in the middle.

Pak Chik: Uncle, a polite form of address for an older man.

Pasar: Market.

Pasar Besar: Main Market.

Petai: Jungle beans, foul-smelling beans in long pods.

Sayang: Sweetheart.

Seri Muka: An amulet used to make the wearer beautiful. Literally: shining face.

Serunai: A flute-like instrument in the *Wayang Siam* orchestra. Its sound has more wail than a flute.

Tahi Itik: A kind of sweet cake native to Kelantan. The name means "duck shit."

Talak: A pronouncement of divorce. Three *talak* make a divorce final, and require another ceremony before the two parties can remarry. One or two *talak* (they are cumulative) don't prohibit the parties from remarrying, and may be revoked.

Teh beng: Iced tea, usually served with a great deal of sugar and condensed milk.

Tikar: Sleeping mat, used on the floor, usually of woven palm.

Tuan: Sir.

Ulu: Literally, upriver. Also used to mean the boondocks, the jungle, Hicksville. Kuala Krai is in the area Ulu Kelantan, upriver for the Kelantan River, and the state's backwoods.

Wayang Siam: The Kelantan shadow play, performed with incised leather puppets, which throw shadows on a screen.

Anak baik, menantu molek: A good child and a pretty daughter-(or son-) in-law; everything one could wish for in a family.

Biar anak mati, jangan adat mati: Let your children die before tradition dies.

Budak makan pisang: A banana-eating child; a naïf, a neophyte.

Chuka diminum pagi hari: Vinegar drunk early in the morning; a description of the bitterness in being one of several wives.

Hangat, hangat tahi ayam: Hot like chicken shit is hot, and cools off very quickly; said of arguments that flare up and are soon forgotten.

Ikut hati, mati; ikut rasa, binasa: Follow your heart and die, follow your feelings and be destroyed; living your life by doing only what you want is disastrous.

Kerbau cucuk hidung: Like a water buffalo with his nose pierced (and led around by a rope tied to it); someone under the power of someone else.

Lain padang, lain belalang: Other fields, other grasshoppers; to each his own.

Makan berkuah ayer mata: Eat your food flavoured with tears; to be deeply sorrowful.

Masam muka macam andam tak suka: As sour-faced as an unwilling bride; sulky and sullen.

Nasi dah jadi bubur: Rice has already become porridge; no sense crying over spilt milk.

Pacat jatoh kelumpur: A leech falling back to the mud; returning to some place you are comfortable.

Rambut dua macam: Hair of two kinds, grey and black; pepper and salt hair; middle age.

Rambut sama hitam, hati lain-lain: Our hair is all black, but each heart is different; one can never know the heart of another.

XIII

Salin tak tumpah: Not a drop spilled (in pouring from a jug); the spit and image of someone.

Seperti ular berbelit-belit: Like a snake rising over its coils; utterly furious.

Sudah terantok, baru mengadah: To look up only after you've bumped your head; locking the barn door after the horse is gone.

Shadow Play

Chapter 1

GHANI'S SECOND WIFE had recently appeared at the home of his first, so no one was completely surprised when he was found dead. There were risks to this kind of announcement, and though no one actually accused his first wife of killing him, sympathy for her had she done so ran high, especially among women.

Ghani played drums in the orchestra of a *Wayang Siam*, or shadow play, backing Kelantan's most popular *dalang*, or puppeteer. Only a few weeks earlier, to the amusement of his fellow musicians, he had begun an affair with a woman in far-off Kuala Krai, where his troupe performed. She peeked into the stage while they were playing, catching Ghani's eye as he had caught hers while taking a quick cigarette and coffee break at her tiny stall set up near the stage.

He was a handsome man, and it got him into a lot of trouble. Women liked his looks: high cheekbones and full lips, almond-shaped eyes and thick black hair. He was tall and rangy for Malay, and muscled, too, spending each rainy season in Singapore working on construction for extra cash.

She was forward, even when compared to the other women who often appeared at the ladder leading to the stage. *Dalang* were well known to be as catnip to a certain kind of woman, and sometimes their accompanists basked in reflected glory. She flirted with Ghani, who then disappeared with her after their performance was over. When the troupe returned to their home base near Kota Bharu a few days later, he'd taken himself a second wife.

He knew he was in trouble, but he hoped it would disappear if he ignored it. After all, he'd be in Singapore for about six months when neither wife would see him, and he hoped that during this time a solution would present itself. It would only upset his first wife, the mother of his two children, to tell her what happened, and so, he reasoned, it would be best to simply not mention it. Besides, Kuala Krai was a long way off in the jungles of central Kelantan, so his new wife really couldn't expect to see him too often. He cheered up considerably after reaching this conclusion, and believed it unlikely he'd be found out.

He was mistaken. His new wife, Faouda, took the bus for a six-hour ride to Kota Bharu, determined to join her new husband and maybe even fight off the first wife. She had novelty on her side, and hadn't Ghani seemed passionately attached to her? Kuala Krai was far from the bright lights of Kota Bharu, and as she understood it, Ghani's village of Tawang wasn't too far from the capital, and near the ocean; in other words, altogether preferable to life in Kuala Krai.

She arrived in Tawang after dark, when the evening's dishes had been cleared away, tired after her trip and hungry, expecting if not a joyous reunion, at least a mildly affectionate one. Ghani's wife greeted her at the door of the small wooden house, clearly having no idea who she was, puzzled to find a slightly disheveled woman trying to put her bags down in the cramped living room.

"I'm Faouda," she announced unbidden, smiling her brightest smile. "I'm sure Ghani's told you." One look made it clear he had not. "We just got married! In Kuala Krai and, of course, he asked me to come up and stay here. Kuala Krai's so far away," she chattered away as her hostess stared at her with her mouth agape. "I knew he was married, but you know how it is." Faouda began to feel uncomfortable. Ghani's first wife, Aisha, was her age, and the children were still quite small. "Well, where is he? Maybe he can clear it up."

Aisha very much doubted he'd be able to do that. At the present moment at least, she had a strange woman sitting on her bags in the living room, and two tired children both frightened and fascinated by her. Aisha's first impulse was to throw this woman, and her bags, down the steps of her house and onto the dirt in the yard. It was probably the best plan, but she was unable to do so. The exacting codes of Malay hospitality were too deeply ingrained in her. Tightening her lips and casting the nastiest look she could muster, she began to make tea and assemble some fruit and cakes.

Both his wives were sitting silently on the porch when Ghani came home, and he had to overcome his immediate instinct to flee. "I didn't want to tell you this way," he began.

"How did you want to tell me?" Aisha hissed at him. With a nervous eye toward the neighbor's houses, he tried to usher both women inside, but Aisha refused to move. "What have you done to me?"

It was hard to explain it in front of Faouda, whom he wanted to throttle. How could she just show up like that? No warning at all! Ghani tried to comfort Aisha without completely alienating Faouda and was therefore a failure on both counts.

"Aisha, you must believe me," he began, unsure of what it was she ought to believe. "I never meant to hurt you."

"Oh my God, Ghani, how could you not hurt me by taking a second wife? What are you saying?"

"I don't really know," he confessed, "I just think maybe I made...a mistake."

It was now Faouda's turn to become infuriated. "Are you saying marrying me was a mistake? Now you regret it?" She burst into sobs, which made Ghani want to strangle her even more.

"Do you want a divorce?" Aisha demanded. "You'd better choose one or the other right now. You can't have both."

Faouda's sobs became considerably louder and more grating.

"Get her out of here," shouted Aisha, collapsing on her sleeping mat in a flood of tears and frustration. "I can't stand it any longer. Shut up!"

Ghani tried hard to think of a place he could put Faouda for a few days until he could convince her to return to Kuala Krai. For the first time, he seriously wondered whether he'd made a mistake in taking a second wife. And five days later, he was dead.

Wayang Siam, The Shadow Play, was performed all over Kelantan during the dry season, when the rice fields are bare and hard and make perfect outdoor theaters. The troupe played for five nights in any one place, and slept on a raised and enclosed stage. Dollah Baju Hijau's troupe, to which Ghani belonged, was in their third day in Kampong Penambang outside Kota Bharu, the center for weaving *kain songket,* a silk-and-gold fabric used throughout Malaysia for weddings and special occasions. The village lay along the main road to Kota Bharu, which followed the Kelantan River to its end. It was crowded with papaya, mango and banana trees and towered over by coconut palms: the trees made the air seem fresher with their thick leaves and dense shade, so different from the slightly fetid air of the city, where trash bins baked all day under the burning sun. Several enormous brick *songket* shops flanking the road dwarfed all the other buildings tucked back among the greenery.

Ghani climbed down from the stage shortly before dawn to relieve himself near the fence and never came back. The next morning, his yawning colleagues stumbled over his splayed body close to the ladder, taking in his torn sarong and gaping chest wound, and the puddle of congealing blood pooling next to him.

"Oh my God!" The other drummer cried out, unwilling or unable to really process what he saw. "Ghani!" The troupe crowded around the body, murmuring and exclaiming, pointing to the machete stuck up to its hilt in the ground, and the blood-soaked towel thrown down beside it. They waited for Dollah, their *dalang* and leader, to step down and comment on the scene. He did so deliberately, being no more familiar with violent death than the rest of the men.

He knelt next to the body and lightly touched the man's cheek. He'd known Ghani since he was an eager boy with a gift for drumming, begging to be allowed to follow Dollah as he played around Kelantan and southern Thailand. Dollah was taken with his enthusiasm and his talent, and promised Ghani's father he would care for the boy on the road. Though Ghani was now in his early twenties and therefore a man, Dollah still felt protective towards him, and had trouble looking away from the body before him. "Call the police," he ordered, not turning his head from Ghani's glazed eyes, his own filling up with tears.

It was his duty to inform his sponsors there had been a murder on their land, and he dreaded it. *Wayang Siam* had something of a wild reputation, mostly having to do with women rather than with murder, but this wouldn't improve it any. He walked reluctantly up the stairs of a large wooden house, the front of which perched high off the ground on stilts to avoid Kelantan's yearly floods. The kitchen in the back sat flat on the ground, closer to the backyard well and chicken coops: the village organic trash collection. The house was painted a light blue, and sported a bit of floral carving over the door. A prosperous village home, comfortable and unpretentious. The lady of the house sat on the porch preparing to leave for work.

"*Abang* Dollah," she said politely, clearly wondering what he was doing here at this time of the morning.

"*Kak* Maryam," he answered slowly. "Something's happened."

She raised an eyebrow, and waited patiently for him to continue. He sat down on the stairs and pulled out a pack of Rothman's cigarettes, offering her one. Most Rothman's smokers were men: women tended to roll their own. Smoking a store-bought filtered cigarette was a bit of a treat, but it signalled that this was clearly going to take longer than she hoped, so with an inward sigh, she smiled and took one. It would help her get through this conversation, coming as it did at a most inconvenient time: she had to get to work to open her cloth stall in the market before the day got underway. She inhaled and looked at him expectantly, willing him to make it brief.

"One of my musicians was killed." He surprised himself saying it so bluntly and his throat seemed to be closing as though he were sobbing. He did not want to lose control, in front of a client no less. It was important he remain calm.

Maryam was still and silent. Had she misheard? Apparently not, since Dollah looked close to tears, which was not like him at all.

She stammered around her reply, not knowing what to say, but feeling she ought to offer something. "Where? When?" she finally managed. Before Dollah answered, she turned and called into the house, "Mamat! Come here."

Her husband emerged from the house, looking hard at both Maryam and Dollah, trying to gauge the situation from their faces. He dropped onto his heels, taking a cigarette out of his own pocket, and lit up. "Well?" He turned to Dollah.

"One of the musicians is dead. I've sent someone to call the police."

"Dead?" echoed Mamat.

"How?" asked Maryam, recovering from a rare bout of speechlessness.

"Stabbed," Dollah mumbled to the porch. "Do you want to come and see…it?" He turned to Mamat, who rose immediately. Maryam followed immediately behind.

"Don't tell me not to go," she preempted. "This is on my property. This was our performance!" She frowned at Mamat. "What will we say? We have guests…" she trailed off as they entered the hastily fenced rice field and saw the clump of men gathered around Ghani. Dollah shouldered his way through and brought Mamat and Maryam up to see him.

Ghani looked younger than he was, and utterly vulnerable, lying on the hard ground. Now he'd reverted to an earlier boyishness, his hair dusty, and his expression vacant.

"Has anyone sent for his wife?" Maryam asked practically. "She needs to know."

"Which one?" one of the men asked.

Maryam gave him an evil look. "Which one do you think?" She had no patience for semantics right now: let them figure out which would be the correct wife to contact. That the question rose so quickly gave Maryam her first inkling of how complicated this man's life might be.

The police arrived, drawing yet another crowd of neighbors, craning to see what was happening. A young policeman stepped from the car, dark-skinned and narrow-faced: skinny, like a kid. He walked over to them, carefully stepping over bumps in the ground.

"What's this?" he asked, immediately branding himself as a stranger to Kelantan by his accent. Kelantanese, a Malay dialect heavily influenced by nearby Thailand, is a riot of guttural affirmatives and glottal stops which makes West Coast Malay seem anemic and colorless by comparison. This boy was clearly from the West Coast. Maryam wondered if he'd be able to understand any of them.

Dollah began the explanation, as slowly and carefully as he could, trying to speak Standard Malay, but forgetting as he got more excited and more involved in his story.

"We were performing here, *Wayang Siam*," he began. "Shadow play. We're playing here for five nights and tonight's the end." He nodded toward Maryam and Mamat. "They've sponsored it, and this is their land."

"Sponsored it?" the boy in the police uniform asked.

"It's my son's circumcision," Maryam added proudly. "This is the celebration. You know," she continued as he looked blank, "you always celebrate a circumcision..." Surely he knew that; he looked Malay, after all.

The boy nodded. "And this morning," Dollah continued, "When we came down from the stage, we found him here. He's our drummer." Dollah stopped, threatening to tear up once again.

"You found him like this?" The policeman squatted on the
ground to more carefully examine Ghani. He put his hands over
Ghani's eyes, a strangely sensitive gesture in an otherwise cold,
professional atmosphere.

"I'm Police Chief Osman," he said, turning the body's head
slightly to get a better look at the wound. "I've just come here
from Ipoh." They all nodded. Ipoh was a large city on Malaysia's
west coast; it explained the accent. "It would be best if you'd all
move away from here for a little while," he suggested, rising.
"We've got to look over the ground."

As the troupe began to drift away, Maryam asked Osman,
"Can I get to work? I've got to open my stall. I sell *kain songket*
in the market and I'm so late already."

Perhaps she'd seemed too cold, she thought, worrying
about her stall when a man had died. But she didn't know the
victim and there was little she could do to help. On the other
hand, she could do a great deal of good at the market where she
belonged. He sighed, and looked around. "Can you open it and
then come back here? Get someone to cover it for you?"

She nodded, relieved, and waved Mamat over to drive her
to the market. Her children couldn't help her: Ashikin, her eldest
daughter, was recently married and no doubt already at work at
her in-laws' *songket* store, and Aliza, her younger one, had left
for school. She wouldn't consider either of her boys to help; she
didn't trust any man's business ability, and her sons had never
done anything to reverse her opinion. Rubiah, her cousin with
a coffee stand on the second floor of the main market, might be
able to help. She'd ask as soon as she opened for the day.

She hopped onto the back of Mamat's motorbike, decorously
arranging herself sidesaddle with a pile of fabric on her lap. The
fruit and palm trees of their small town gave way abruptly to
Kota Bharu's dark, cramped Chinatown, pushed hard against
the river as though space were at a premium, though there was
plenty of it. Three-storey shop-houses further narrowed the
road, blocking the light, giving a barrack-like atmosphere to
this brief stretch. It was Maryam's least favourite part of the city;

though the downtown around the crowded market was hardly more attractive, its energy and constant activity made up for its lack of aesthetic as far as Maryam was concerned. For she was born a market woman, and this was her element.

Maryam strode into the *Pasar Besar*, a cavernous two-storey building in downtown Kota Bharu, and the nexus of its busy commercial life. She sold cotton batik sarongs made by her older brother, and more importantly, *kain songket* woven in her own village, the heart of the *songket* world. She'd inherited her spot in the cloth section from her own mother, in the centre of the market's frenzied activity.

She brought down the plywood planks with which she closed her stall at night, and restacked the batik to make a seat for herself: *songket* was far too expensive to sit on. She extracted her cache of hand-rolled cigarettes from the folds of her sarong, placing them conveniently near for easy access, set out the tin plate she used for an ashtray as well as her box of matches, checked the cardboard box she used as a cash register, and went to work.

Like many of her fellow businesswomen, Maryam eschewed frippery, both physical and behavioural. She was plain-spoken— in business only, of course, since Malay courtesy demanded a more roundabout approach to things—and busy. She dressed practically, in a batik sarong and long blouse, a *baju kurung*, and kept her hair wrapped under a cotton turban. However, a pragmatic approach to work attire did not mean a lack of jewellery, and Maryam was almost never seen in public without a respectable number of bangles and small but heavy earrings. She had thick black hair with just a few touches of grey (which she removed when they got out of hand) and beautiful large, brown eyes with sweeping lashes. Her face was round and pleasant, with a small nose and wide lips, and she had grown a bit stocky as she moved into middle age.

She was determined and energetic: the primary support of her family, as were almost all the market *Mak Chik,* or aunties. These older women dominated the economic as well as the family life of Kelantan, and went about their business with the no-nonsense attitude of people aware of their own worth. Kelantanese men were famous for letting their women make money while they sat in coffee shops talking politics. Mamat was himself an accomplished coffee-shop lawyer, a mainstay of his favourite establishment, and a prodigious drinker of the sweet, milky coffee beloved in Kelantan.

Maryam called to customers, waving them over to buy her cloths. She'd promised that kid—Osman, was it?—to be back as soon as she could, but what could be the harm in making at least some money today? She'd missed the early morning hours, and once she went home, she'd miss the rest of the day. She wasn't sure to what purpose, since she was no policeman and had no idea what happened or why. Just a few sales, and then she'd go upstairs to the prepared food area on the second floor and find Rubiah, her cousin, though more like her sister and best friend.

Asking her next-door stall owner to watch her stall for a moment, she ran up the stairs to Rubiah's coffee stall. It was quiet: the lull between breakfast and lunch, with only a few men sprawled on stools flirting with younger women stirring their pots.

"Guess what?" Maryam dropped onto a chair in front of Rubiah's minuscule counter. "You won't believe it!"

"Tell me," she leaned towards Maryam, her eyes alight, her hands still polishing some glasses. Rubiah was of an age with Maryam, and they resembled each other with stocky builds, snub noses and large brown eyes. Rubiah's were hidden behind thick wire-rimmed glasses, which gave her an academic air, and her turban was unwound, draped around her shoulders rather than covering her hair. "What happened?"

With a cup of coffee laden with sweetened condensed milk comfortably in her hand, Maryam told Rubiah what had happened earlier in the day, weaving a dramatic tale of death and betrayal. She'd caught the mention of a second wife, which provided a sterling motive for murder. She sorrowfully related her impression of the new police chief, an untrained, unsure kid, thrown in over his head in a state where he couldn't understand the local dialect. How did the authorities think he'd be able to tackle this job?

"I promised this kid policeman that I'd come back after I opened my stall. Could you look after it?" Rubiah looked around her tiny store as if to calculate what she might lose by abandoning it.

"We'll split the afternoon's money. Take some of your cakes with you," Maryam cajoled her. Rubiah was renowned for her baking. "Maybe you can sell some downstairs. I really need the favour," Maryam pleaded.

Before she'd finished the sentence, Rubiah had already started closing shop, gathering her cakes to bring downstairs. "Go on, go on," she waved at Maryam. "Don't worry."

Chapter 2

OSMAN WAS RUNNING HIS investigation of the scene with as much bravado as he could muster. He was new at his job and new in Kelantan: he'd done remarkably well in his two earlier postings, and his superiors were ready to see what he could accomplish on his own. The Malaysian police made a point of stationing more senior people away from their homes, in order to avoid entrenched favouritism. Osman was nervous: at any moment he might be found out and people would laugh at him, a *budak makan pisang*, a banana-eating baby, thinking he could pass himself off as a police officer. Even worse, he could barely understand a word people said when they spoke Kelantanese, as they all did, though he tried to look thoughtful when he heard their answers.

This was Osman's first posting out of his native Perak. His mother had not taken the news of his transfer to Kota Bharu well, though Osman was delighted when he heard: he was young for a police chief and excited about the responsibility. His mother, however, feared her son would fall in love with a Kelantanese girl, or worse yet, under her spell, and never return. She had other plans in mind for him, beginning with marriage to a nice Perak girl, preferably a distant cousin, and many grandchildren she could oversee. She warned him often and in detail about remaining aloof from the local women and the benefits of keeping his mind on his work.

His career to this point had gone very well indeed, and he was confident he could handle any crimes he found in Kota Bharu, which he expected to be of the lost goat variety, or maybe an exciting quarrel turned violent, where he could witness, and tame, the renowned Kelantanese temper. He hadn't counted on murder. There probably hadn't been a murder in this area for years, and now it had to happen to him. He looked morosely around the dried field and beaten dirt for a clue, the mark of a shoe, a scrap of cloth. Nothing. It was the end of the dry season, and the ground was baked to a hard finish.

He squatted together with Dollah, trying to get some background which might illuminate Ghani's murder. Using one of his juniors as an interpreter, it was painfully slow going, compounded by Dollah's reluctance to air Ghani's private affairs to the police.

"He played with me since he was a kid, maybe eight or nine," Dollah reported to Rahman, the interpreter, darting an occasional look at Ghani. Dollah was a small man, even among Malays, with a large head and hands and a surprisingly deep voice. He looked to be in his forties, with slightly slanted eyes and a wide, heart-shaped face. When not performing, Dollah was soft-spoken and courteous, betraying nothing of the over-sized personality he displayed as a *dalang*. Seeing him talk, it was hard to imagine him as famous, the centre of gossip and scandals surrounding successful performers. He seemed like any villager, trying to say as little as possible.

"He played with me in the dry season, and went down to Singapore in the rainy season to work on construction jobs, so he wasn't here for about half the year." Dollah thought about what to say next. "He's from Tawang, not too far on the other side of Kota Bharu; we're all from around there. His wife lives there and they have two children." With that, he appeared to be finished, and commenced looking at the sky.

"What's the wife's name?" Osman asked directly. It was a simple question, and he felt sure Dollah would understand him.

"Aisha." Dollah did not look down from the sky.

"Did anyone go for her?" Osman asked, turning to the group of musicians talking behind him. One nodded. "Should be here soon, *Che* Osman."

Maryam arrived home to find the investigation grinding to a halt. Osman seemed to have run out of questions, and Dollah had never intended to give any real answers. Maryam went to make coffee immediately, hoping to grease the wheels of police work and get them off her property as quickly as possible. It looked awful, a dead body, police everywhere, musicians milling around. "This kid can't handle it," she whispered to Mamat in the kitchen. "He'll never find out what happened. He can't even talk to anyone! He can't understand us." She shook her head ruefully. "I'd say it was horrible to have this happen at Yi's circumcision, and, of course, it *is* horrible," she added hastily, while Mamat smiled. "But Yi's going to think it's really exciting."

"I know," Mamat replied, watching Maryam add the syrupy milk to the coffee and mix it. She loaded a tray with coffee and cups and handed it to him. "He'll never stop talking about it," Mamat finished as he walked outside, Maryam following with a large collection of Rubiah's cakes she'd had the foresight to take from the market, and they set everything down on the porch.

The musicians talked animatedly among themselves, hoping to go home soon and leave this behind them. Osman wondered sulkily if he would ever learn much Kelantanese, or ever solve this crime, and then Aisha appeared, her pretty face blotched with red, her eyes puffy, stepping out of the police car looking wildly around.

"Where is he?" she looked straight at Osman, who rose awkwardly and ducked his head.

"*Chik* Aisha. I am so sorry…"

"Where is he?" Her voice rose an octave, threatening to break glass on the next sentence. Maryam walked with her as Osman led them to Ghani's body, now covered with one of Mamat's sarongs. Aisha's hands shook and though she controlled her tears, her lips trembled and she swayed slowly.

"Breathe!" Maryam urged, praying Aisha wouldn't faint. When Osman drew back the cloth, it was clear he had taken some pains to straighten out the body, and make it more decent for Aisha's view. It wasn't the best way to preserve clues, Maryam thought, but it was a nice touch for the widow.

Aisha stared hard at Ghani, biting her lips, unable to speak. Maryam murmured to her, comforting her as best she could, though there was really nothing to say. Aisha nodded finally, saying curtly, "It's him."

On the porch, with a coffee cup balanced in her hand, Aisha stared at Osman as he talked, as if unable to make sense of where she was and why he spoke to her. Maryam took over: someone had to, or she feared they might stay all night and she couldn't wait to have everyone leave.

"*Chik* Aisha," she began with a significant look at Osman, "when did you last see your husband?" Aisha saw Dollah, and tried to smile. "Saturday?" Dollah nodded.

"Did you come here to see him?" Maryam probed further. She really didn't need Osman to tell her what to ask: the questions seemed obvious.

"No." She looked at Maryam as the silence grew longer. Finally she added, "I have two kids at home. Why would I come to visit him?" She sighed, her shoulders slumping. "Can I go home now? I have so much to arrange…" Her eyes filled with tears, and Dollah took her arm.

"Can I take her home now, *Che* Osman? Look at her, she needs to get back."

Osman agreed, looking preoccupied, and turned back to the corpse. As the new widow left, he squatted again by the corpse with one of his men. "What do you think made this wound?" he mused.

Rahman reached out a tentative hand, not quite touching Ghani's chest. "A knife? This one, I'd say. And whoever did it wiped it clean with the towel and stuck it into the ground. I don't think we'll find anything about it."

"I'm afraid you're right," Osman said softly. The handle gleamed, and he had no doubt the blade would, too; the fact that it was sitting in the ground wouldn't help the search for fingerprints either.

"Everyone has one," Rahman sighed. "It won't narrow the field down at all."

"Whose is it though? Someone here?" He waved over some of the musicians. "Is this one of yours? Does it come from your stage?"

The other men stared silently, as though they had never seen one before, but the oldest among them nodded. "Well, all old knives look alike, they're nothing special. But we had a couple with us—we always do, we always need them—and this could be one of them."

He turned to one of the younger men and instructed him rapidly. He left at a trot for the stage and jumped up the ladder to go inside.

"He'll look," he advised Osman. "Just wait a moment." He smiled, and offered his hand. "*Pak Chik* Mahmud," he introduced himself. Osman smiled and clasped his hand, each of them wrapping their two hands around the other's.

"*Che* Osman, Kota Bharu Chief of Police." It sounded odd to his ears. "From Perak."

"Ahh," Mahmud smiled, as if this explained a great deal. The younger man returned and spoke volubly to Mahmud for a minute or so, while Osman waited. "It could be. We usually keep three or four around, and there are three there now. I wish I could swear to it," he shrugged, "but all I can say is, 'It could be.' It's a beat-up knife, and one beat-up knife looks much like another."

Osman thanked him, and became more depressed by the moment. "Take it away," he ordered Rahman, "and make sure you keep the towel clean, too." He himself turned to leave. Maryam was standing right behind him.

"I need to talk to you," she informed him. "Come over here with me." She motioned him to sit next to her on the high shaded porch with fresh coffee in front of them while the remaining musicians began disassembling the stage and the fence around the field.

By evening, there would be nothing left.

"*Che* Osman," Maryam began, flicking the ashes from her cigarette through the floorboards. "I see you may have a problem. Now, don't be angry with me, I'm talking to you like your mother, which I could be, you know."

Osman suddenly keenly missed his own mother far away on the west coast. She was a strong-willed woman who brooked no opposition, and he was very close to her. He was relieved to be drawn into Maryam's orbit and receive unquestioned orders. He sat up straighter and listened attentively.

"Now, this has all taken place at my home, and I feel responsible for it. Not that I did it or anything like that." She looked sternly at him to banish that thought from his mind. "But it was a performance I sponsored, and it's my land. I must see it solved." She paused momentarily. She could not admit her sudden elation at the prospect of taking over an investigation. She'd be just like the detectives she watched on television, solving crimes and ordering around her subordinates, a particularly seductive aspect of the plan, and Maryam concentrated all her will on overcoming Osman's. "I'm going to help you, because I think you need help. You can't really ask anyone about this: you can't understand Kelantanese well enough, and besides, no one will tell you anything if they can help it. Me, though, they can talk to: I'm only a *Mak Chik* and everyone will talk to someone like me."

Osman nodded automatically.

"So," she continued, expertly flicking her cigarette butt onto the hard-swept ground below, "I'll go and ask the questions. You can tell me what you think I should ask," she added graciously, since she didn't intend to let this kid ever tell her what to do, "and I'll let you know what I find out. Then you can do your police...

stuff. I think that should move things along faster than if you try to do it yourself." She smiled modestly at him. "I've got to talk to my daughter for help at the stall, but it shouldn't be a problem. And if I need a ride, I can always ask you, right?"

Osman automatically nodded again. Her personality and natural command seemed to take over, and he tried manfully to shake it off. "Now, *Mak Chik*," he began, determined to re-establish his authority, "It's nice of you to offer to help…"

"Offer to help?" Maryam echoed, expressing both sarcasm and disbelief, leavened with a touch of irritation. "Do you take me for some bored housewife with nothing else to do?"

In fact, Osman did just that, but he wisely refrained from admitting it. He began explaining himself, realizing immediately it was a mistake, but too late to change direction. "No, indeed. I meant only that we police, we have methods, and you know, it's my job to do this. Why, you could get hurt!"

"I think it's more likely for you to get hurt, *Che* Osman," she retorted, staring at him with narrowed eyes. "I'm offering to help you when you need it most. Well…" She stood up and dusted off her sarong with sharp slaps. "If you don't need any help, I'll leave it to you. Good luck." Disobeying all precepts of Malay courtesy, she turned and strode into her living room, leaving him alone on the porch.

He stood, looking disconsolately at the police hat he held in his hands. He'd corrected her attitude and warned her off the investigation. It was the right thing to do, he assured himself, but he'd offended her. That was bad enough; he was well brought-up, and pained to think Maryam would think him rude, and he feared he might have lost a valuable ally. He began to leave, dragging his feet as he came down the steps, hoping to be called back and be convinced to accept her help.

He looked back hopefully while idling on the stairs, but the living room seemed empty, and no one called to him. He trudged slowly through the yard, head down, proud to have asserted his authority, anxious about having spurned such a perfect surrogate mother.

"*Che* Osman!" Mamat hailed him before he reached the road. Osman lifted his head hopefully. "Good luck!" Mamat smiled at him. "It looks like a tough case, but I know you'll solve it."

Osman's face fell. "I think I've insulted *Mak Chik* Maryam," he admitted glumly. "She offered to help, but I, well, you know," he stammered, "I can't let her take such chances."

Mamat watched him quietly.

"It could be dangerous," Osman continued, justifying himself. "I mean, how could I place a *Mak Chik* in danger, right?"

"Well," Mamat observed mildly. "She's a lot more than she seems. I mean, not just a *Mak Chik* who's never been outside her village. She's got a lot of know-how. But," he clapped Osman familiarly on the shoulder, "you're the professional! I know you'll do well."

Osman sighed deeply, but didn't walk away.

"You have work to do, *Che* Osman," Mamat assured him. "I won't keep you any longer." He turned and strolled back to the house, examining the chickens pecking at the ground near his feet as though he'd never noticed them before.

"*Pak Chik* Mamat," Osman called after a few moments. "Wait a moment."

Mamat turned with a bland smile. "Yes?"

"Perhaps I should talk to *Mak Chik* Maryam again. I mean, I wouldn't want her to be angry with me."

"Ah, don't worry, *Che* Osman," Mamat assured him. "She won't be angry—I know she'll understand. You're a professional, after all. No, put that thought out of your mind. You have your work to do."

Osman began to sweat slightly in the hot sun; he turned his hat around in his hands. "You know, it might be a generous offer. I mean, it might be helpful. She could go and talk to people…"

"Do you want to come upstairs and talk to her again?" Mamat asked him kindly.

Osman nodded, more like a schoolboy than ever.

"Come on," Mamat invited him up the stairs and sat him back on the porch. Maryam was in the kitchen.

"He's back." Mamat leaned in over the stairs. "Come out front and talk to him."

"Why?" Maryam asked innocently. "Hasn't he got to get moving on this case? Why's he hanging around here?" She sniffed in irritation.

"He's just a kid. He's afraid to make a mistake. Come on, Yam, go back in. He's really dying for you to help him."

Maryam got up slowly, holding her hip as she did so. "You know, I have a pain right here. I should rest, really, not run around trying to solve other people's crimes. Especially," she grumbled, "for ungrateful policemen who can't even speak Kelantanese."

She gave Mamat a sudden grin of pure joy. She'd not only gotten just what she wanted, she was about to be begged to take it. She walked slowly and majestically out to the porch, where Osman sat ready to plead for her help.

Chapter 3

"**H**E JUST LET YOU TAKE over like that?" Rubiah was incredulous. "I mean, after all, they are the police."

"He's a kid," Maryam replied, somewhat dismissively. "Believe me—he was happy enough to have some help. He's in over his head here."

Maryam seemed slightly irritated to be questioned on this topic: she'd already made her views on Osman perfectly clear and expected Rubiah to share them on general principle. Rubiah, drawing on vast experience with Maryam, retreated, and silently lit her cigarette, waiting for her orders to be issued: they were sure to come within moments. She was not disappointed.

"This Ghani had a second wife," Maryam resumed. "We ought to go to Tawang to see the first wife, at least. It's going to be awkward asking her about any others."

"Can't be helped," Rubiah answered briskly. "If you're going to ask anyone about this, the wives have to be first. Who's more likely to kill him?"

"True," Maryam agreed immediately. "I could see killing Mamat if he took a second wife. Thank God, I haven't had to deal with that."

"I know, poor thing. There could be others reasons to kill him, I guess, but he's just a young musician: why else would anyone hate him?"

Maryam shrugged while studying a plate of Rubiah's rice cakes before her. Kelantan boasted a profusion of local specialties, and Rubiah was an expert in nearly all of them. They were chewy and sweet and rich, redolent of coconut milk, and most were brightly coloured with hues not found in nature. Maryam chose a fluorescent, layered rectangle topped with coconut cream and chewed it ruminatively. "This is going to be a mess, I can see it now." She prepared to rise from the porch. "We might as well get going," she informed Rubiah. "We aren't solving anything by sitting around here. Go get dressed," she ordered, "meet me back here. Remember, the people we're going to see will have to respect us!"

They chose carefully for their first foray into detecting. They fairly shimmered with gold chains, bangles and earrings, calculating the sheer quantity of precious metal would intimidate their witnesses into speaking the truth. Kelantan women wore much of their wealth in gold jewellery, and its profusion on its owner offered an excellent barometer of the family fortune. Maryam painstakingly fixed her hair into a proper bun on the back of her head, covering it with a chiffon head cloth. She wore a sarong of the best quality Kelantan batik which her older brother Malek had made, and a heavily embroidered *kebaya*. Rubiah broke out all her jewellery, one of her best sarongs and a matching over-blouse. They looked like prosperous, solid citizens: pillars of Kelantanese society and arbiters of Kelantanese morals. Just the kind of *Mak Chik*, Maryam thought, that people would instinctively open up to, as they would to their own mothers.

Tawang was a small town on the way to Bacok, a large seaside town. It lay untidily along a paved road, surrounded by rice fields and palm trees of various types, heavily shaded but forlorn at the end of the dry season, the fields baked hard and dusty. Ghani's house was well in from the road, smaller than most: unpainted wood with a thatched roof. The tiny pounded-earth yard was vigorously swept to keep any vegetation well away from the house, banishing the snakes who hid there to a safe distance. The house was in a state of disarray: clothing bundled in the middle of the one large room, *tikar*—woven palm sleeping mats—rolled and stacked in the corner, and the mistress of the house busily wrapping a few pots and plates in newspaper.

Maryam called from the bottom of the ladder leading to the house. "Good morning! Is anyone home?"

Aisha poked her head out the door, her eyes widening at the spectacle below. "*Mak Chik!*" she stammered. "What are you doing here?" Then, remembering her manners, she scrambled to her feet.

"Come in, come in, don't stand out there in the sun. Please." She ushered them into her small house and cast frantically around for a chair; the small couch was wrapped in newspaper and lay on its side, ready to be taken away.

"No, please, don't trouble yourself, *Chik*," Rubiah soothed, "We will sit here," and they lowered themselves to the floor, tucking their feet under their sarongs, offering the fruit they'd brought with them. "We don't want to interrupt you…"

"No, no, not at all," Aisha bent over her tiny stove in the corner, already making coffee for them. "All I have out is coffee," she apologized. "The tea's already packed."

"Coffee's even better," Maryam assured her. "Going somewhere?" she then asked, craning her neck to take in all of the room.

"Home to my parents," she explained, her face hidden by her hair as she bent over the cups on a tray. She was slightly built, with an expressive face and large eyes. "I can't manage here on my own with two kids. My parents live close by, and they have room for me. I'm lucky." She came back to them with cups of coffee on a worn wooden tray and their fruit set nicely into a large dish. "My kids are with Ghani's parents right now; my mother-in-law's got them so I can pack. My brothers are coming to get my stuff later." She waved her hands over their cups. "Please, drink."

They sipped their coffee slowly. "You know, *Chik* Aisha," Maryam began slowly, "we're helping the police, asking questions. Helping to find out what…happened. After all," Maryam picked up steam, "It happened at my house, at my performance, so to speak."

"Yes, how awful," Aisha murmured.

Maryam was stunned. Was Aisha really commiserating with her because the performance was ruined, when it was her husband who was killed? Rather cold, Maryam thought, shooting Rubiah a penetrating look. Or was that just a strange overabundance of courtesy?

"Yes, indeed," she continued, trying to understand Aisha's expression, which was blank. "So anyway, I feel as though it's my business too, and well, it's sometimes difficult for the police to talk to people, so I thought *Mak Chik* Rubiah and I could help. We too want to find whoever would do such a thing, such a vicious thing, to your husband."

"So you're working for the police," Aisha said slowly.

"Yes," Rubiah jumped in, "unless you'd prefer to talk to them, and, of course, you could…"

"No, not really," Aisha said, almost dreamily. "It's easier to talk to you, *Mak Chik*." She folded her hands in her lap and waited.

Maryam took a fortifying sip of coffee and steeled herself for tears. She composed herself to look as sympathetic as possible. "How long have you been married, *Chik* Aisha?" she began gently.

"Five years. I have two kids, four and two."

"And you're from here too, aren't you?"

"From Tawang? Yes, of course. I've known Ghani since we were little."

Maryam nodded, encouraging her to talk about her life.

"Well, Ghani started playing with *Pak Chik* Dollah since he was small—he always loved playing the drums. He didn't really go to school, me neither. But I can read and so could he. His father was worried about him travelling around and getting into trouble, and *Pak Chik* 'Lah promised to watch out for him. He's been everywhere," Aisha was picking up speed now, speaking more fluently, and had stopped staring at her lap and was now talking to both women directly, "Patani, Kuala Krai," here she grimaced, "Bacok, all over. *Pak Chik* 'Lah is very popular, the most popular *dalang* in Kelantan. You knew that, right?" She smiled, and Maryam smiled back.

"Anyway, I was around sixteen and Ghani's parents came to mine and asked for me, to marry him. I always liked him. He's very handsome; used to be." She rose and pulled a frame wrapped in newspaper out of a bag and pulled the paper off. "This is when we got married," she explained to the women. "See?"

Maryam and Rubiah leaned over a color photo of two teenagers in their wedding finery: both wearing light blue *kain songket*, which to Maryam's expert eye was certainly of acceptable, if not top, quality. They were both solemn-faced, as Malay wedding portraits always were, and they could see here that Ghani had been remarkably good-looking: his cheekbones were high and his nose chiseled. Aisha too looked fetching, with large eyes and a round face, but the eye was drawn to him.

"You look lovely here," Rubiah said sweetly. "Oh, he's handsome, yes, but look at you!"

Aisha was self-deprecating, "Thanks, but I'm just saying, he was always noticed, and it's gotten him into a world of trouble now."

Rubiah cocked her head. "Now?"

"Yes, now!" Aisha's cheeks were turning red. "He just married a second wife, and look what she's done!" Rubiah looked shocked and Aisha continued. "Don't you think she killed him when he told her to go back to Kuala Krai? She knew she lost. She came here, you know. She just showed up one night, it was just a week ago, can you believe it? Just showed up here and dropped her stuff on the floor here and said 'Here I am!'

"'Who are you?' I asked her, and she said 'Oh, I married Ghani, didn't he tell you?' 'Of course he didn't tell me. Why should I believe you?' I thought, 'Now he's gotten himself into trouble, and it won't be so easy to get rid of her.' That's what I thought. And it's been even more trouble than I thought it would be: he's dead, and she killed him."

Aisha sat back on her heels and looked satisfied; she'd said what she wanted to say. Maryam had laid a pack of cigarettes out on the floor and gestured for Aisha to take one. They all lit up, and Aisha tipped her head back to blow smoke at the ceiling.

"Ghani was weak, you know," she said philosophically, "but I didn't expect anything like this. She must have been at him. He couldn't afford a second wife: we can barely make it as it is, even with him working in Singapore. But this woman wanted a husband. I think she just wanted to get out of Kuala Krai. It's a dump—so far away in the jungle and all that."

Maryam would not have said it so bluntly, but she shared the sentiment. Kuala Krai was far from Kota Bharu and the coast, deep in the rainforests of central Malaysia, and though Maryam had never been there (why would she—there wasn't anything to see) she imagined it as a small, gloomy place, hemmed in by overgrowth and claustrophobic in the extreme. She could easily believe someone who lived there would be desperate to leave and clutch at any straw to free herself from the jungle vines dragging her back upriver.

"I think she killed him after she realized he wasn't going to let her stay here," Aisha continued.

"Where did she stay when she was here?" Maryam interrupted. "I mean here in Tawang?"

Aisha thought for a moment, and shrugged. "Not here. I don't know. Maybe in someone's house?"

"Any ideas?" Rubiah asked her. "I think we want to track down where she was."

Aisha narrowed her eyes, whether in thought or suspicion, Maryam couldn't tell. "I don't know," she repeated, gritting her teeth slightly.

Maryam nodded, and backed off her questions. She would visit Ghani's mother, and it would be much easier to talk about this with his mother than his wife.

"Did you ever go and see him when he played?" Maryam asked gently.

Aisha nodded without speaking. "Before the kids were born, I went all the time. Not so much now: I'd need to find someone to take care of them or take them with me. It's such a big job, you know."

"Did you go to my house when he was playing? It's not so far away."

"Did I kill him, you mean?" Aisha snapped. "No. He was my husband. And I didn't visit them when they played at your house." She looked as though she might begin to cry. "I never thought it would be like this. I never thought he'd actually marry someone else. I never thought he'd even go around with anyone else. I thought he loved me."

Maryam patted her arm and smiled sympathetically. Mamat, her own husband, was a very handsome man, and even now, with his hair graying and his face ageing, she still thought him well worth noticing. She saw other women's eyes follow Mamat as they walked through the market, but she believed he wouldn't betray her. Still, all women said a man was only as faithful as his opportunities, and there was little collective confidence in any husband's ability to resist an intriguing offer. How would she feel if he took another wife? Would she kill him? She really didn't know. If Aisha had killed Ghani, Maryam conceded she had excellent reason.

"I'm sure he did love you," Maryam said quietly. "You know, men are so…unthinking sometimes. It doesn't mean that much to them."

Rubiah nodded sagely, and she and Maryam began murmuring their thanks and their preliminary leave-taking phrases, when Aisha unexpectedly began to cry.

"Just a week ago he was still here, and I didn't know anything about this wife," she nearly spit the word, "from Kuala

Krai! Everything was fine! Now I know he betrayed me and he's dead and I'm a widow with two children living at my parents' house. I can't believe it. My whole life is ruined because of her. She married him and then she killed him, and I'm the one suffering for it."

She buried her head in her hands and jerked her shoulders away from their comforting hands. "No, just leave. I'm sorry to be rude," she said, wiping her eyes as Maryam and Rubiah tried to talk to her, to tell her it would be all right. "I just can't talk anymore. I'm sorry, very sorry. Another time."

She tried to smile as they left and squatted in her doorway, knuckling her eyes. "Please forgive me," she called after them.

Chapter 4

"OH MY GOD! I feel so sorry for her," Maryam said softly, leaning towards Rubiah's ear.

"Oh, I know," Rubiah agreed passionately. "That poor girl. What she's going through, I don't even want to imagine. What a pity."

"I don't know how I'd deal with it myself. She's being so brave," Maryam marveled. "You've got to admire it. Respect it. Unless of course..." She paused, and stopped walking. "Unless, of course, she killed him herself. Which I wouldn't blame her for, I can tell you that." She resumed walking towards the main road, stepping around a variety of fruit trees planted at cautious distances from the houses: banana, papaya, and mango. "I'd feel sorry for her if she did it. I would."

"Would you keep it from the police?" Rubiah pressed her. "Just tell him you couldn't find anything?"

"Are you suggesting it?" Maryam asked her, avoiding her eyes.

"I don't know." Rubiah was honest. "I don't know what I'd think after all is said and done. Being made a second wife is a bitter drink to swallow. Who knows what it could drive you to do?"

They walked in silence for some moments, each contemplating the private hell of a husband suddenly appearing with a second wife. "We should see both sets of parents, as long as we're here," Maryam pulled herself together. "It can't be too difficult to find them."

The stopped at a small coffee shop on the side of the main road, where a small group of men sat on the tiny bench at the counter. Maryam and Rubiah smiled at the owner, washing the used coffee cups. "Excuse me, we aren't from here, and we're looking for *Che* Ghani's parents. Do you know where they live?"

The owner looked up from his cups and saucers and gave them a long look. "The late Ghani?" They nodded. "Why?"

"Well," began Maryam, "we're helping the police, you might say, looking into this unfortunate occurrence."

"Helping the police?"

"Yes, *Abang*," Rubiah moved in. "You know how it is. It's so difficult for people to talk to the police, and at a time like this, of course, you don't want to make things even more difficult for them, isn't that true? It's so much easier to talk to us, you see, two Kelantanese people, not official, just trying to help."

He put his hands on the counter. "So tell me, *Kak*, why the police let you do this?" His grammar and his accent were noticeably coarser than their own.

Rubiah was insulted. She'd offered such a smooth and polite speech, and she was interrogated as though she weren't a well-dressed and well-spoken *Mak Chik*. She unconsciously rearranged her headscarf to make sure her earrings and necklaces showed to advantage—and in the bright sunlight they were blinding—to show this man who he was dealing with.

"Sometimes, *Abang*, even the smartest people need help, and if they're really smart, they try to find the right person to the job." She shook her wrist slightly so her bangles tinkled softly. "We are the right people and, of course, we are perfectly ready to help."

The man looked back and forth at the two of them, registering their dress, their jewellery and their natural imperiousness. He was slow to acknowledge his defeat. "I've never heard of that," he grumbled. "I'm just trying to make sure no one bothers the family: it's a painful time for them. People coming from outside; I don't want to tell you where they live and then you'll disturb them."

"Disturb them?" Maryam asked, speaking more softly as she became more irritated. "Do we really look as though we came out here to enjoy ourselves disturbing them? God forbid!

"And so, *Abang*, I ask your help, where can I find them?"

"Alright," he ended ungraciously. "The house toward the end of the alley, on the left," he pointed with his chin. "Over there."

Thanking him sweetly, they walked down the narrow opening between two houses, shaking their heads in contempt. The nerve of him, treating them like teenaged girls out to make mischief.

Ghani's parents' house was easily identified by a very pretty older woman sitting on the porch with two small children. The children were playing in the shade as their grandmother sat silently watching them.

"Hello," Maryam called from the bottom of the steps. The grandmother looked at her dully, not even rousing herself to a smile. She had a finely sculpted face, with high cheekbones and large, almond-shaped eyes, and her hair was pepper and salt: what people called *rambut dua macam*, or two kinds of hair, black and grey. Ghani must have gotten his looks from his mother, Maryam decided, remembering the wedding picture she'd just seen. Ghani's mother nodded at Maryam, not answering. Maryam pursued her introduction.

"*Kak!* I am *Kak* Maryam, and this is *Kak* Rubiah." They both smiled. "It was at my house that this so unfortunate… thing…well, tragedy happened, during the performance. We are helping the police, *Kak*, and asking some questions. I'm so sorry to bother you."

They waited for her reply. It was hot and unshaded where they stood, and they were beginning to perspire. She continued to look at them, and after what seemed to be several minutes, but was probably much less, she said "Yes? At your house?"

"Yes *Kak*," Maryam answered vigorously, anxious to be out of the sun, "at my house. And we're looking into it. Can we talk to you?" It was as close as Maryam could come to asking for an invitation without being terribly rude.

"Come up," the woman answered dully, remembering her manners. "Please, get out of the sun." She stood up to greet them and disappeared into the house to make some coffee, gesturing for her guests to make themselves comfortable on the porch. It was so cool and dark out of the blazing sun, it took a few moments for their eyes to adjust. Ghani's two children sat solemnly watching them, their eyes large, their hair pushed back from their foreheads and some cooling white powder rubbed on their cheeks and foreheads. Rubiah tried to coax them closer, but they wriggled farther away and she let them be.

Ghani's mother came out with a plate of cakes, no doubt brought by the neighbours, and coffee. She served them from the tray and urged them to eat and drink. She ran her hand over her face and watched them.

"Aren't you drinking, *Kak*?" Maryam asked.

She smiled silently and shook her head. Maryam introduced herself and Rubiah, offering the most pertinent details, like what they sold in the market and where they hailed from.

Their hostess nodded slightly, and Maryam feared she would never speak. "It's nice that you're doing this," she said quietly. "I am *Kak* Hasnah, and that was my son. These are his children," she made a sweeping gesture towards them. "I still can't believe it. Poor boy. Too many problems with women," she unrolled some homemade cigarettes from her sarong, just as Maryam so often did, and she recognized Hasnah as a kindred spirit. Hasnah spread her cigarettes on the porch and each woman took one and lit up.

"Always with women. I worried that it would catch up with him in the end. I told him so. His father told him too, but you know how young men are. All men, really. They don't think woman trouble is trouble until it's too late, and that's just what happened to my son."

"Is he your only son?" Maryam asked, grateful that Hasnah was now talking.

"Yes, the only one. I have three girls, also, but Ghani was the oldest and the only boy. I'm glad the rest are girls. Less trouble and more sensible."

"Kids," Rubiah interjected. "They can break your heart." All three mothers sat silent for a moment, considering the truth of this.

"Did you know about his new, um, that is…?" Maryam was strangely reluctant to come to the point.

"That he got married again?" Hasnah asked. "Of course, I knew once she showed up here. How could he be so stupid? This girl, this Faouda, showed up right at his house, to his wife. Can you believe it? He came running over here with her after Aisha threw them out, or her out anyway. Late at night, woke us up. 'Are you kidding?' I asked him. 'You married someone in Kuala Krai? A second wife? What in God's name do you need a second wife for?'

"Naturally, Ghani had nothing to say." Suddenly, Hasnah, seeing the two children listening with interest, turned to the inside of her house and called, "Ijan! Come over here and take the kids inside. They could use a nap, right?" She smiled at them. Ijan came to the door and smiled shyly, gathering the children with her to take inside. "My youngest," explained Hasnah. "Still in school."

"Such a pretty girl," enthused Rubiah. "She looks just like her mother—*salin tak tumpah*, not even a drop spilled."

"Thanks," said Hasnah shortly. She tapped the ash over the railing. "Anyway, Ghani couldn't really explain. 'I didn't know she'd come here,' he tells me. 'You really married her,' I said, 'and you didn't think she'd show up here?'

"Oh, I was furious, I tell you, and so was my husband. 'What have you done?' his father asked him. And Ghani had nothing to say. He needed a place for this girl to stay; it was so late at night.

"'Not here,' my husband told him. 'She can sleep by the side of the road for all I care. Why don't you divorce her right now?' he asked him. The girl starts sniffling. It was like TV here, shouting and all in the middle of the night. I could have killed Ghani myself right then. Two little kids, you've seen my grandchildren, and you marry someone else?"

Maryam and Rubiah clicked their tongues and commiserated. Men.

"*Ya*, well then, he left with this girl. I think he might have gone over to his auntie's house, my husband's sister. She lives over there," she gestured vaguely away from the main road, "with her family and my husband's mother.

"Maybe Ghani tried to talk his grandmother into keeping her for one night. But let me tell you, this girl was angry when she left here. She thought Ghani would be thrilled to see her, and I guess she thought his family would celebrate when she got up here, but instead, I told her she ought to go right back to where she came from.

"What could my son have been thinking? To do that to your own wife. You know what we say about a second wife: *cuka diminum pagi hari*. It's a bitter drink to swallow." She stared at the trees outside the house.

"Our proverbs tell us a lot about life, if we listen to them," Maryam agreed. "That's why we say *biar anak mati, jangan adat mati*: let your children die, but not tradition." Maryam pulled herself up short. She was horrified at her lack of tact: to talk about dead children, even as a proverb. She blushed scarlet, and put her hands together under her chin. "Oh *Kak* Hasnah, I didn't think. I didn't mean…"

"I know," Hasnah answered tiredly. "It's just a proverb."

"No, I'm so sorry. What must you think of me?"

She shook her head. "You mustn't worry. I know what you meant, and you're right. We can learn a lot from the old ways."

Maryam cleared her throat to begin again, admonishing herself to watch her tongue. "It's so difficult, *Kak* Hasnah," Maryam sympathized, but continued. She thought for a moment. "Ghani left the day after that to play, didn't he? At my house?"

Hasnah nodded. "He did. That girl wasn't around. I think she may have gone home to Kuala Krai right away. That's what Ghani told me, that he divorced her with one *talak*, and she went home. Aisha came over with him, so it looked to me as though it was all right.

"'You're sure she's gone?' I asked him when I could get him alone for a minute, 'You're sure this is over?' He said it was. He said he was going to register his *talak* in Kota Bharu, but I don't know if he did or not. I don't know if he ever had the time to do it." She sighed, and sat silently.

"Did Aisha ever go to visit him when he played?"

She nodded. "Sometimes. Sometimes I'd keep the kids when she did. You know, they were close. It was a good marriage. Maybe she went to check up on him too, I don't know. She didn't stay all night or anything; there wasn't any place for her to be. She'd come home late and sleep here with the kids, then take them home in the morning."

"How about last week?" Maryam asked.

"You think she went to your place to kill Ghani? She didn't."

"Was she there?" Maryam pressed.

"Are you going to ask the rest of the troupe whether she turned up there? Is that what this is about?"

"No, no," soothed Maryam, trying to slide away from an argument. "Just asking."

"I'm tired," Hasnah announced. "I've got to look after my grandkids now." She stood up and tried to fix a polite smile on her face, but failed. Maryam and Rubiah thanked her profusely, and backed away down the alley.

"She was there," Maryam told Rubiah as they walked away.

Rubiah nodded. "Of course. The other musicians will confirm it, I guess. Do you want to see the auntie? Maybe she knows where what's-her-name, Faouda, went."

Ghani's auntie and her elderly mother were busily working in the kitchen when Maryam and Rubiah appeared. Their house was a traditional one, built on stilts in the front, with a ground level kitchen in the back. There was no running water in the area, and two pottery jars of water sat on the floor next to a charcoal brazier and a large plastic bucket of rice. The younger woman was slicing onions, and the older one shelling *petai*, jungle beans in large pods.

They looked up to see their well-dressed visitors and quickly stood, flustered to be visited in their working clothes: faded sarongs, the younger woman in a T-shirt and the older in a well-worn cotton blouse.

"We're sorry to walk in on you like this," began Maryam, wishing for the first time in her life that she was wearing less jewellery. The younger woman stood up, vigorously brushing her hands against her sarong, and whipped the dishtowel off her shoulder. She smiled shyly.

Maryam introduced herself and Rubiah, and the woman's face fell. "I am *Kak* Nurhayati, and this is my mother," she said stiffly. Her mother watched them all without rising, her face now expressionless. "I'm Ghani's aunt," Nurhayati added. She watched Maryam without moving.

Maryam cleared her throat and once more explained herself. "*Kak* Hasnah said that Ghani may have brought, um, that girl, to stay here," Rubiah broke a long silence. "We thought that might be important, you know."

Ghani's grandmother made the decision to speak. "That horrible girl. I told him," she said, ostensibly addressing her daughter, "I said, 'what have you done, you stupid boy! Are you leaving your family for her?'"

She turned for a moment and tore apart a pod, sending *petai* spattering over the ground. "'Just keep her here for the night, *Nenek*,' he said, 'I'll send her home to Kuala Krai tomorrow.' 'You will, will you?' I told him. 'You think she'll go? She came all the way up here to find you and make your family miserable.'"

"He told me he was sending her back the next day, so I said I'd keep her for that night. But I told him, 'Don't fool around with me, Ghani. Right after breakfast she's out of here, I mean it. If you don't come back here for her, I'll push her out onto the road.' Didn't I, Yati?" She turned to her daughter. "I didn't want any part of it, but I didn't want him wandering around all night with her trailing behind him complaining for the entire village to hear."

"She wasn't happy," explained Nurhayati.

Her mother snorted. "Not happy? I'll say. She was furious: *seperti ular berbelit-belit*, like a snake rising over its coils."

Maryam and Rubiah had squatted down in front of the older woman and, at this point, Nurhayati did too. Maryam produced a pack of Mamat's Rothman's cigarettes, and offered one to each woman. Nurhayati haltingly accepted one, and her mother reached behind her to pull out the ingredients for a betel quid.

"I prefer this," she explained, smoothening out the leaf and cutting off slices of the betel nut. "I never got used to cigarettes; too modern for me." She smiled, revealing the blackened teeth and red gums of the betel chewer, and methodically added some tobacco and lime to the bundle she rolled up and stuck into her cheek next to her back molars. This completed, she continued.

"She started to complain to me, after Ghani left, but I told her straight out, 'Don't talk to me about Ghani. He's my grandson. What do you think you're doing here? You just go to sleep and get ready to leave in the morning, you.'" She chewed placidly and then spit over her shoulder. "And loud? I was so embarrassed. Everyone could hear our business, especially in the middle of the night like that. Goodness, what a disaster!"

Nurhayati suddenly remembered her manners. "Tea, coffee?" she asked rising, but Maryam and Rubiah begged her to sit down instead. "Don't trouble yourself, please! We've just had tea at your brother's house. Really, we don't want to bother you!"

She allowed herself to be convinced, and squatted on her heels, holding the cigarette between her thumb and forefinger and taking a deep drag. She took over the narrative from her mother, who was for the moment immersed in her betel. "I gave her a cup of coffee in the morning. Ghani came over early to get her, and when I saw him, I gave him a smack on the side of the head. Idiot! Too good-looking for his own good." His grandmother cackled sadly at that.

"Always been a problem. Anyway, he took her with him, and that was it. I hear he was over at his parents' house later in the day, so I guess he got rid of her and went home to make up with his wife. We never saw him after that." Both she and her mother became silent, hearing the finality in those words.

"Never again," echoed his grandmother, rubbing her eyes with a dishtowel.

"Find out who did it," his aunt urged them. "He didn't deserve it."

Maryam nodded. "He didn't," she said. "Did she go right back to Kuala Krai?"

Nurhayati shrugged. "I don't know. I didn't see her again, and I never asked anyone. How would we know? Once she left Tawang, she could have gone anywhere." She thought for a moment. "I think she killed him."

Her mother gave her a searching look. "Probably. Who else would want him dead?"

Maryam did not want to interrupt, but could imagine that Aisha might want to kill him herself for bringing home another wife. Still, Aisha was a girl from here, surrounded by her family, and this other wife was from far away and no one knew her. It would be infinitely more convenient if she were the killer, since no one Maryam ever met would be very sorry about it. Indeed, it would be an object lesson in second marriages and being far too forward for Malay courtesy, and would no doubt be passed down from mother to daughter for years to come.

"You don't know anything about where she might live in Kuala Krai, do you? Did she say anything about it?" Maryam probed.

Nenek shook her head. "She didn't say much after I finished talking to her, let me tell you." Maryam could well believe it.

"She said something about living a little outside of town, didn't she, Yati? Let me think. I know she said something." She spat again and frowned slightly as she thought.

"Kampong Kedai Lalat, wasn't that it?" Yati asked. "She said it as though we should know something about it. I guess it's a big deal in Kuala Krai." She rolled her eyes. "Are you going down there to look for her?"

"I guess we'll have to," Rubiah answered morosely. She did not care for travel, and Kuala Krai was a lot farther than she cared to go. The jungle, she thought: bound to be hot, steamy and oppressive. No doubt wild animals and venomous snakes lurked in the underbrush, waiting to take a bite out of unsuspecting women from Kota Bharu. Not a pleasant prospect, but she knew Maryam would never let them skip that part of the investigation.

Maryam rose, feeling it in her knees as she stood up. "Thank you so much for talking to us," she said with feeling. "You've been very kind." Rubiah gave her thanks as well, and the two women smiled and nodded at them, and turned back to their cooking.

"Do you think they'll find out who killed Ghani?" Nurhayati asked her mother. Her mother shrugged, looking hard at the *petai*, afraid to lift her eyes up lest she start crying and find herself unable to stop.

Chapter 5

"**D**O WE HAVE TO SEE Aisha's parents today?" Rubiah asked. "Can't we come back tomorrow? I don't think I can stand listening to this story again right now. It's so sad."

Maryam weighed their options. It was getting later, and she was reminded that she needed to get dinner started. She was hot, and emotionally exhausted from these conversations: she needed to think them through. Yet they were already here and if they left now, they'd just have to return tomorrow morning. "Let's finish up here. One night without home cooking won't kill anyone. We can pick up dinner from the stalls on the way home."

Rubiah needed convincing. "I can't stand listening to these stories anymore. I need to hear something cheerful."

She completely understood how Rubiah felt. "We've got to be more determined, more professional." She fixed Rubiah with a stern eye. "After all…" She paused. "I won't let that Police Chief think I lost interest as soon as it got a little difficult. I said I would do it, and I will," she said stubbornly.

"OK, OK," grumbled Rubiah. "Let's go," she added with a regretful sigh. "We'll see how Aisha's family is taking it."

Aisha's family was not far away: both Ghani and Aisha's families were spread throughout Kampong Tawang. Her parents lived at the end of the village, bordering on the still-dry rice paddies; the view from their porch over the flat fields was pleasant, especially as the sun set. Two men, recently bathed after a hot day's work, lounged in the shade, each with a cup of coffee in front of him. Maryam called before she reached the stairs, announcing her arrival.

The older man, Aisha's father, rose and invited them up. He turned and called into the house for his wife, who met them at the door, smiling politely. "Come in," she welcomed them. "You must be the *Mak Chik* from Kampong Penambang, helping the police." She laughed at their expressions. "Don't be surprised. You know how it is in a village: the news travels fast. Please sit down, make yourselves comfortable. I'm *Kak* Azizah; this is my husband, *Abang* Ramli, and my son, Ali."

Everyone smiled and sat down, and almost immediately, a teenaged girl appeared with a tray of cold drinks and cookies. "It's so hot in the afternoons now," Azizah said, urging them to eat. "I can't wait for the rainy season to start. It's dusty, too, isn't it?"

They agreed it was. Rubiah now felt completely reinvigorated: some sugar, something cold, and she was now ready for action once more.

Azizah continued. "Aisha will be moving back here tonight. They're going to get her soon." She waved towards her husband and son. "And then she and my grandchildren will live here with us. It's so difficult for her," she said sadly. Ramli, Aisha's father, grunted, signalling that this was women's talk and he would stay out of it.

"Is Aisha your only daughter?" Rubiah asked.

Her mother laughed. "Oh no, I have three younger daughters and three sons. Seven, altogether. One son is married, everyone else lives here. Ali's the oldest—after Aisha, of course. So now we'll have three more. Well, it might be a bit crowded, but we don't mind. I mean, it's our grandchildren, and it will be nice to have Aisha back." She looked sad, having said this, but tried to be as pleasant as possible.

"How difficult," Maryam commented.

"Yes, but who would have thought something like this would happen? Poor Ghani." Her husband looked disgusted, and Ali grimaced. Azizah ignored them. "And Aisha a widow so young. Ah well, at least she is so young, her whole life ahead of her." The women all smiled at the platitude.

"Did you hear anything? I mean, about Ghani?" asked Rubiah, unwilling to mention a second wife.

"You mean the new wife?" Ramli growled, looking over at his wife. "Of course, we heard. Everyone heard."

"When did you know?" asked Maryam.

"When?" Ramli repeated. "When? I guess the day after he brought her back. That next morning, Aisha came over here with the kids and told us what happened. I wanted to go out and find him right away, but Aisha said he was sending her back to wherever she came from."

"Kuala Krai," his son interjected helpfully.

"Yeah, Kuala Krai. I didn't actually see her. Didn't want to."

"Well, what for?" Azizah explained. "By the time we heard about it, Aisha said she'd already gone back. And then Ghani came to get her."

"I took him aside." Ramli leaned forward toward Maryam. "I told him, 'I'm watching you now.' I said, 'You'd better straighten up if you know what's good for you. How can you treat my daughter that way?' He didn't have much to say for himself. Apologizing all over the place. Said he didn't know what came over him. Didn't know why he'd done such a thing."

Ali gave a short, mirthless bark of laughter. "I know why."

A forbidding look from both his parents quieted him. "He did apologize," Azizah added. "Though I was so disappointed in him. What good is an apology when he just married someone without thinking like that? I mean, what does that say about him?" She shook her head regretfully.

"It says he's a fool," Ramli interjected. "It says he doesn't think at all. It says he hangs out with all kinds of women and doesn't realize what's going to come of it."

"Yes, yes," his wife hurried to stop him. This was clearly a well-trodden road for them in the past few days. He would not be hushed.

"You know, *Kak*," Ramli took a deep drag on his cigarette and fixed her with an intense stare, "I've known Ghani since he was born. We both have; our families are from this town and we grew up with his parents." His wife nodded.

"He was a good-looking kid, a nice boy always playing the drums and wanting to play with Dollah Baju Hijau, the famous *dalang*. He started travelling with him when he was still little. So cute, right?" He looked at his wife, who nodded once more. "Always a sweet kid, but a little girl-crazy. I thought that would stop once he got married, had children. You know, it often does." They all nodded.

"And it did, really, for years. He and Aisha were happy together, she always liked *Wayang Siam*, and she'd go and watch him. She was really proud of him, I could tell." He smiled briefly. "But this! I tell you, *Kak*, I was knocked over. I couldn't believe it! I felt as though I didn't know anything about him. I'm not naïve about the world, you know. I know what happens. But I didn't see it coming with Ghani."

He pulled thoughtfully on his cigarette, tapping the ashes through a small gap in the porch flooring. "I have four daughters," he told Maryam and Rubiah. "How do you think I felt to hear this from my oldest? Well…" He nodded, looking over at Ali slumped in his chair, "I wouldn't want to hear one of my sons did it either, you know. I think it's wrong, it's selfish." He frowned. "But…" He paused for a moment, "I don't think I'd want to kill him. A son-in-law…" He shrugged ruefully. "*Rambut sama hitam, hati lain-lain*: all our hair is black, but our hearts are all different."

Maryam nervously approached her next question. "Did Aisha go to see him a lot?"

"Not so much since the kids were born. It's difficult. Sometimes, though, she'd have one of her sisters go and stay with the kids and she'd go over with her brother to see him. She liked watching it." Her father took a sip of coffee and waved his hand at them, inviting them to drink.

"Did she go this week?"

He looked hard at her. Aisha's mother twisted her hands in her lap and looked down at them. "*Ya,* she went the next night, I think; I don't remember when exactly." Maryam did not believe that. "Her brother took her. She went to see him since they made up."

He'd told her only because he thought someone else would, and then it would seem even worse. Surely, if Aisha were there, the musicians—and Dollah himself—would have seen her. This was a much smarter way to deal with it: Maryam had to give Ramli credit for it.

She nodded politely. "Did you go with her?" she asked Ali.

He was silent for a moment, clearly willing his father to answer for him. Finally, grudgingly, he nodded. "I have a motorbike," he mumbled.

"Did you go during the performance?"

He was very still for a moment. "Of course," he said shortly. "She liked watching it."

"Did she see Ghani? I mean, did both of you see him?"

Ali glared at her, not knowing what to answer. "Well, she must have," his father came to his aid. "She went to see him."

"Could she see him while they were performing?" Rubiah asked innocently.

Ali gave her a look of pure hatred. "Sure. She looked in the back of the stage."

"Did you go with her?"

"No, I went to drink some coffee. I didn't need to see him."

"Wouldn't it be easier to see him after the performance was over?" Rubiah asked.

All three stared daggers at her, but no one said a word. "I mean, if she wanted to talk to him, surely it would be easier…" She seemed to run out of steam.

Ramli stood up. "Thank you so much for coming here to see us," he said. "You probably want to go home to make dinner and see your families, and we wouldn't want to keep you. You are very kind to look into this and bring the killer to justice, and we thank you for all that you are doing."

This formal speech announced their departure: in the nicest possible way, they were being thrown out. Maryam and Rubiah smiled as best they could and thanked Azizah for her hospitality. They backed off the porch and walked quickly over the pot-holed path to the only slightly less pitted main road to find a taxi to take them home.

Chapter 6

"HAVE YOU EVER THOUGHT about taking a second wife?" Maryam asked Mamat as they readied for bed.

He laughed. "Don't I have enough to deal with now? How could I possibly deal with another wife?"

"No, really," she said seriously. Although Maryam had no mean opinion about her own looks, especially when she was younger, Mamat had always been remarkably good-looking. Girls would turn to look at him as he walked down the lanes coming home from school, and more than one of her friends had confessed a serious crush before her engagement was announced.

Mamat, unlike Ghani, didn't take much advantage of it as a boy; he was a sober youth with a great deal of responsibility. His father, a law clerk, had fallen into drink and gambled away the family's rice lands. His mother was a *songket* weaver, but found it difficult to support all nine of her children when her husband not only brought in very little money, but lost all they had at the mah jongg table. As the eldest, Mamat went to work early to support the family and helped raise all his younger siblings. He'd won awards in grammar school, but couldn't afford to go on to high school and settled quickly into an early adulthood.

Maryam occasionally worried he would want to relive his youth now that he had some time to relax. He was still, she believed, a very handsome man, even with his hair turning gray. Sometimes she'd see him walking into the *Pasar Besar* and she'd lose her breath and blush like a girl to see her husband of over thirty years. What if some younger woman took a shine to him, and chased him? Would he be able to resist, or would he take whatever he found on offer? She'd certainly thought about it before, but her full day hearing about the tragedy Ghani had brought upon himself made the possibility seem all the more real.

"*Sayang*, what's bothering you?" he asked her, putting his arm around her shoulder. She shook off her thoughts.

"I'm just worried. I've seen what happened here with him taking a second wife, and I sometimes wonder whether you'll want to do that: I mean, you know, you had to work so hard as a kid, will you want to…fool around now the way you couldn't before?" She buried her head in his shoulder, embarrassed to have said as much as she did, but wanting reassurance just the same.

He threw his head back and laughed. "Are you serious? You are!" He drew her hair back from her face. "Why? What's wrong?"

"Nothing's wrong, I'm just concerned. Are you getting… bored?"

He smiled again, as though he would burst into laughter at any moment. "Bored? You drive me crazy! What other woman would be out investigating a murder, and intimidated the whole police force into letting her do it? That's why I love you." He leaned back on the bed, still holding her hair. "Come here," he said softly. "I'll prove to you I'm not bored."

The next morning she was shy in front of Mamat, though she scolded herself for unbecoming maidenly modesty. She was the mother of four children, and had been married to Mamat nearly thirty years! Yet when she looked at him and remembered their lovemaking of last night, she felt like a girl again, as she did when they were first married, and her own passion surprised her. Now she tried to hide it by keeping her head down as she made *nasi kerabu*: wrapping blue-tinted rice, vegetables and bits of fish in a banana leaf, as lunch for her two youngest children to take to school. Mamat seemed to know what she was thinking, and grinned at her; she lightly slapped his arm. "You can see I'm busy," she reprimanded him. "What are you looking for?"

He smiled again and wandered off to find coffee and take some rice for his own breakfast. Ordinarily she would be leaving for the market around this time, but today she and Rubiah planned to visit Kuala Krai to see Faouda. Mamat announced he would go with them. "It's OK with me if you ignore me," he said through a mouthful of rice, "but I'd feel better if I were there, just in case something happens."

Maryam agreed. "I'm leaving plenty of *nasi kerabu*; no one will starve if we don't get home for dinner."

Osman had been prevailed upon, or rather, ordered, to have them driven to Kuala Krai: it was such a long trip, and difficult for them otherwise. The young police chief obeyed Maryam when she commanded him, but after she left, and he felt her spell lifting, he couldn't understand why he acted so spinelessly around her.

He railed at himself for allowing her to take over the investigation, and yet, he admitted to himself, he was relieved by it, too. He'd been ready for all kinds of robbery and domestic mayhem, but he hadn't counted on murder so soon! And Maryam at least seemed unfazed by it, while he was hourly becoming less sure of himself.

He longed to speak to his own mother. She'd tell him how to resist the pull of a domineering older woman—as long as he continued to listen to her. Or she might read something into it, and take it as an indirect criticism. He winced at the thought, and decided not to risk it.

His lack of volition led directly to Rahman, his junior officer, sitting quietly behind the wheel of their one unmarked car (Maryam had been very specific about that) waiting to drive her wherever she wanted to go.

She and Rubiah bundled into the back seat, to enjoy the rare treat of a private car. Mamat sat up front with the driver in a fraternity of silence.

None of them had ever been so far as Ulu Kelantan. Maryam and Rubiah looked out the window with undisguised fascination, as the coastal plain began to disappear and the darker jungle began to close in on them. The road from Kota Bharu headed south, following the Kelantan River to its source in the central mountains of the peninsula. Towns were now farther apart, and rice fields became oil palm plantations, which alternated with untamed forest. The blacktop shimmered in the heat, even though the tangled greenery formed deep shadows on either side of the road. The air seemed even more humid, heavier, and the land somehow sinister. There were fewer cars down here: Kuala Krai was the last real town in Kelantan before you entered the nature preserve in central Malaysia, and it was unfamiliar terrain to anyone brought up on the flat and crowded coast. It looked deserted to their eyes… and vaguely malevolent.

It was several hours before they arrived at the last railroad stop in Kelantan: the end of the line. The town of Kuala Krai itself was heavily Chinese, an anomaly in Kelantan. Most Malays lived in villages surrounding the small, dilapidated town centre. The town pushed up against a high limestone cliff which was visible everywhere; a menacing presence, it loomed over the horizon, closing in the view, trapping the light, rendering it all the more claustrophobic.

Maryam and Rubiah got out to make inquiries about Kampong Kedai Lalat and to freshen up before stalking their prey. They entered a small coffee shop half filled with Chinese merchants drinking coffee and eating savoury pastries. The two visitors drank cold soda out of the bottle, afraid to eat any of the food, lest it be made of pork. They felt uncomfortable. In Kota Bharu, they never went into Chinese restaurants. (Actually, women rarely went into coffee shops at all; this was Mamat's turf.) But Kota Bharu was overwhelmingly Malay, and there were plenty of food shops to suit them. Maryam became aware that although she was still in Kelantan, it was not the Kelantan she knew. She was glad for the company of Mamat and Rahman, which somehow (she couldn't explain the particulars, even to herself) made her feel safer.

They left Rahman with the car, and walked towards Kampong Kedai Lalat: an unkempt village on the outskirts of town. The paved road gave out quickly after downtown, becoming cratered dirt. It would be hellish driving; even walking required a good deal of attention. They passed an anemic market selling small heaps of vegetables and fruit past their first blush of youth. A meat stall displayed a few joints of goat covered in flies, and some *ikan bilis*, dried anchovies, in a disorderly pile on a slab of wood. Maryam and Rubiah exchanged horrified glances.

Kedai Lalat was surrounded by vegetable plots, oil palm and rubber plantations. When they saw the mosque they peeked in to see a few older men relaxing in the forecourt. It was a small wooden building painted white with green trim, with a hand painted sign in Arabic script announcing "Prayer Room Kedai Lalat."

"This must be it," Rubiah said doubtfully.

Mamat walked in and began talking to the men, all of whom began explaining something with great enthusiasm. Maryam and Rubiah couldn't hear the discussion, but it was just as well. "It's weird here," Maryam whispered to her cousin.

"I told you I didn't want to come," Rubiah whispered back.

"You never want to go anywhere," Maryam countered, and began examining the houses nearby. Most were small and unpainted, maintained as well as could be expected. There were pots of bright flowers set at the bottom of the stairs, and most had lace net curtains in the glassless windows. People tried to make things tidy and even pretty. Unlike Kampong Penambang, the houses were huddled together around a common yard, rather than each with its own. Perhaps there were snakes, and the houses crowded together for safety. Or perhaps they stood together to ward off the encroaching jungle. These were not pleasant thoughts.

Mamat emerged through the door and pointed further down the dirt path. "Down this road." The sun came between the leaves overhanging the alley, providing a bit of shade and flickering shadows when the breeze blew. They fetched up at a large house made of wood with a roof made of tile rather than thatch, which displayed some level of prosperity. They could hear a radio playing Malay pop songs inside. Chickens wandered around the yard, as did three goats who ambled over to examine them immediately, butting softly against Mamat.

Maryam called out a hello from the bottom of the steps, and a neighbor poked her head out of her window. "*Mak Chik* Maimunah isn't here," she offered. "She's at the market down the road. You know; you must have passed it coming in here."

"Selling vegetables?"

The woman nodded emphatically. "That's her. She's got eggplants today. I saw her leave. Do you know her?"

"Not really," Maryam answered vaguely. "But thanks! We'll go and look for her." She smiled, and the woman left the window. "Oh my God!" Maryam hissed to Rubiah. "That market is a disgrace!"

"Well, it isn't Kota Bharu," Rubiah sniffed, "they aren't used to what we have." She nodded complacently. "You can't expect them to keep to the same standards." They came back upon the ragged little market. Mamat immediately hared off to find a coffee shop: even such a small and deplorable *pasar* would no doubt have accommodations for coffee, since husbands had to wait *somewhere*.

Maryam searched for eggplants. Sitting behind a pyramid of them, on a chair made of several folded sarongs, was a woman Maryam's own age, dressed in plain batik with a matching *baju kurung*, long sleeved tunic, her sleeves rolled up to her elbows and a cotton turban over her hair, just as Maryam dressed for the market. She was immediately cheered; this was a woman they could talk to. She and Rubiah bent down in front of the vegetables, examining them.

"*Kak* Maimunah?" Maryam introduced herself. "We're here looking for Faouda: do you know her?"

Maimunah's face clouded. "Who are you?" she asked sharply.

"Do you have a moment?" Maryam looked around, reluctant to speak of this in front of everyone else present. "Could we go somewhere and talk, please?"

"About what?"

"Well, Faouda."

Maimunah rose, and asked the woman next to her to watch the eggplants for a few minutes, and gestured for Maryam and Rubiah to follow her. She walked swiftly and silently back to her house and waved them up the stairs. The three sat on the porch; Maimunah offered neither drinks nor cookies.

"I don't wish to be rude, not at all, but as you see, I am in the midst of work here, and I'm not sure what your business is." She leaned back against the wall and produced her home-rolled cigarettes from the folds of her sarong. She passed them around, and waited expectantly, clearly counting the seconds until she could get back to work.

Maryam respected her businesslike approach: from the turban she wore to the cigarettes she carried, she could have been Maryam herself. Maryam gave the most concise possible explanation of their quest. "...and after the third night," she finished, "one of the musicians was killed, and I understand he took *Chik* Faouda as a second wife. So we're looking for her, to see what it was about."

Maimunah nodded. She relented somewhat, and asked, "Would you like something to drink? I'm sorry I didn't ask before."

"No, no, please," Rubiah said hurriedly. "We can't keep you from your stall. We work in the market in Kota Bharu ourselves, so we know how it is."

"Alright," Maimunah lit her cigarette and passed them the matches. "It isn't a really nice story, though. I've been married about thirty years, maybe?" They nodded: so had they all. "A few months ago, I noticed my husband was acting strange; staying out late, couldn't find him during the day, kept complaining about how tired he was.

"Well, naturally, I suspected something, but I didn't know what to do exactly. I kept a sharp eye on him, as much as I could, anyway, and then all of a sudden, he comes home one night and tells me he's taken a second wife." Her guests both gasped with dismay. It was a middle-aged woman's worst nightmare.

"Now, mind you, my husband is in his fifties, and we have children who are already married. He's getting ready to be a grandfather, so what does he need a young girl for? More kids? We already have five, and my eldest daughter is having a baby."

"Congratulations."

"Thank you. So, he brings home Faouda. I thought she was a nasty piece of work, but, of course, I would, wouldn't I? He tells me he's rented a small house down the end of the road for her and that I should learn to treat her like a sister." She snorted. "Right. He was crazy for her for the first three months or so. Like a buffalo led by the nose: *kerbau cucuk hidung.*

"It was so hard," she said calmly. "He gave her almost all the money every week, and I had to make do with what I earn to feed myself and the kids. He just didn't care." She looked bemused, and Maryam whispered, "I'm sorry." Maimunah shrugged.

"What can you do? You just have to keep going and hope for the best. And I did just that, *Kak*; I kept my mouth shut and waited. And what do you know? He got tired of her, just as I thought he would. One day, he came back here and started complaining: she didn't know how to save money, she didn't know how to cook, she always wanted to go out to the movies, she wanted to have a baby.

"She was a young girl; of course she wanted these things! And you're an old goat, I thought, and have no business having a baby who'll be younger than your first grandchild. But I bit my tongue, as we women often do. I smiled and made him dinner, and he was glad to be back. *Pacat jatoh kelumpur*, like a leech falling back into the mud. He couldn't have been more relieved.

"Two days later, Faouda shows up after dinner and starts yelling at him. All the neighbors could hear! Oh my God! You know, I decided to stay out of it. I had nothing to gain by jumping into the middle."

"That's true," Rubiah agreed solemnly.

"You're right," Maryam chorused.

"So," Maimunah flicked her cigarette over the side of the porch and lit another immediately. One of the goats came by to investigate. "My husband says to her, 'I divorce you with three *talak*.' Three *talak* at once. That's great. I'm happy. And he stomps out of the house right then and there to see if there's anyone around to register it. She can't believe it. She's standing there with her mouth open. What happened?"

Maimunah laughed. "A man his age, how's he going to keep up with her? He's exhausted, and besides, does any man like spending that much money? Especially after he's decided he doesn't want what he's bought." All three laughed at the folly of men and the naïveté of young women.

"She looks at me, like she's going to cry, but there's no sympathy for her here. I told her, 'Go get your stuff out of the house and go back to your parents. I've had enough of you to last me forever!' She pouts for a minute and then I give her a little push to guide her to the door, you know." She nodded, smiling slightly. "That was it, really. By the next morning, she was gone, and the next week I heard she married a musician from Dollah Baju Hijau's troupe. Fast work, wasn't it?" She shook her head, wonderingly. "Is it even legal?" she asked. "You have to wait before you marry again, don't you?" She shrugged. "Well, it isn't my problem. Anyway, she went up to see him in Kota Bharu and I heard the first wife wasn't happy to see her. I'm not surprised.

"I heard in the market…you know. It's big news around here, you can imagine. Everyone's talking. I heard he divorced her right away and sent her packing back from Kota Bharu in only a few days. I haven't seen her, and I don't think I will. It's fine with me. I'm done with her."

Maimunah paused. "You might see her parents, if you want to. They might know more than me. Don't know if they'll want to talk though; it isn't very flattering for their daughter, and they're probably hoping for another husband for her."

"So she's back with them now?"

Maimunah shrugged. "I don't know. I don't care either, as long as she stays away from me. But you could find her mother if you want to: they live on the other side of Kuala Krai, nearer the Kota Bharu road. Kampong Gelap. Just ask when you get there, *Mak Chik* Nah." Maimunah rose, anxious to get back to work. "If you don't mind…"

"Of course," Maryam agreed hurriedly, and rose immediately. "You must get back to work. Thank you so much for talking to us." Maryam and Maimunah clasped both their hands together and Rubiah followed. They walked with her back to the market, where she resumed her spot and dived back into her vegetables.

Chapter 7

THEY DECIDED TO BRING Mamat with them. "You never know," Maryam said firmly, now hot on the scent. "What if we need him? And if we don't, they'll give him some coffee…"

Mamat rolled his eyes. "Is that what I am?"

Maryam gave him a suddenly blazing smile. "No, that's not all you are!"

He laughed, and walked self-consciously behind them. "No, don't turn around! I'm just here. *Kerbau cucuk hidung.*"

"You know, that's just what the first wife said about her husband and Faouda," Rubiah twisted her head to look at him. "But you, at least you're being led around by your own wife. I mean your real, proper wife: it's an improvement."

They approached Faouda's parents' home, set in a more sparsely populated hamlet than the one they'd just left. Fewer trees, and more dust; the houses were farther apart and scrub plants grew onto the road. Nothing blocked the view of vertical limestone cliffs, dotted with vegetation. To Maryam's eye, it had all of the drawbacks of the rainforest and none of the advantages: no shade, no green, but a feeling both ominous and lonely. Maybe she was just too used to the coast to understand living upriver.

It was a smaller house than *Mak Chik* Maimunah's, and its roof was thatched. Maryam judged the inside had two rooms: a front room and maybe a small bedroom. A shed in the back served as a kitchen. Rather than real stairs, it had a ladder leading up to it, and a tiny porch; and on the porch sat two women, their legs hanging over the edge, weaving palm leaf mats. The older one looked up inquiringly.

"Hello, *Kak*!" Maryam greeted her effusively. "We are looking for *Chik* Faouda's house."

The woman narrowed her eyes at Maryam. "Who are you?"

"Us?" she asked brightly. "We're here from Kampong Penambang, near Kota Bharu. Is this her house? I mean, is this her parents' house?"

The woman nodded and stood. "What do you want?" she asked bluntly.

"Well," Maryam bustled over to the bottom rung of the ladder. "You know the performance where the tragedy occurred? That was at my house. For my son's circumcision." She smiled and bridled a bit. Mamat was stunned: he'd never seen her perform like this. Rubiah was not stunned at all. "So, we're helping the police. It's so much easier for people to speak to us," she gestured at Rubiah. "Two *Mak Chik*, you know," she smiled a conspiratorial smile at the other woman: they belonged to the same sisterhood.

"We're trying to find out more about this, and of course, *Chik* Faouda." This was far more polite than she needed to be, since Faouda was a good deal younger than she was, but better to be overly polite than chance an offense. "She married Ghani and we thought it would be best to talk to her. She might know something, or have heard something, isn't that possible, *Kak*?"

The woman stared at her. "You want to talk to Faouda?"

"Yes, I do," Maryam nodded and smiled.

"That's me." The younger woman stood up, her face expressionless. "It's alright, *Mak*," she said to her mother. "I have nothing to hide." She turned again to Maryam, "You might as well come up," she said resignedly.

Mamat made his excuses, and disappeared down the road. Maryam felt it most likely they'd find him at the first coffee shop they passed. She and Rubiah sat down on the porch, which was now full with four women sitting on it. Faouda's mother sat in the corner, slowly weaving her palm mat but listening intently.

"I am so sorry," Maryam began, "It must be terribly hard for you."

Faouda nodded. "Yes."

"What a shock."

"It was."

"How long were you married to Ghani?"

"Not too long."

"Where did you meet him?"

"In Kuala Krai. They were performing, and I met him there."

"When was that? About three weeks ago?"

Faouda shrugged. "Maybe."

"What happened?"

"Happened?"

"Well, you aren't married to him anymore. What happened?"

"He divorced me."

"In Tawang?"

"Yes."

"Why?"

"Why what?"

"Faouda," Maryam was quickly becoming exasperated, "you aren't answering anything. Would you rather not talk to me?"

"No, it's OK."

"Then please help me understand what happened."

Faouda shifted uneasily, squinting into the sun. Her cheeks were wide, with a few shallow pockmarks sprinkled along her cheekbones. Her lips were thin and straight, her chin pointed and her hair pulled back in a tight ponytail. In the morning light, with no makeup, she looked plain, but Maryam could see how makeup would improve her: smoothening her skin, widening her lips and defining her eyes. She'd still have a slightly vulpine look with her small eyes and long nose, but some men liked that.

"He divorced me because his first wife wanted him to, and he was too scared not to listen to her."

Faouda leaned back against the wall of the house and began a litany of complaints about her treatment at Ghani's hands. She hadn't been welcomed, she'd been divorced as soon as she turned up to see him, and (Maryam guessed this was her primary grievance), everyone blamed her for the situation when she felt Ghani was as much, if not more, responsible.

"You know," Faouda said, warming to her theme, "he took me over to his *Nenek's* house, where they treated me like dirt. That isn't fair, is it?" Faouda tossed her head and narrowed her already narrow eyes. "How could I have been so stupid?" she asked Maryam.

"Well, haven't we all been stupid about men?" Maryam replied, and the two other women nodded. "That's just the way it is. You don't have to feel that you've been any worse than any of us. It's just bad luck, that's all. Not stupid."

"I'll get married again," she vowed, glaring at the trees around the house.

"Anyone in mind?" Maryam tried to keep it light.

"Not yet," she answered shortly.

Maryam took a deep breath and asked, "What happened with your other marriages?"

"Is that any of your business?" Faouda asked crossly. "What's that got to do with anything? Or just nosy?"

"I'm just asking," Maryam explained. "I'm sure everything went well, but I don't want to leave anything the police will then want to know more about."

The implied threat hung in the air as Faouda debated what to do. Her first choice would have been to tell Maryam and Rubiah to go to hell, but she rejected that early in her deliberation. She decided it was better to tell this old *Mak Chik* than have police show up. Everyone would talk about that, and she'd had enough of being the most interesting topic in all of Ulu Kelantan.

"My first marriage," she began crisply, "was for two years. We just couldn't agree, couldn't get used to each other. No children, either, and so we decided to divorce. I was what, eighteen?" She turned to her mother as if seeking confirmation. Her mother nodded.

"The second was with *Abang* Yahya. He was a lot older than me, and had a first wife and kids. It just didn't work out. Too old. He was always tired, and didn't want to spend any money. It just wouldn't work for me. Better to end it quickly than drag on something that doesn't have a future, isn't it? That's all. No one's dead, if that's what you're looking for."

Maryam nodded. "The next one should be just right," she said sweetly. "Someone closer to your own age, a nice man."

"Yeah, well I thought it might be Ghani, but it wasn't. What can you do?" she ended on a philosophical note. "I keep hoping. Maybe a widower or someone divorced, like me. I don't think I want to be a second wife anymore. It's just not good for anyone, know what I mean?"

They all agreed fervently. It wasn't good for anyone: not for anyone female, at any rate.

"Good luck, Faouda," Maryam rose to go, Rubiah close behind. "Thank you for talking to me. It's very kind of you. I won't keep you from your work."

Her mother rose and asked, as though it had just occurred to her, "Won't you have something to drink?"

"Oh, thank you *Kak*, but perhaps another time. We can't trouble you anymore!" Rubiah smiled as widely as she could, and she and Maryam ducked their heads, clasping the hands of first Faouda and then her mother.

"Oh, one more question," Maryam asked suddenly. "When did you get back from Kota Bharu?"

"I left right away," Faouda answered quickly, looking at her mother, who nodded and leaned over her weaving. Maryam nodded, and she and Rubiah climbed carefully down the ladder, fearing the humiliation of pitching headfirst into the dirt. Luckily, they made it down without a scratch.

Chapter 8

"**A**ISHA," MARYAM sat with her on the porch of her parents' house, "We know you were there. Why don't you tell me about it?"

Aisha looked tired, like she'd been crying for the past ten days; and perhaps she had. Her hair was pulled back in a severe bun, and she wore no makeup or jewelry. She looked at Maryam and then drew her hand down her face, as if erasing something from her cheeks. She continued to do it throughout their discussion, and Maryam found it unnerving, as though Aisha were slowly taking leave of her wits.

"Where?"

"At the *Wayang Siam* performance before Ghani passed away."

She sat stonily. "You're wrong. I wasn't there. I told you."

Maryam spoke to her as sweetly as she could. "Your brother Ali was seen there, Aisha. Did he have a fight with Ghani?"

"I didn't know," she said petulantly. "I'm not feeling too well, *Mak Chik*. I've been to the *bomoh*, I've had spells and God knows what else, but it doesn't seem to work."

"I can only imagine how unhappy you are now," said Maryam, and she could. If this were her daughter, her beautiful

Ashikin, she'd be wild with worry and helplessness. "It will pass, you know, it always does."

Aisha nodded. "That's what people tell me." She plucked at her sarong. "You know, Ghani was too young to die; he still has small children." She rubbed her eyelids almost absently. "He didn't have a chance to really live yet, *Mak Chik*. And someone else killed him. Not me." She seemed to drift off.

"But Ali…"

Suddenly, she was all attention. "Ali didn't do anything. Why don't you go to Arifin's house down the road?" Maryam tried to recollect who that might be. "The man who plays the gong in the orchestra," Aisha said impatiently. "Didn't you talk to him?"

Maryam shook her head. "Not yet."

"He was always jealous of Ghani. He thought his wife liked Ghani, maybe something was going on. It wasn't though: his wife likes to flirt sometimes, but she'd never go farther than that. And I used to think Ghani wouldn't either. I was wrong, wasn't I? Anyway, he used to argue with Ghani all the time, even came over here once to yell at him."

"Well," she turned to Maryam, "Why don't you ask him and leave my brother alone? I've had enough. I can't even think about something happening to Ali. Just leave it alone, *Mak Chik*, please."

Aisha rose and drifted into the house without a word. Maryam sat for a moment, wondering what had happened to her, when her mother came out the door.

"Don't be angry at Aisha," she said, brushing her hands on her sarong and taking a quick look into the house again. She sat down next to Maryam and produced a cigarette immediately: this was clearly her smoking break. They lit up.

"She's been like this for about a week. I'm afraid, *Kak*, look at her. She's in a fog. I took her to the *bomoh*, I had the *imam* come and pray over her, I don't know what to do and that's the truth."

"It's so hard to be a mother," Maryam sympathized. "When something doesn't go well for your children, you wish you could take their place."

"In a moment," her mother agreed. "Don't listen to what she's saying right now. She's not thinking."

"Is it true that Arifin came to their house to yell at Ghani?"

"Oh, that's true enough!" Her mother laughed softly. "You should have seen it: his wife hanging on his shirt and sarong trying to pull him back to the house, him dragging her through the village. I thought she'd pull the clothes off him.

"It was nothing, you know. Ghani didn't do anything with the wife. That time, anyway," she ended sourly. "Women turned out to be the death of him."

"What do you mean?"

"What do you think I mean? That second wife, she killed him. That was a disaster from the start. Of course she did." She took a deep drag on her cigarette.

"I don't know if it was even a real marriage! She married Ghani so soon after her first divorce."

"I wondered about that," Maryam answered.

Hasnah shrugged. "You see how Aisha mourns for Ghani. She'd never hurt him. Scold him, yes, but kill him? Never." She flicked her cigarette over the porch and rose to return to the house. Her break was over.

Maryam rose too, ready to leave. "*Kak*, one more question, what about Ali?"

She walked into the house. "He didn't do it," she called out to Maryam, "the second wife, or whatever she was, did it. Believe me."

Chapter 9

MARYAM HAD ONLY BEEN back at work for the better part of the morning. Her daughter Ashikin had taken over the stall, and Maryam trusted her business instincts, having trained her herself, yet she couldn't stay away much longer.

"Did you think I sold all our *songket* for nothing?" Ashikin admonished her when she saw her mother arrive just as she was taking down the planks from the stall. "Don't you trust me?" Ashikin was a renowned beauty in Kampong Penambang, small and slender with large doe eyes and thick shining hair. She had delicate eyebrows and a straight nose, high cheekbones and a perfect, dazzling smile. When she was annoyed, however, as she now was, she sounded exactly like her mother: Maryam was amused to see herself so accurately reflected.

Maryam smiled placatingly. "It is my stall," she said as sweetly as she could, climbing up on the folded sarong before Ashikin could get up. "I trust you completely. Completely. But I miss the market. And hearing all these stories about the murdered boy…" She lit her first cigarette of the day, "It's pretty depressing."

Ashikin was interested in spite of herself. "What have you found out, *Mak*?"

Maryam grunted and flicked the ash into her dish she'd put into her lap. "A second wife is a disaster, that's what I found out."

Ashikin leaned against the stall and took one of her mother's cigarettes. "We knew that."

Maryam nodded, and rearranged some cloth while explaining the details to Ashikin: anyone could have done it, and everyone had a reason. Some had more than others, but all were workable.

Ashikin listened intently. "Poor guy. He really screwed everything up."

"Ghani, you mean? Naturally! Have you ever heard of someone taking another wife and it worked out really well?"

Ashikin shook her head. "I hope Daud never does something like that."

"He won't. He's crazy about you! As he should be." Maryam liked her new son-in-law, but felt strongly Daud was lucky to have Ashikin, and she hoped he continued to realize it.

"*Mak Chik!*" The owner of a stall a few feet away strolled up to her, lighting the first cigarette of the day. "Did that woman find you?"

"What woman?"

"There was a woman here only yesterday looking for you. She asked for you particularly."

Maryam was mystified, and shook her head. "Looking for *songket*?"

Her neighbor shrugged. "I guess, I don't know. She asked if she could find you at home and I said maybe, but your *songket* was here. She said she'd be back."

"What did she look like?"

She shrugged again. "Young, I guess, kind of pretty, not too tall. Nice figure, though."

It was Maryam's turn to shrug. "She'll be back if it's important."

The first morning shoppers began trickling into the market, and Maryam and Ashikin bent their energies toward attracting customers and making the first sale of the day, which would set the tone for all sales to come.

"Look at this *songket*," Maryam called out to a woman slowly passing by, eyeing the fabrics lining the aisle. "Beautiful. Look at that work! I've got the colours you want, and the quality, too!"

The woman stopped uncertainly, fingering some of the *songket* sarongs piled invitingly on the edge of the counter. Ashikin immediately whipped open the cloth the woman had touched, displaying it temptingly to her.

"Beautiful, isn't it?" Ashikin murmured encouragingly. "I love that colour myself." The woman laid her hand on the *songket*. "A special occasion?" Ashikin asked.

The woman nodded. "My niece's wedding. I've got to get clothes for a few people, you know how it is."

"Of course, we do," Maryam soothed. "It's the same for all of us, isn't it? You'll like this fabric, and not too expensive. But," she added earnestly, "excellent quality. Look closely at the gold work. Well done, eh?"

"And not too flashy. Very tasteful, this sarong. You've got a great eye," Ashikin said approvingly. "You'll be very happy with cloth like this. Do you want to see any other colours? You can compare." With a deft twist, Ashikin took another cloth and settled it on top of the first. "This way you can really see what you want."

The woman stepped back a step to consider. "Do you think maybe something lighter? More, I don't know, pink instead of more red? Or do you think pink will look too washed out?"

"For you?" Maryam asked. The woman nodded.

Maryam looked for a few moments. "I like the red. More sophisticated. Too much pink is a young girl's sarong. It isn't good for women like us."

The sale was finally made, after much conversation and bargaining. By the time the woman left, the market was packed and had reached full volume. Maryam was completely engrossed in business when *Che* Osman appeared in front of her. For a brief moment, she couldn't quite place him, and wondered at a man wandering around the market alone. It was a rare sight, since Kelantanese believed men had little business sense and invariably overpaid: a man alone in the market was a fruit ripe for the plucking.

Then she recognized the patch on his shirt and his West Coast face with its expression of intent concentration mixed with utter incomprehension. "Police Chief Osman," she greeted him politely. "How nice to see you here. Shopping?"

He made a face. "No. I came to see you."

She raised her eyebrows.

"To talk about the case," he said impatiently. "I don't know what you've been doing." He tried not to whine.

"Well, that's easy," Maryam gave him her full attention, trusting Ashikin to handle everything else. "I went to see the widow and her family…"

"Can we go somewhere else? It's so noisy here."

Maryam shrugged. "Upstairs? You can have some coffee." Maryam had rarely witnessed a male activity which did not include copious cups of coffee.

Osman followed her upstairs to Rubiah's stall, which was thankfully empty. Rubiah smiled at Osman and put out a selection of the house specialties and three cups of coffee.

Osman hovered over the plate of Kelantanese cakes. "Some of these don't look very familiar," he said doubtfully.

"They're good, try them," Rubiah encouraged him. "No one's died yet."

"I didn't mean that," he blushed. "What's this one?"

"*Tahi Itik*," Rubiah laughed. "Go ahead," she urged. "It's sweet!"

He put the rice cake topped with golden coconut cream in his mouth gingerly, and then smiled. "It's good, thanks!" He raised his head and looked both Maryam and Rubiah in the eye.

"Don't worry," Maryam assured him, "Rubiah's my cousin. She's been with me on all our investigating." Now she got down to business; neither she nor Rubiah had all day. "Anyway, you wanted to know what we found out."

He nodded silently and brought out a small notebook and pencil. He composed his face into an expression of both industry and lofty authority, and nodded at Maryam to speak. She began to outline all that they'd done, all the places they'd been.

"But," she wrapped up efficiently, "that still leaves us a lot of people with a decent motive to kill him: two wives, two parents-in-law and brothers, maybe ex-husbands…and there are probably more! And all because of getting married again." She glared at Osman.

"*Mak Chik*, I'm not even married once. Don't look at me like that!"

"Just keep in mind, when you get older, what that can lead to," she warned him. "Look where it got Ghani," she warmed to her subject, but Osman held up a placating hand. She rolled her eyes, but changed the subject.

"Well, anyway," she continued. "Faouda's back in Kuala Krai. She says she went home right away by taxi, but you should check that out." Osman lifted his head from his notebook and looked at Maryam.

"Yes," she nodded at him, "you should have your men check the taxi drivers who go to Kuala Krai and see if anyone can remember taking her, and when. That way we'll know if she stayed up here longer than she's admitted to."

"It could be important," Rubiah added, nodding at Osman and looking pointedly at the pad he held. He began writing furiously again.

"So, we're going to keep looking: I think tomorrow we'll go to see the musicians he played with. There's certain to be gossip." She looked at Osman over the rim of her coffee cup.

"So, *Che* Osman, will you help us out here? Can you send someone to check the taxis? It's always going to be the same people going back and forth to Kuala Krai, heaven help them. What a trip! Have you ever been there?"

Osman shook his head. "No, I've only been in Kelantan for a month or so."

"Well, take my word, you don't want to go. It's so far! And there's nothing there, just jungle and these rocks…" She stopped herself in mid-sentence. She began again, seeking a more diplomatic tone. "Though, of course, I'm sure the people from there really like it. But for someone from Kota Bharu, well, it's kind of…rough."

Maryam stood up to indicate the interview was at an end. "Please excuse me, *Che* Osman; I must get back to work."

"You can stay," Rubiah invited him, "and finish your coffee." And spill the details of your life, she forbore to add, such as why aren't you married yet? What does your mother think about that? She smiled at him, and his defences began to drop. "Have some more cake," she urged him. "Do you need a home-cooked meal? You look as though you might," she said casually. "Here, sit for a minute, and eat."

Maryam thanked Rubiah, and walked swiftly down the stairs to get back to work. Osman stayed with Rubiah and ended up sampling her wide variety of cakes and answering all her questions in commendable detail. He found himself so full, he could barely stagger back to the office.

Chapter 10

OSMAN RAGED AT HIMSELF. He *knew* he should ask the taxi drivers about when Faouda returned to Kuala Krai. He *knew* the wives and their families were the most likely suspects. He was, after all, a policeman, and so far, a successful one. He could have gone to talk to them all himself, but when Maryam informed him she was taking over, he simply nodded and took notes like a schoolboy. And now she was telling him what to do and to let her know when it was finished.

This might be his first major posting, but he was the police chief here and he intended to make it known. He would not be underestimated. He slapped his hand on his desk for emphasis, and then called in one of his men and ordered him to check the taxi drivers going to Kuala Krai. He felt better. He had taken control of his own investigation.

Rahman was hot, tired and discouraged. He was the most junior policeman in Kota Bharu, and always chosen for the least thankful tasks. This morning he wandered amid the chaos of Kota Bharu's small taxi and bus station, looking for a driver plying the Kuala Krai–Kota Bharu route who might recognize the blurred black-and-white picture of Faouda he clutched in his increasingly sweaty hand.

Osman had handed him the fax of Faouda's identity card photo with a flourish, proud of himself for getting it from the Kuala Krai police. "Here it is," Osman crowed, waving it above his head before slapping it into Rahman's palm. "Go and find out who drove her down to Kuala Krai and what day they did it. And if you can't find a taxi driver, start on the bus drivers."

Rahman nodded glumly and walked over to the open square. He looked at the picture himself and found it unidentifiable: at certain angles, it looked like nothing more than blotches of black and gray. He squinted at it, trying to form the shapes into animals or perhaps trees. Finally, he tore himself away from his game and plunged into the crowd.

He began with taxi drivers, identified by their routes painted on the side of their cars. He had found three so far, none of whom were anxious to talk to him and who took a long look at his damp paper and shook their heads. When he pressed them, they shrugged. Most of them were in their twenties and thirties, slightly older than Rahman himself, and they looked at him like amused older brothers watching him play pretend. This did not improve Rahman's mood, and he made several promises to himself to remember these faces and make their lives hell when he moved up in the department.

Finally, luck broke his way. Another driver was leaning back against his car, smoking a cigarette, looking bored and calling out without enthusiasm to passing passengers. "Kuala Krai, Kuala Krai, Kuala Krai: Jeram, Jeram, Kuala Krai."

Rahman reflected that when heard it said that quickly and that often, the syllables stopped making sense and sounded like gibberish. He broke through a knot of people bargaining for another taxi and leaned next to the driver, passing him the picture. "Know her?" he asked. He hoped the grainy photo would be more evocative to someone who'd actually seen her.

The driver looked at it, moving it closer and farther from his eyes to focus it. "Not much of a picture," he commented.

"I know that. Do you recognize her, though?"

"Maybe."

"Maybe?"

"It could be."

"What does that mean?"

"I took some people down to Kuala Krai a few days ago. This could be her."

Rahman's heart leapt. "When?"

"Monday morning."

He was disappointed. Faouda was supposed to have left on Friday. "Are you sure it wasn't Friday?" he pressed.

"Of course, I'm sure. It was first thing Monday morning. Really early, like 6:30. I was just about to go and get some coffee and they came over to me."

"They?"

"She and a guy. They wanted to leave for Kuala Krai right away. That's why I remember them, otherwise I wouldn't. I don't pay much attention to passengers, but it was so early, so I did."

"Did they say anything about what they were doing?"

He shook his head. "No, they slept most of the way. Tired, I guess."

"The guy, an older guy?"

"No, like me maybe. Not old."

"Were they married?"

"How would I know?" The driver was getting impatient now. "I was just driving them. I'm not the religious police. Why are you asking about this, anyway?"

"We're trying to find her."

"What's she done?"

"Nothing, we just want to find her."

"You want to find her for nothing? Well, that's a change."

"Never mind that. Thanks! You've been a great help."

"Do I get a reward or something? I mean, I did help you."

That was true enough: he should have known this was coming. He brought out his notebook and began copying the driver's name and address. "I'll ask my boss," he said resignedly. "We'll see. Thanks." They shook hands, and Rahman trotted back to the station.

Rahman burst into Osman's office, brimming with success. He'd found the driver, identified the suspect and already shredded her alibi.

"Great work!" Osman congratulated him. "This is a big break. Monday, huh? So right after the murder: that really changes the whole game, doesn't it? And another guy. This is a breakthrough." He rose from behind his desk and clapped Rahman on the back. "I'm impressed!"

Rahman beamed. At last, he was being noticed. It would be, no doubt, the beginning of a storied career.

Osman walked straight to the market, but Maryam wasn't there. "She may be at home," Ashikin told him, sitting on her mother's pile of batik. "She's working on your case. Try her there." She was polite, but Osman felt she wanted him to leave: he wasn't good for business. He looked at her for a moment, without speaking. "Go to my mother's house," she urged him, a bit less patiently. "Go on!"

"I'm going, thanks," he said sulkily. Why were Kelantanese women always telling him what to do? He didn't think his mother had much to worry about as far as the women here were concerned: all any of them had done so far was boss him around like a little boy. Even Maryam's beautiful daughter treated him like a raw recruit in a backward platoon. He'd positively welcome seduction and a brush with black magic, but no one seemed interested enough to be bothered. He left the market looking downcast and commandeered a car to take him to Kampong Penambang.

Maryam and Rubiah had planned to go to Dollah Baju Hijau's house in Kubang Kerian on the other side of Kota Bharu, but instead, Dollah came to her.

He smiled at her from the bottom of the steps. "*Kak*!" he cried, "I'm here to help you."

Mamat greeted him immediately on the porch. "Come on up! Have some coffee! So early for you to get over here!"

Dollah came up and sat down next to Mamat, while Maryam disappeared into the kitchen. "I just wanted to help," he explained, accepting one of Mamat's cigarettes, listening for the welcome clink of china meaning coffee was on its way. "I know how hard you're working to find who did this, and I want to make sure I give as much help as I can."

Mamat approved this praiseworthy hope and welcomed the opportunity to chat with Dollah before Maryam and Rubiah took over. He was fascinated by him: this small, unassuming, ever so soft-spoken man held audiences in the palm of his hand. Mamat didn't see it when speaking to him. A nice man, polite, but not magnetic. What happened when he started performing?

"How did you begin as a *dalang*?" he asked. He was looking for some of the spark here in the house that he saw onstage.

"As a child," Dollah began, not at all reluctant to talk about himself, "I just loved watching the plays. My father wasn't a *dalang*: he was just a farmer. But I'd go every night to watch, and make my own puppets out of banana leaves. You know, carved them into characters, put handles on them." He laughed. "I played for my friends where older *dalang* were performing. One of them saw me: he was angry at me for trying to steal his audience. He told me, 'I'll train you. If you're going to play, you might as well do it right.' That was a great thing for me. I stayed with him for a few years and followed him back to Patani. I studied there.

"I play more Thai style, more modern. Sometimes I even add characters from TV. Like Lindsay Wagner. I have one of her as the Bionic Woman." They both laughed. "The Bionic Woman" was wildly popular on Malaysian TV. "In colour," Dollah added slyly. "When I came back to Kelantan, my troupe wore uniforms, green shirts, so we were a team, you know. That's why I'm called 'Dollah Baju Hijau,' Dollah Green Shirt.

"There's a lot of competition between *dalang*, but whenever we have a performing contest, I always win. Why?" he asked rhetorically, "Because people like my style. I try to be funny and entertaining and bring things in that are modern. Some people want to look back to the way things were, but in entertainment, you have to give people what they want. *Ya*, it can be a hard life," he said philosophically, shaking his head slowly, "but I can't imagine doing anything else."

"They say women always chase a *dalang*," commented Mamat.

Dollah laughed, a huge laugh from a small body. "It's true!" he chortled, "It really is. Well, now of course, I'm older. I'm on my fourth wife. Not all at once, though. I've met all my wives at performances. They all saw me and wanted me. Even the one I have now. She was just a girl and her father came to talk to me about marrying her. I never thought about it, just been divorced, you see. I thought to myself, here's a nice little girl. She wants me: what am I waiting for? I think I may be done with getting married all the time. *Ya*, getting older and settling down." He seemed vastly amused by this.

"Some of the spells we use to bring an audience also bring women. It can get mixed up. I always carry some amulets, *Seri Muka*, to make me attractive. To audiences, I mean." He patted his pocket. "I sell them, too, to people who need them." He cast a significant look at Mamat, who blandly looked back. "And women follow an entertainer. I don't know what it is exactly."

He leaned back and stared off into the middle distance. "They like excitement. Someone new who's been around. A voice they like, someone to make them laugh. Romantic, that's it. They like a bit of romance. You see the women peeking in the back of the stage. Not only divorcees—young girls, too." He lowered his voice, "Like for Ghani." He looked disapproving.

"Of course," he added virtuously, "we don't use black magic or anything like that: just spells to draw the audience. We get trouble from the Ministry of Religion when they say we're not Islamic. I say we are! We're Muslims, good Muslims." Dollah was deeply engrossed now. "Our spells and magic have been with us for a long time, since our ancestors' time. We call upon Muslim spirits: *jinn*, everyone knows that. We don't fool around with spirits we don't understand, you know. You must be careful."

Mamat nodded. He was sure they did have trouble with the religious authorities, but it didn't seem fair. *Wayang Siam* was a Malay tradition. He couldn't see anything wrong with it.

Maryam and Rubiah entered, bearing coffee, Malay cakes and fruits. "*Pak Chik!*" Maryam greeted him effusively. She was surprised that he was so anxious to volunteer to speak to her since all her other witnesses avoided her to the best of their ability. She and Rubiah distributed refreshments and then sat down themselves.

"I'm here to help you," Dollah told her with a wide smile. She returned one with slightly less wattage.

"Thank you, *Abang* Dollah. It's so good of you."

He nodded. "I have an idea."

She waited.

"I'm thinking," he said, leaning back. "I don't really know how to say this…"

"*Abang* Dollah, you know you can speak frankly to us."

He smiled. "Perhaps poor Ghani's passing didn't necessarily have to do with his marriages. Maybe it had to do with *Wayang Siam*."

"*Wayang Siam*?" Maryam said blankly. "How would that be?"

"You know, some *dalang* are very competitive. They can't stand another *dalang* being more popular than they are. They're very proud. I don't know if it could lead to something terrible."

Maryam stayed quiet, waiting to hear. So far, it didn't make too much sense.

"I was first chosen to go on a tour of America and England. Yes, because I was the most popular *dalang* in Kelantan, and they wanted me to bring the art to these other countries. But my father asked me not to go: he said he'd miss me, and I couldn't break a father's heart, could I?"

Maryam shook her head, still unsure where this was leading.

"I had to turn it down," he took a sip of coffee and carefully picked out a cake. "I couldn't go. I told the university, 'My father doesn't want me to go. I'm a grown man, but can I break my father's heart?' They understood, and they picked someone else in my place. Well, he got ideas."

"Ideas?" Maryam asked, passing a cigarette to Rubiah and taking one for herself. They both lit up.

"That he was the best *dalang* in Kelantan. He began to believe he was a more important *dalang* than I was. He wasn't, he isn't, I mean, but he's a very jealous man when it comes to me. Could that have driven him to undertake such a terrible deed?" He paused for effect. "I don't know. Could he have, God forbid, mistaken Ghani for me in the dark?"

He shook his head sorrowfully. Maryam was doubtful: Ghani was several inches taller than Dollah, and broader too, but perhaps, in the black of night, an attacker might not have noticed.

"You might want to look into it. I'm not accusing him, you understand; not at all. I just want to make sure you have all the facts in front of you, and that nothing is hidden."

"Thank you, *Abang*."

"Do you know this *dalang*? From Kampong Laut—Hassan. You might want to talk to him and see if there's anything suspicious. I hope not," he said, pious as an *imam*, "but I can't keep secrets in a situation like this."

"Of course, you can't, *Abang* Dollah. It would be wrong. We'll have to go to see this Hassan, and find out what we can. Can you do me a favor, *Pak Chik* Dollah? Can you give me the names of your musicians so I can talk to them?"

He nodded. "Can you write them down now?"

Maryam began taking dictation. "By the way," she said innocently, "did you notice anyone coming to visit Ghani, either during the performance, or maybe afterward? Anyone at all?"

Dollah seemed surprised to have been interrupted in his list of names and addresses. "Well," he stammered. (And did he blush? Maryam thought he might have.) "Well, no. Not really."

Maryam stayed quiet. There was something more here: Dollah was usually the soul of poise.

He began again. "There might have been. Sometimes women peek in the back." He looked meaningfully at Mamat, willing him to remember their earlier conversation. "It's common; they want to see the troupe." This was modesty on his part: for the most part, women looked to find the *dalang* himself.

"Did you recognize anyone peeking?".

"It's dark," Dollah made his excuses, "and, of course, I'm performing, not looking around the back."

Maryam nodded. "I understand, *Abang*. But is it possible you might have noticed either Aisha or Faouda talking to Ghani?"

Dollah thought for a long moment. The silence stretched, but Maryam was determined to have him break it first. "Now that I think of it," he said firmly, having decided to speak, "I think Faouda was there one night."

"Faouda? And you didn't say anything?" Maryam was shocked.

"*Kak* Yam," Dollah began seriously, "I'm not sure, and I don't want to get someone innocent into trouble. If I did, you know, *if* I did, it was early in the evening, before the performance actually began, I think."

Maryam nodded. "I'll ask the musicians. Perhaps they had more time to look around."

"They would have," Dollah agreed.

"And Aisha?"

"What about Aisha?"

"*Abang*," Rubiah took over. Perhaps another voice might jog his memory. "Did you see Aisha at any of the performances? Visiting her husband?"

Dollah drank coffee, lit a cigarette, and stared at it as if he'd never seen one before. At last, he said reluctantly, "Aisha might have come to see Ghani; I think I may have seen her talking to him."

"Which night?"

Dollah shrugged. "Perhaps one of the musicians can remember more precisely. I have such a bad memory for times and such. I wouldn't want to give you the wrong information."

"You've known Aisha a long time, haven't you?"

"Since she was a kid, like Ghani," Dollah admitted. "I know what you're thinking, and yes, I do like her, and she didn't deserve what happened to her. She's a nice woman and a good wife and mother. Ghani was crazy to do what he did, everyone agrees on that. But in the end," he emphasized, "in the end, he was married only to Aisha. I think he learned his lesson, poor kid. It's a shame he was killed just as he began to make it up to her. But the intention, was there, and that's what's really important."

With this sermonette, Dollah rose to leave. "Let me know when you've spoken to the other men," Dollah asked Maryam. "Let's talk again soon, yes, *Kak*?"

"We will call on you, *Abang*, and thank you for your help," Maryam answered sweetly.

When Dollah could no longer be seen down the road, Maryam, Rubiah and Mamat stayed on the porch, not allowing any of the refreshments to be wasted while they debated Dollah's motives for disgorging his information.

"It's strange, isn't it?" Maryam mused, "Dollah's just dropping over to tell us about that other *dalang*. Dollah must really have it in for him."

"Maybe he just wants to make sure he tells you all he knows," Mamat weighed in with a man's perspective. "You know, he wants to be careful, but he can't keep it from you. Like that."

Maryam snorted. "I don't think it's a delicate conscience, if that's what you're saying, *sayang*. It must be something else." She threw her head back and let smoke rise towards the sky. "How do you feel about visiting Hassan, the other *dalang*?" she asked Rubiah and Mamat. "It's a great day to cross the river."

Chapter 11

THE TRIP TO KAMPONG LAUT was a scenic one, requiring a ferry ride across the broad Kelantan River. The ferry was wide and flat, able to carry people, motorbikes and livestock. Maryam, Rubiah and Mamat stood in the corner, next to the ferryman poling them across. The several chickens in bamboo cages squawked wildly the whole trip, drowning out any other sounds and making conversation impossible. Maryam spent the time admiring the strength of the river and its wide mouth, flanked by greenery, looking cool in spite of the afternoon's heat.

A small battalion of motorbikes waited on the Kampong Laut side of the river to pick up passengers. Each got on behind their separate drivers, the ladies carefully tucking their legs to one side holding the seat for balance, and most emphatically not the driver. Here as in most villages, the road was more a series of slaloms around potholes than a straight line, and the driver spent much of the ride with one foot on the ground to balance in the endless curves.

Hassan's house was much larger and more imposing than they'd expected; wider than most of its neighbours, with a solid tile roof and a deep veranda. The back of the house had its own permanent stage, allowing the *dalang* to put on his own performances without waiting for a patron to sponsor him. He must have brought some money back from his tour of America, Mamat mused, admiring Hassan's good business sense.

They called up the stairs, and a small, wiry man came to the door, dressed only in a sarong, holding a cigarette. He looked at them expectantly.

"We're here to speak to *Chik* Hassan," Mamat called up. "Is he here?"

"That's me," Hassan welcomed them. "Come on up."

They trooped up the stairs, coming into a well-furnished living room with obviously new couches and chairs arranged around it. Hassan picked up a short-sleeved shirt and put it on without buttoning it. A little girl wriggled against the doorjamb, and he sent her off to order tea and cakes.

"What can I do for you?" Hassan asked expansively. "Looking for *Wayang Siam*?"

"Well, sort of," Maryam began.

Hassan waited to see what she meant.

"I wonder if you've heard," she looked at him, "about the tragic death of one of Dollah Baju Hijau's musicians." He nodded, and said nothing.

"Well, they were performing at our house when it happened. We're helping the police now, trying to find out what might have happened."

"You know what happened," Hassan informed her. "He was killed, wasn't he?"

"Yes, I know. I didn't mean that really. I meant, who killed him?"

"Why are you asking me?"

Maryam had a premonition she was now on very thin ice, and she tried to think of a polite way to say it. "As another *dalang*, I wondered if you might have heard any gossip, or known anyone who might have had a grudge…"

"You mean, if I had a grudge?"

"No, no, not that."

"Dollah sent you here, didn't he?" Hassan was getting red in the face.

"No, he didn't." Maryam was getting flustered. Had she been led into the middle of a feud between two *dalang*? She shot Rubiah an imploring look.

"No, not at all," Rubiah loyally jumped in. "We're just asking. *Dalang* are such a close knit group, we thought..."

"You thought nothing of the kind!" Hassan leapt out of his seat. "Dollah sent you here to make it seem as though I would kill someone in his troupe! What kind of people are you?"

His wife came in with a tray of cups and cookies, and he gestured for her to go back into the kitchen. "Not for them! Take it back! These people aren't guests; they're coming here to accuse me of murder."

He turned back to his three uninvited visitors. "How would I have anything to do with it? You think I run around Kelantan looking to kill musicians? Are you crazy or what?" He was now in a fury. "What is your name?" he bellowed.

"Maryam," she replied meekly. This didn't seem real.

Mamat moved between Maryam and Hassan and tried to soothe him. "Now, *Che* Hassan, there's no need..."

Hassan ignored him completely. "Maryam," he repeated at a scream. "From where, Kota Bharu? You aren't from around here."

She nodded. Mamat again tried to quiet him, placing a calming hand on Hassan's shoulder. "*Abang*," he began in a soft voice, "please. To talk to a lady like this, my wife, in fact, it just isn't right. She isn't trying to accuse you of anything."

Hassan wrenched Mamat's hand from his shoulder, nearly separating it from the wrist. He turned to him, nearly spitting with rage. "Don't lecture me about what's right, my friend. You have no idea what you're doing here." He turned back to Maryam.

"Get out!" He pointed dramatically to the door. "How dare you come here and talk to me this way? Accusing me of things with no basis in fact. Are you and Dollah trying to plot against me? He's always been jealous of me, but who are you? Have you no shame at all? Aren't you embarrassed?"

They rose to leave, and as Maryam began to go down the stairs, Hassan gave her a slight but well-directed push. "Now go! Get out of here! Go back to your friend and tell him you failed!"

Maryam stumbled down the stairs and landed on her face in the dust at the bottom. Mamat was stunned by this turn of events: he'd never seen this kind of outburst in a Malay household, and he stood for a moment trying to take it all in. He suddenly turned and pushed Hassan hard, back into his living room where he lost his footing and fell back hard against the brand new sofa.

The ring of the open-mouthed and silent neighbors seemed unable to process what they had just seen. Not one of them tried to help Maryam until Rubiah ran down the stairs to lift her up. Her clothes and face were covered in dust. It was in her mouth, in her hair: she tried to brush it off her clothes but it stuck. She began to weep silently. Mamat clattered down the stairs in a fury, knowing it was best to get her out of there as quickly as possible, and he and Rubiah led a quietly sobbing Maryam down the road, tears making wet tracks through the dust on her face.

At the first turn in the road, when Hassan and his neighbors could no longer see her, they stopped and began cleaning her off in earnest. They could still hear Hassan haranguing them, describing her as an old woman from Kota Bharu in the pay of his rivals to discredit him. He, Hassan, would never let that happen. He was a great *dalang*, one who had been to England and America, who went to the university to speak to students. He'd fix her and her *dalang* boss.

Maryam was completely humiliated. She was now filthy, unkempt, her hair coming out of its pins and powdered with dirt, her mouth dry with dust, her clothes gritty and streaked. "What happened?" she sobbed. "What did I do?"

"I think we got into the middle of some feud," Mamat said as he tried to wipe off her face. "I can't believe Dollah would have done this to us on purpose."

"It sure looks like he did," Rubiah said, whacking Maryam's clothes with her headscarf. "I like Dollah, too, but I've got to say, I think we were set up here."

"I want to go home," Maryam tried to get her crying under control. "Everyone on the ferry will be staring at me," she said, and began crying again.

"No, they won't," Rubiah scolded her gently. "You think they have nothing better to do than to look at you? Nonsense! They have work to do themselves. They're busy. Come on," she signalled Mamat with her eyebrows. "Let's go home and you can get cleaned up. You'll feel so much better, and you can forget about this Hassan. Who is he, anyway? A bad-mannered lout."

They began walking three abreast with Maryam in the middle. "We'll walk back to the ferry, *sayang*," Mamat told her. "Are you hurt?"

A bruise was blooming on her arm, and although she couldn't see it yet, she was sure there was another on her leg. "I'll be alright," she said tiredly.

The walk was long and hot, and in spite of what Rubiah had told her, people stared all along the route to see a *Mak Chik* so disheveled. Maryam tried to keep her eyes trained on the horizon, so as not to meet anyone else's, and pictured in her mind arriving at her own house, taking off these clothes and washing off. Looking like a normal person again, instead of one who fell face first into the dirt from the height of several steps.

The ferry trip and walk back to Kampong Penambang was a nightmare Maryam chose to forget. She washed her hair twice when she got home, and scrubbed her face and brushed her teeth with a vengeance.

She silently sat down, now clean and dressed and looking once more like herself, to prepare dinner: carefully chopping the vegetables in the kitchen, speaking to no one. She could not stop picturing herself, a well-upholstered middle-aged *Mak Chik*, flying down a flight of stairs in full view of Kampong Laut. She saw it even more clearly when she closed her eyes.

The rhythmic thunk of her knife drowned out all other noises, but when she paused, she heard a stuttering, stumbling voice at the door, and recognized with a sinking heart it was Osman. Mamat stuck his head in the kitchen door, his face full of sympathy and concern, and asked her to come into the living room: she had guests. She smoothened down her clean blouse and sarong, washed her hands, and ascended with no enthusiasm whatsoever to greet her visitor.

If possible, he looked more uncomfortable than she did. "*Mak Chik*," he began, "I have some news."

Maryam's younger daughter went to the kitchen to prepare coffee, and Maryam sat quietly and listened.

"We have found the driver who took Faouda back to Kuala Krai! And she didn't go on Friday: she went on Monday. He remembers her because she went with a man, early in the morning, around 6 a.m., he said. So, *Mak Chik*, she was here in Kota Bharu when Ghani was killed, not back in Kuala Krai."

Maryam tried to work up some enthusiasm. "That certainly makes a difference, doesn't it?" she said. "She's a real suspect now. And who was the man?"

Osman shrugged. "We don't know yet. But we'll find out!"

Maryam nodded and made herself smile. "Of course!"

"And something else." Now he looked embarrassed, and looked down at his fingers clasped in his lap. "I'm sorry."

"Sorry about what?"

"Well, I don't know what to say."

Maryam was becoming exasperated. "What is it, *Che* Osman?"

"I got a complaint," he said miserably. "From *Che* Hassan, in Kampong Laut. He came to the police station and said you were harassing him, accusing him of murder, getting yourself involved in some vendetta between *dalang*. I calmed him down, and took down his statement. What have you done, *Mak Chik*?" He looked as though he might cry himself.

Maryam closed her eyes, and her feeling of vertigo returned. "I haven't done anything," she said wearily, turning from the

Mak Chik who ordered Osman around with so little effort to a sore and tired woman who needed to sleep. She no longer looked so formidable.

"I just went to talk to him because *Abang* Dollah came here this morning and told me there was some jealousy between them, and that Hassan could possibly have acted on this jealousy."

"You believed *Pak Chik* Dollah?"

"I don't know if I believed him." She was silent for a moment. "I just thought I needed to check it out. I couldn't just leave it alone."

Osman nodded. "It's a shame. You have to be careful. Maybe," he stammered again, "Maybe you should leave some of this to the police, *Mak Chik*. Things might get dangerous. I can't have you getting hurt."

Now she bristled. "I know that. There's been a murder, how much more dangerous can it be? Don't worry about me." She glared at him. "I'll be careful. I'm going to speak with *Abang* Dollah about it too." She stood up, wanting to get this over with. But her manners won out, as they always did. "Would you like to stay for dinner, *Che* Osman? Relax here for a while and dinner will be ready in a bit."

She walked into the kitchen, overwhelmingly relieved to be alone, even if only to chop onions and grill fish. She needed some time to think.

Chapter 12

ASHIKIN STOPPED IN the next morning on her way to the market. "Your policeman stopped by yesterday, and I told him to look for you at home. Did he find you?" she twitted her mother.

"Yes," Maryam said, without looking up from her morning coffee.

"For a policeman, he takes orders pretty well," Ashikin commented.

Maryam smiled a small smile. "I know! He's dying for someone to tell him what to do."

"That'll do him good when he gets married," Ashikin said as she ducked out the door to go to work. She backtracked momentarily. "*Mak*, that woman was by again, looking for you."

"Who?"

"You know, the one who came before, the *Mak Chik* told you…"

"Oh yes. Who is it?"

"I don't know her. But she wanted you. I thought maybe she was looking for *songket*, but she seemed, I don't know, nervous, sort of. Kept her headscarf up high and didn't look like she was shopping."

Maryam thought for a minute. "If she comes again, send her here. I can't imagine who she is."

Ashikin nodded, and bounced down the road, full of energy and good humor, and Maryam morosely compared it to her own state of mind: she had bruises on her leg and arm, she was humiliated and frightened, she'd lost her confidence. All because some guy, some little guy smaller than she was, pushed her down the stairs. The enthusiasm she had for her project evaporated when she hit the ground in Kampong Laut. She could still taste the dust in her mouth.

She should be more determined than ever to solve this crime, she told herself firmly, instead of hiding in her living room hoping not to show her face outside all day. It was unlikely that *everyone* in Kelantan heard about what happened, and it would only make sense to get back to work and interview Dollah's musicians. No more interviewing other *dalang*, she vowed: they probably all hated each other, and maybe with good reason. It was best she stayed out of the way.

Mamat wandered into the living room, holding his own cup of coffee, and sat down across from her. "Let's get going," he said in a determinedly cheerful tone. "Don't you have work to do? Let's go," he urged, "I want to come with you and see what they say. I'll get a taxi for the day, so you don't have to stay out in the sun."

He was trying his best, she knew that. She was grateful to him for pretending he was deeply interested in this and willing to spend the money on the taxi to keep her comfortable. She burst into tears: "I don't deserve this! I'm a meddling old woman!"

"You? Never!" He sat down next to her and put an affectionate arm around her shoulders. "You're running the whole police department here: you can't stop just because someone tried to push you down the stairs. That just shows you're onto something, doesn't it? People get angry when you get close to their secrets, Yam. You've got to expect it: it means you're on the right track." She lifted her head to look at him.

He nodded at her, and put his hand on her cheek. "I think so, you know. I was thinking about it last night, after I got past wanting to wring his neck."

He smiled. "Now, someone with nothing to hide, someone completely innocent, would he have flown into such a rage? I don't think so. He'd just listen to you and shrug his shoulders. The way he acted, Yam—now I want you to think about this—isn't it way out of line? A complete overreaction, wouldn't you say?"

She nodded mutely. It was, of course: Malays did not, as a rule, push people down the stairs, ever. Especially respected *Mak Chik* accompanied by their husbands. Yes, it was strange indeed.

"And," Mamat continued, "going to the Kota Bharu police station to complain? He had to travel there: it's practically a whole afternoon's work. Why bother? Only if you have something to hide," he concluded, looking pleased with his deduction. He leaned back on the couch and took a long drink of coffee. "Yam," he said, looking proud, "you're onto something. You can't stop now."

"You really think so?" She was beginning to feel alive again, although it was just a small jolt.

"Yes." He nodded. "There's something going on here, and you've got to find out what it is," he said portentously. "Though we shouldn't go right back to him. I couldn't take it. Next time it'll be him and me rolling in the dust." He smiled at her, underlining his chivalry. "You want to see the musicians, or you want to go back to Kuala Krai? Which are you up for?"

Before she could answer, Rubiah was up the stairs and ready to go. Usually, Rubiah had to be coaxed to travel anywhere, but she'd made up her mind to support her cousin, and was now unstoppable.

"You're up, good," she said briskly, walking straight through to the kitchen to get some coffee. "Where to today?"

"We were just talking about that," Mamat announced in a raised voice. "Kuala Krai or the musicians."

Rubiah had already heard the details of Osman's visit last night. Maryam's younger daughter, Aliza, had overheard the conversation and reported it without delay to her aunt. Aliza was lively and mischievous, taller than most girls, and graceful. Her wealth of wavy black hair and slightly slanted eyes gave her an exotic Chinese look. Rubiah was proud of her niece for taking the initiative: that girl had brains and courage, Rubiah thought, as well as an insatiable curiosity which would probably get her into trouble.

"Which is it?" Rubiah asked, coming back into the living room. "I think maybe Kuala Krai." This was nothing short of astounding, coming from Rubiah. She gave Mamat a significant look when she thought Maryam wouldn't see. "I heard Faouda was here when Ghani died," she continued blandly. "And besides, I'm sick of *dalang* right now. I need a break, after yesterday."

She shook her head sadly. "What's become of manners, I'd like to know? I've never seen anything like it, and I don't want to ever see it again." She sat next to Maryam and fixed her with a steady eye. "So, what do you want?"

"I'm thinking Kuala Krai again. I don't think I want to talk to anyone with anything to do with…"

"*Wayang Siam*," Rubiah finished for her. "I'm glad, I have to admit. I don't feel like it either."

"I'll get a taxi," Mamat rose.

"No!" cried Maryam. "Let the police drive us. I'm not slinking away like I'm afraid to talk to them anymore."

"Right!" said Mamat. "I'll get the police here to call them. Get ready to go, then."

Faouda was not glad to see them again. They tracked her down at a local market doing her family's grocery shopping. Maryam came up quietly behind her as she considered a purchase of papaya, discussing the rising cost of fruit with the seller. She squatted in front of a hillock of fruit, her headscarf casually thrown around her shoulders, her simple brown sarong with its border of white fish hitched up on her calf, showing her dusty rubber flip-flops.

"*Chik* Faouda!" Maryam greeted her happily. "How nice to see you here."

Faouda swiveled her head quickly, startled to hear her name. Her expression became sulkier when she beheld Maryam and Rubiah standing behind her.

"What are you doing here again?" she asked ungraciously.

"We came to see you."

"Why?"

"Come, we'll talk when you're finished buying." Maryam directed a dazzling smile at the papaya seller, who smiled back and tried to speed up the selling process. Faouda rose reluctantly, shoved her fruit into a plastic bag, and started walking away.

"Why are you unhappy to see us?" Maryam asked with great good humour.

"Who says I am?" Faouda flipped her hair. "I'm delighted."

"Really? That's good. Then why so sulky, *masam muka macam andam tak suka*: as sour-faced as an unwilling bride?"

"I'm not sulking," Faouda retorted, looking even more put out. "I just don't know what you're doing here. Do you like Kuala Krai that much?"

"Of course we do. Now Faouda, where can we sit down and have a nice little chat?"

Faouda stared at her as though she didn't understand what had been said.

"A coffee shop?" Maryam answered for her. "Excellent idea. There are always coffee shops around the market. Aren't you the clever one?"

Looking as though she had just sucked on a lemon, Faouda was led under the awning of a small shed next to the market. They sat at a tiny table and ordered iced coffee with plenty of sweetened condensed milk and some packets of sticky rice. Maryam's mood continued to improve.

"So, tell me Faouda," she said familiarly, after a long restorative sip. "Who's the man you were with in Kota Bharu?"

Faouda blanched and sat silent.

"Come, talk to me, or else you'll have to talk to the police. It won't be as much fun."

"It isn't any fun talking to you, *Mak Chik*!"

Maryam remained positively jovial. "Well, perhaps you think that now, but just wait till you talk to them. You'll long for me."

Faouda sipped her coffee.

"We've had a hard trip from Kota Bharu, and I want to get back there by tonight. We don't have forever." Maryam gained in confidence with every word. She believed she was on the verge of a breakthrough.

"He's a friend."

"A friend?"

Faouda nodded.

"He stayed with you in Kota Bharu?"

She remained stubbornly silent.

"Faouda, I'm asking you a question." She put on her sternest mother voice. "Did you stay with him?"

She nodded unwillingly.

"So you didn't go back to Kuala Krai right away, like you said."

She looked hard at Maryam and then looked at her lap.

"I really need you to answer me," Maryam prodded her.

"No," she said shortly. "I stayed in Kota Bharu for a few days."

"Till Monday?"

She nodded.

"With this friend?"

She nodded again.

"Faouda," Maryam said, leaning back in her chair. "I can't go on this way: I ask a question and you answer with one word or just a nod." Rubiah nodded her agreement and raised her eyebrows meaningfully at Faouda.

"I'm a lot older than you are," Maryam continued, "and I just don't have the patience. Are you going to talk, or not? Because if not, I might as well go back right now." She started to collect her bag and rise.

"OK," Faouda capitulated. "He's my husband now."

Maryam was astounded. "What?"

"You heard me. We're married. We got married in Kota Bharu. So it's totally alright that I was staying with him."

Rubiah nodded. "Yes, it's alright you were staying with him, that's true." Kelantan had very strict laws about unmarried couples being together unchaperoned at all; staying together was out of the question. "But how, when…"

"I knew him here, before I married Ghani," Faouda preened, smoothing down her sarong and tossing her head ever so slightly. "We were talking about getting married; teasing really," she said deprecatingly, "and then I met Ghani."

"That was fast," Maryam said as neutrally as possible.

"Sometimes love is fast," Faouda answered self-righteously. "Anyway, he heard I went up to Kota Bharu to stay with Ghani, and he followed me up there." Her eyes danced: she clearly thought this terribly romantic.

"He was looking for me in Tawang, and someone there told him I'd gone to Kota Bharu to go home. And he found me at the taxi station! Can you believe it?"

"Amazing. He was your *jodoh*: your fated love. Wonderful."

Rubiah couldn't tell whether Maryam was being polite or sarcastic. Either way, it didn't look as if Faouda would notice.

"I know!" Faouda said excitedly. "He doesn't have any children either, so we're both starting together. I mean, it's just the two of us!"

"It is great," Maryam smiled. "Where did you meet him?"

"Oh, around here. You know, Kuala Krai. In town."

"And you knew him while you were still married to that older guy?"

"It wasn't like that," Faouda said hotly. "Not at all. I met him then, but nothing happened. We just talked. And then I got divorced and I went back to my parents' house. Well, you know the rest. Before anything could happen, I met Ghani. But he wanted me, my husband, and he came up to look for me."

"When did you get married?"

"That day!" Faouda said proudly. "That very day! In Kota Bharu."

"Fabulous," Maryam enthused. "A real fairy tale. So romantic." She lit a cigarette. "So you spent a honeymoon in Kota Bharu, did you?"

Faouda smirked, "You could say that."

"And you came home on Monday morning?"

She nodded, and reached for one of Maryam's cigarettes. "Early in the morning on Monday. He had to get back to work."

"What does he do again?" Maryam asked guilelessly.

"I never told you," snapped Faouda. "He drives a truck. Lumber."

"Why are you still living at your mother's house?"

Faouda made a face. "You know how people talk. What would they say if I came back divorced and remarried in the same week? Even you're thinking it, don't deny it. We wanted to keep it quiet, and then announce it in a few weeks.

"He's gone now anyway, driving wood over to Kedah. It takes a while, you know. They drive through Thailand," she leaned forward, confidentially. "Up through Kelantan through Patani," she sketched a map in the air with her finger, "and across to Perlis and Kedah. Very rough driving, so it takes a while." She seemed happy enough to talk now.

"Your mother knows." It was a statement rather than a question.

"My parents know. His parents know. That's all for now, till we get a place to move into. I'm just waiting. I can be patient."

"Marvelous." Maryam smiled at her. "So, you've been divorced and married twice in the past…what? Month, is it?"

Faouda gave her the dirtiest of all possible looks.

"Don't you need to wait three months after a divorce before you're married?"

Faouda rubbed her ankle, not taking her eyes off it. "Is it even legal if you haven't told the authorities about your marriages? I don't know. What do you think?" she asked Rubiah.

Rubiah shook her head. "Can't be," she answered shortly. "Why, if she were pregnant now, who'd be the legal father? It's hard to know..."

"It isn't any of your business," Faouda interrupted, furious. "Just butt out, OK?"

Maryam and Rubiah exchanged skeptical looks. "Tell me, when you were up in Kota Bharu, did you take in any *Wayang Siam*?"

Faouda's face went red, or rather, redder. "You think you're tricking me. Well, you aren't. I know what you want. You want to say I killed Ghani. Well, I didn't. So go look somewhere else."

"I'm just asking if you saw any, that's all."

"No!" She was now as sulky as she had been at the beginning of the conversation. Maryam sighed. It was too much to be expected to cheer her up twice within an hour. She'd had enough of Faouda for one day.

"OK. You're sure?" She and Rubiah prepared to leave.

"I'm sure," said Faouda with infinite bad grace. "Have a good trip back."

Chapter 13

DOLLAH VOLUNTEERED TO gather all the musicians at his house for Maryam's convenience. Maryam suspected they'd already coordinated their stories and didn't want to make it even easier for them. She declined his offer, preferring to see each in his own house, his own environment. She and Rubiah slogged through seven different towns, and in six of them heard the same story. They loved Ghani and couldn't imagine how this happened. His wife Aisha was a lovely girl and they didn't know Faouda, but believed her capable of this crime. They weren't sure if they saw Hassan or any of his troupe, but he, too, could easily have done it. And then they kept their mouths firmly shut.

At the seventh one, where they arrived hot, slightly bedraggled and ready for an argument, luck was with them: they met the one musician who would speak honestly with them. The oldest of the troupe, the one who played the flute-like *serunai*, was a round-faced, affable man, living in a small village not too far from Dollah's. His house was new, made of plywood, and sparsely furnished. His wife was at home cooking, while several grandchildren played under the house, out of the sun.

He invited them in, and showed no signs of the nervousness that plagued all his colleagues. "It's hot out there," he said genially, "you must be exhausted. Come, sit down," he motioned to the couch. He called to a grandchild and gave him some instruction, and then bade his guests relax. His wife excused herself to return to the kitchen.

"Have a cigarette. Have you been to see everyone else?" He laughed. "Oh my, what a day. You must have covered twenty miles!" He laughed again. "What can I do for you ladies?"

"*Pak Chik* Mahmud," Maryam had checked his name before they reached the house, to guarantee she had it right. "Thank you for seeing us." By now, it felt as though they had memorized their lines and were going through a meaningless ritual.

"Of course, of course. It's such a terrible shame, poor Ghani. Such a young man, he didn't deserve to be cut off so soon. And with little children left alone!" He shook his head, sadly. "I'd like to see whoever did this be caught, you know. I really regret what happened. I'm sorry he's gone." He sat quietly for a moment. "A tragedy," he whispered.

"I know," Maryam sympathized. "Did you see anything, *Pak Chik*, anything at all the night Ghani passed on?"

He nodded as he spoke. "There was a lot going on that night. I don't know why that night more than any other, but there you are. You know Ghani and Arifin, the gong player, they don't get along." Maryam nodded. "They argue a lot. Arifin's jealous of his wife and thought Ghani tried to get her away from him. A month ago, I would have said it was nonsense, but after Ghani took a second wife, I'd have to think about it again. Well, that doesn't matter. Ghani was teasing Arifin, and Arifin always takes the bait. They finally had some words, and Dollah told them to shut up.

"Anyway," he continued as Maryam and Rubiah leaned forward, not wanting to miss a word, "During the break, I went down, you know, and Ghani was at the back of the stage arguing with Aisha's brother."

"Was Aisha there?"

"I don't know. I didn't see her, just her brother. But I wasn't really looking around either. I just wanted to take care of my business and get back."

"Did anyone else see them?"

He thought for a moment. "I don't think so. The coffee stalls were against the other side of the field, so you couldn't see from there. There are usually some little boys hanging around the back of the stage looking in, but not during the break, 'cause there's nothing going on. I mean," he said, after brief consideration, "some of the others may have seen it, or heard it, but I don't think the audience would have."

"Could you hear them?"

"Not really, but I could see them, and given all that happened, I didn't really need to hear them to know what the argument was about. Ali, that's Aisha's brother, was furious at Ghani, and Ghani was arguing back, and before I went back, Ali had taken a swing at him. Ghani pushed him away and went back up."

The grandchild returned carrying icy bottles of Green Spot Orange soda and a small bag of cakes. Mahmud's wife came in with some glasses and plates.

"This is such a treat on a hot day," Maryam told him gratefully.

He laughed. "Drink, drink, please!" He took a swig himself and then continued his story. "Ghani came up and sat down, he sat next to me, you know. We always keep a few knives around, you need them to cut things and make repairs. Anyway, one was lying around in the middle, on a pile of clothes, and Ghani got up and put it down next to him. 'Just in case,' he said to me. 'He's really mad.'

"'You don't really think he'd do anything,' I said to him. 'He's a hotheaded kid, but Ghani,' I said, 'you really deserved it this time.' He knew he did, he was sorry. 'I know,' he said to me, 'but I'm going to keep it next to me just in case.'

"I kind of forgot about it, because he didn't mention it again, and after the performance, Ali was gone. So I figured it was the kind of argument young men have: it gets hot very fast and cools off quickly. The next time I saw a knife like that," he said sadly, "was in the ground next to Ghani. I still can't believe it."

Maryam commiserated. "I know how much you feel, a young man like that. Was Ali the only visitor Ghani had? Was anyone else at the performance you noticed?"

"Not to see Ghani."

"Who did they want to see?"

"*Dalang* go to each other's performances, you know, to see what's going on. Steal a few tips from each other, too, no doubt."

Maryam began to feel dizzy. It couldn't be. "I thought Hassan was in the audience that night. Do you know him?"

"Yes," Rubiah answered tersely.

"Yeah, he and Dollah are rivals, though for my money, Dollah's better and more popular. But Hassan got to go to America, and he never lets anyone forget it. He and Dollah argue a lot, but really *Kak*, I don't think Hassan would have any reason to argue with Ghani. Ghani was just a musician. Any argument here would be *dalang* to *dalang*, do you see?"

"How about the second wife, Faouda, was she there too?" Rubiah asked, thinking it would have made the performance pretty crowded.

"Not that I saw. But again, *Kak*, I wasn't looking. Anyone could have been there, but if they didn't stick their nose into the stage, I wouldn't see them. I'm sorry." He smiled.

"No, you've been so helpful," Maryam thanked him. "And now, we don't want to bother you anymore. Thanks again." He waved them out the door, and they walked to the road to find their car. Rahman was waiting for them, melting in the heat. He had retreated from the car to the slight shade of a small outdoor coffee shop and was passing the time gossiping with the proprietor.

"Ready?" He leapt to his feet.

As they climbed into the car, he blasted the air conditioner. They took deep breaths of the icy air and sighed: it was heavenly.

Chapter 14

"**W**ELL," MARYAM TOLD OSMAN, "You aren't going to believe this."

"You may be right," Osman said without enthusiasm. She seemed pretty cheerful, he had to admit. He leaned back in his chair behind his desk at the police station, and Maryam recounted all she had found out from Dollah's troupe. Osman was fascinated by it all. "So, Ali was there," he mused, stroking a nonexistent moustache. "Well, that's something. What about the second wife?"

"That's more complicated," Maryam said sadly, wishing the whole case were more straightforward, and she could solve it right now. "She's married again."

"What? How?"

"Right here in Kota Bharu. Do you know," she looked at him sternly, and he secretly quailed, "she's been divorced and married twice in just a month? Can you believe it? What wouldn't she do?" She tightened her lips in disapproval. "And, guess who else was there?"

"Who?" he said dejectedly.

"Hassan!"

"Hassan! The one who came here to complain, that Hassan?"

"The very same. Think about it. All his complaining about me, and pushing me down the stairs, and he was there! I think it's very suspicious."

"Very strange indeed," Osman said, sitting up straight.

"He must have been sure that no one saw him when he complained like that. Because now that I know he was there, what does he really have to whine about? He was there on the night of the death and should be investigated."

"Absolutely," Osman agreed. "Though, of course, we don't know if he stayed after the performance."

Maryam was momentarily nonplussed. "Well, I'm trying to think how to find that out. We've got quite a crowd..."

Osman nodded. "Is that all?"

"Do me a favour," she asked in a businesslike way. "Can you find out Faouda's new husband's name, and where he works? We'll need to talk to him."

Osman nodded automatically. Maryam wondered what, if anything, he did when she wasn't there, but she kept that conjecture to herself. "And also," she continued briskly, "you should send someone to question Aisha's brother, Ali. I can't get to see him, and he might know something."

"Of course," Osman pondered. "He'd have an excellent motive."

"I know," Maryam nodded slowly. "Look, Aisha's not well, she's wandering."

"What?"

"Her wits," Maryam explained. "Her wits are wandering, poor soul. And no one wants me to talk to Ali. So you've got to get him and bring him here. Then we can talk to him here."

"You're sure he was there at the performance?"

"That's what I was told. By several people."

Osman squirmed slightly and blushed. "I don't think I want to bring him here," Osman said uncomfortably, unwilling to disappoint Maryam, yet unwilling to follow her directions either. "It sends the wrong message: we don't just drag people into the station."

He seemed to gain confidence as he spoke. "No, *Mak Chik*, I'll go with you to see him at his house. He'll have to speak to us, he can't refuse the police." He rose quickly, pulling himself up to full height. "I'll get things ready."

Maryam eyed him closely. She thought she might have seen a flash of self-confidence there, a bit of a backbone. "I'll just run over to the market, it's so nearby. Just send someone, if you don't mind," Maryam added graciously, "to get me when you're ready."

She gathered up her bag and left the police station. Why waste time here when she could make sure the stall was all right? She had perfect faith in Ashikin, but maybe she could help out.

The market was busy, and Ashikin had left her seat made of folded batik and was on the floor, working two customers at once. Maryam overflowed with maternal pride: just look at her, she thought. What a businesswoman!

Maryam immediately began handling one of the customers, giving Ashikin a brilliant smile. This customer, a harried young mother with two toddlers, was looking for low-end merchandise: two cotton sarong for everyday use. Maryam opened the fabrics as though she were throwing out a fishing net: they unfurled from their folded state and landed perfectly on the shelf.

"Here are a few you might like." Maryam displayed them with pride. "Good colours for you: red and blue are always nice. Here, look at this pattern: very finely drawn, isn't it?"

The woman nodded and grabbed hold of a wandering little boy.

"I see you don't have much time," Maryam sympathized with a grin. "I'll try to make it easy for you." She picked out two from the several she'd shown her. "What about these? Do you like them?"

The woman ran her eyes over the fabrics. "Nice," she commented. "From around here?"

"My brother makes them," Maryam said proudly. "I only sell Kelantan sarongs here: none of that factory-made cheap stuff. It's not worth buying, you know: the colours fade and the fabric's thin. This one will look just as bright a year from now!"

Her customer nodded vigorously. "You're right. I won't buy those sarongs. They've turned into rags before you know it! And with these two, you can see I can't go shopping all that often."

They laughed together. "Well, how much are they?" she asked.

Maryam named her price: the correct one, plus a little something for bargaining. While they haggled, she wrapped the sarongs in a newspaper, knowing it was harder for a customer to refuse an item she wanted when it was all wrapped and ready to go. She thanked the woman for her business and watched her frog-march her two kids out of the market before they could grab anything off the shelves.

"Sell anything?" she asked Ashikin.

"Two *songket* sets. Pretty good, isn't it? A bridal party, getting married in two months. Took forever to choose the colours, but bought in the end."

Maryam beamed with pride. "Good," she said shortly, imbuing that one word with a world of parental approval. "I'm waiting for the police to come and get me." Maryam lit a cigarette and gave one to her daughter. "We're going to talk to a suspect."

"Wow."

"Wow nothing. I just couldn't get to see someone, so I'm going together with the police. Otherwise, how am I supposed to talk to him?"

"What would the police do without you, *Mak*?"

"Nothing, probably." Maryam was disappointed, frankly, in how little they seemed to have done. Osman often looked as though he hadn't moved a muscle between meetings with her. Maybe that glimmer she noticed earlier would grow, she thought charitably, and Osman would begin working on his own.

Suddenly, a woman appeared in the midst of milling shoppers, walking swiftly down the aisle of the market, looking neither left nor right, paying no attention at all to the fabrics heaped on either side of her. Just as Ashikin had described her, she had draped a white chiffon headscarf over her head, with the flowing end held over the lower half of her face, eyes locked on Maryam as she approached.

"It's her!" cried Ashikin, nudging her mother in the shoulder. "That's the one I told you about."

Maryam jumped off the stall shelf to stop her as she walked by, reaching out her arm and saying, "I'm *Mak Chik* Maryam. Were you looking for me?"

The woman stopped and looked intently at Maryam, saying nothing. She almost began to speak, then abruptly stopped herself, glared at Maryam with what looked like hatred, and continued her march out of the market.

"What was that?" Maryam asked, confused and maybe a little frightened. "Did you see the way she looked at me? I don't even know her."

"That was strange," Ashikin agreed. "What did she want?"

Maryam shook her head, and continued to look out the entrance to the market as if following the woman, who had already melted into the chaos on the street. There were a great many strange people walking around, she thought, and why any one of those would seek her out especially was a mystery. "Does it have anything to do with Ghani?" she mused to Ashikin.

"I can't imagine," Ashikin replied, lighting a cigarette for each of them. "She was odd, that's for sure." She tried to keep her unease out of her face, where she knew her mother would immediately spot it, and turned away towards the crowd of shoppers, distracting herself from the woman and what it might mean.

Maryam, too, dived back into her work, fearing to upset Ashikin if she reflected on who it might be. Perhaps another message for her, silently ordering her to leave the case. Such a strange way of sending it. Glancing at the door, she saw a young policeman jogging uncertainly down the aisle towards them. "Here's my date," she told Ashikin jauntily, and went to meet him.

Chapter 15

MARYAM ONCE AGAIN arrived in Tawang, this time accompanied by the chief of police. She felt quite professional, and oddly excited. "*Kak* Hasnah," she called from the bottom of the steps. Osman stood quietly next to her.

Hasnah appeared at the doorway, her eyes widening when she saw Osman in his uniform. "*Kak* Maryam," she said slowly, her eyes moving back and forth between Maryam and Osman. "Please, come in and get out of the sun."

Osman carefully untied his policeman's shoes at the top of the stairs and sat next to Maryam on the porch. "*Mak Chik*," he introduced himself, speaking slowly and clearly, "I am Osman, the Chief of Police in Kota Bharu."

"Ah," said Aisha's mother, nodding. "I see."

He smiled his most winning smile. "You know *Mak Chik* Maryam is helping us…"

"Coffee?" Hasnah interrupted, and leaned into the door to order one of her children to prepare something. "Yes?" she returned to Osman.

He smiled again, tamping down his impatience. Village life had its own rhythm, and there was no use trying to rush it. "I am here with *Mak Chik* Maryam. She is working with us." Maryam was proud to hear it put so officially. She looked approvingly at him.

"So," he continued, "we'd like to speak to Ali."

"Why?" she asked Maryam in rapid Kelantanese. "What does he want with Ali?"

"Don't worry, he only wants to ask some questions," Maryam answered soothingly. "Really, it's all for a good reason."

Hasnah sniffed. "I'm not so sure." She turned back to Osman. "What do you want to ask him?"

This is what Osman had feared: people would speak to him and he'd be unable to understand. Maryam rescued him as she saw him hesitate. "Just questions, right, *Che* Osman?"

"Yes," he answered firmly. "I have some questions for him."

The coffee and cakes appeared, and Hasnah appeared to throw herself into serving with a vengeance. "Have something to drink. Please," she invited them. "It's so hot, isn't it?"

Maryam nodded politely. "Yes, indeed." She agreed. She let Osman ask again for Ali, maintaining her own status as a friendly neighbour rather than a member of officialdom.

Ali came slowly and unwillingly out to the porch, clearly resentful. His mother watched him anxiously. "What is it?" he demanded. "Why are you keeping me here?" He saw Maryam and a sour smile twisted his face. "I should have known. Why are you doing this? Is this any of your business?"

"Yes," Maryam answered calmly. "It happened on my land."

"So what?"

"So I want to see justice done."

"You don't think Ghani might have deserved it?"

Osman raised his eyebrows and shot Maryam a quick look. She was more than happy to engage in a philosophical discussion: it made a nice change.

"He deserved something, for sure: believe me, Ali, I'm no fan of taking another wife. I don't think any woman is. But death: don't you think it's a touch harsh?"

"Look at my poor sister."

Maryam shook her head sadly. "Oh, I know. I'm heart-broken to see it. Has anything worked?"

"No," he answered morosely. "She's confused." He paused and rubbed his forehead. "We're all sick. It's as though we've all lost our wits, just like Aisha."

"Really?" Maryam was curious. "Since when?"

Ali shrugged again: now that Maryam looked closely at him, and at his mother, she thought they did look pale, although it could be grief alone. She looked over at Osman, whose face mirrored her own concern.

"A few days. I think my parents are sick because of watching Aisha. They can't bear seeing their daughter suffer like this. Who could?" Hasnah looked at the porch, lost in her own reverie. "Aisha's not here now. She's at Ghani's parents," Ali added.

Maryam shook her head in sympathy. "I can't imagine. You know, time may help. It may be the only thing. And she's still very young. She could remarry."

"Or she could spend the rest of her life wandering around the house with only half a mind."

Hasnah rose abruptly and walked into the house, clearly unable to listen to the conversation. Osman watched her go with a concerned frown.

"I hope not," Maryam shuddered. "It's too sad to think about."

"Well, she's my sister, so I've got to think about it, don't you see? That's why I argued with Ghani."

"I understand, but by then, he'd already divorced this girl and was back with your sister. And sorry, too, I heard."

Ali nearly spat. "Sorry! That's really nice. He broke Aisha's heart, and I wanted him to know it."

Maryam nodded encouragement. "And what did he say?"

Ali's shoulders slumped, and he suddenly looked tired.

"Some coffee, Ali?" she asked. He nodded. She poured him a cup from the tray in front of them, and he sipped it thoughtfully.

"Where were we?" She affected forgetfulness and Ali eyed her suspiciously. "Ah yes, what Ghani said to you." She settled back for the story.

He squirmed for a moment and then began talking. Amazing the power of mothers, Maryam thought. An older woman could command most younger men with just a stern look. It was perhaps the only benefit for a woman getting older. Of course, it could also have been Osman's quiet but official presence next to her; she was surprised at herself for thinking this.

"First, he started apologizing," Ali began, still sulky but coming out of it. "He kept telling me he agreed with me, it was his fault, he didn't know why he'd done it. He said he loved Aisha and the kids, would never leave her, blah blah blah. He told me he thought he'd been bewitched: Faouda must have put a spell on him and that's why he married her. Then when he came back to Kota Bharu, he was too far for the spell to work and he woke up.

"That's what he said, 'I woke up when I came home, and I couldn't believe it was me who married Faouda. Ali, maybe it wasn't me, because I love my family, and now that I'm cured, it will be fine.'

"'Right,' I told him, 'it'll be fine until the next time, and then the whole thing will start all over again. What are you going to do about it?' I asked him. 'You can't have this happen every time you go away, you know. Why don't you go to a *bomoh* yourself and get a talisman? Or better yet, Aisha can get one to make sure you stay faithful, what about that?'

"That's when he got mad. 'You're trying to have me bewitched all the time?' he asked me. 'I won't have a life of my own? You just shut up about *bomoh*,' he told me, 'I don't want to hear it.' He was shouting by now: scared, I think, that we'd have all these spells on him and he'd be totally in our power. Which is crazy, of course; that's not what I was talking about at all. 'Stay away from me!' he said. 'You're trying to kill me!'"

Maryam sat up at this. "He said that?"

"Of course, *Mak Chik*, he meant you're trying to kill me with spells and sorcery, not with a knife. Because I wasn't: I didn't have one or anything."

"That's quite an argument," Maryam commented. "Was Aisha there with you?"

Ali was silent. Maryam surmised she was, and Ali didn't want to give her away. The silence grew, and Ali realized he'd not spoken for too long to have 'No' be a credible answer.

"You know," he began slowly, trying to see his way out of the thicket, "she didn't have anything to do with this argument."

"She wasn't there when you were talking to Ghani?"

"No." Now he answered promptly, not making the same mistake twice.

"Where was she?"

"Around," he said vaguely. Maryam stared hard at him until he decided to amend his answer. "Look, she wasn't part of the argument."

"Where was she?"

Ali answered with a hint of desperation in his voice. "She was standing a little way away."

"So she heard the whole thing."

Ali nodded miserably. "She did. I didn't want her to."

"What about Ghani?" He shrugged and stared at the floor.

"Ali," she said sternly. "Do you want to tell us, or shall I leave and you can speak to *Che* Osman here yourself?"

Tears came to his eyes. "*Mak Chik*, I made everything worse. I meant well, but I made it worse and it's all my fault." He began crying in earnest.

"What?" Maryam asked, both alarmed and elated at the thought of an explanation at last.

"Aisha heard it all, like I told you, and she tried to stop the argument. And Ghani yelled at her and said, 'I won't spend the rest of my life bewitched by you and your family. I said I loved you, I said I was sorry, and now your brother wants me to just *alangkah leher minta disembeleh*: stretch out my neck and ask to have it cut? Are you going to put spells on me whether I know it or not?'

"'I won't have it,' he said to her. 'Maybe it would be better if I just left. I can't live like this.' And he pulled his arm away and ran back to his drums. She stood there crying into her hands, and I knew it was all my fault."

"Oh my God!" Maryam was at a loss. No wonder Aisha was so beside herself.

"She was so angry at me," Ali sobbed. "She said I'd ruined her life. I'd made her children fatherless. Why did I even get involved, she asked me? She sat on the ground in the back of the stage and just cried. I was ready to do anything to make it better, *Mak Chik*, you must believe me."

She nodded. "I do. What happened next?"

"She wouldn't leave," he wiped his nose with his sleeve, and tried to dry his eyes. "She told me to get away from her. By this time, the break was over and the performance had started again, so she couldn't go in and talk to him. Besides, I don't think he was ready to talk to anyone right then. I told her she should just go home and talk to him tomorrow, but she started hitting me. So I walked to the front and tried to watch. I couldn't go home without her, *Mak Chik*. I couldn't leave her there."

"Of course not," Maryam agreed, passing him some paper napkins from the tray. "Here, blow your nose." She waited until he was finished. He looked like a woebegone five-year-old. "So when did you leave?"

"Not for a while."

"For a while?"

He wiggled again. Finally, the truth, she thought. "Not till after the performance ended. Aisha tried to talk to him."

"What did he say?"

"She said he told her to leave him alone. That he'd divorce her if she went to the *bomoh* and put a spell on him. He said they could talk when this run was finished. She was crying and crying. I took her home on my motorcycle." He looked miserably at Maryam and Osman, his eyes moving from one to the other. Osman now seemed a strangely sympathetic presence, and Maryam could see how people might open up to him, once he could understand them. "I walked it out to the main road so it wouldn't wake anyone."

Osman smiled kindly, as though he had just heard what he'd been waiting all his life to hear. "Thank you, *Che* Ali," he said calmly, rising slowly from the porch. "You've been a great help." He touched him briefly on the shoulder, a small but strangely comforting gesture, and with that, he was down the stairs, waiting for Maryam at the bottom.

Chapter 16

MARYAM LEFT HER HOUSE early the next morning, even before the children had gone to school. She was completely exasperated: as her investigation progressed, she seemed to add suspects rather than eliminate them. With every step, she seemed to be farther from a conclusion.

Something wide and flat seemed half buried under the stairs, and she bent over to throw it away. It wasn't that big, true, but some poisonous snakes weren't that big either, and she wasn't going to provide camouflage for them. "Goodness!" she cried. Her middle finger was bleeding, punctured by a spiny thorn, deep and clean. She pulled out the whole package, and picked it apart gingerly.

She found a spine which she thought might be from an *ikan keli*, a poisonous catfish, stabbed through the head of a crude wax figure of a woman. A rolled paper with drawings on it, a spell no doubt, ran through the figure's torso. Nails were driven into the doll, through the head, chest, arms and legs and, of course, the poisonous spine through the forehead. It was wrapped in a white shroud, covered with a broad banana leaf.

She examined it blankly at first, then with mounting horror. It was an evil spell, perhaps even a death spell. The wax

figure was clearly meant to represent her, to add *jampi* as supernatural assistance to the more practical poisonous spine. She
felt a sudden prick of fear: was the poison active and even now
coursing through her blood?

She looked up at the stairs, thankful that it was she who
found it, rather than her children. She tried to stay calm.
"Mamat!" she cried.

He came calmly to the door, holding a cup of coffee.
"What?"

"I…I think I've found a *jampi* under the stairs," she began.
"A spine from an *ikan keli*," she ended vaguely. Her head was
beginning to pound, whether from fear or a poison, she didn't
know. Maryam bent over and closed her eyes, tamping down the
panic rising within her. "It's all in my head," she told Mamat,
who was now next to her holding her arm. "I'm imagining it.
There's nothing wrong with me."

She opened her eyes to find herself stretched out on the
ground with Mamat leaning over her. "Don't worry, *sayang*," he
told her, "Aliza's getting a taxi right away." He ran his hand over
Maryam's forehead; it felt cold to Maryam, like cool water over
hot sand.

"What is it?" she murmured to Mamat, "Poison? Black
magic?"

"Never mind," Mamat told her. "Here's the taxi. Rubiah's
here, too." He tried to maneuver her upright, but Maryam
seemed slippery, without strength. "Come on, Yam," he urged,
"try to get up."

She was dizzy, unable to focus: her legs felt weak and
rubbery. They half-dragged Maryam to the car, while Aliza
stood at the taxi door sobbing. "Don't worry," Mamat told her as
they got in. "Get Yi to school and you, too. It will be fine." They
were gone in a moment.

It seemed hours before they pulled up in front of the
English Doctor's dispensary; Maryam now slurred her words
and her eyes drooped. Rubiah restrained her own dread, and
Mamat concentrated only on getting Maryam in front of a

doctor. Rubiah ran forward to the receptionist, "Please! We need help immediately! Hurry!"

The girl had never seen a *Mak Chik* in such a state. She whisked Maryam into an examination room, where a middle-aged English doctor and a Chinese nurse bent over her solicitously.

"What happened?" asked the doctor, shining a light into Maryam's eyes.

"This." Rubiah offered him the bundle. "She pierced her finger on this spine. *Ikan keli*, do you suppose? Is it poisonous?"

The doctor examined the spine very carefully. "It looks like it. We see some fishermen in here occasionally with these. Painful. Very rough."

He listened to Maryam's quick breathing. "*Mak Chik!*" he called out. "*Mak Chik*, can you hear me?"

Maryam opened her eyes lazily, looking at him without focus. "Yes, I hear you," she said softly.

"Excellent," he pronounced. He turned to Mamat. "She's very lucky the spine's dried out a bit. Less harmful. Still, painful. Who did this?"

The doctor's rapid-fire delivery distracted Mamat. "I don't know. She found it under the steps to our house." He thought for a moment. "Thank God neither of the kids picked it up," he breathed fervently.

The doctor nodded and prepared an injection. "This will keep her going. Energy. Very important in cases like this. I think she'll be all right, but we'll keep her here for a while. Let her sleep. Keep an eye on her. Has enemies, does she?"

Mamat looked doubtful at first, and then increasingly uncomfortable. "I don't know. Maybe. I mean, enemies who would do this?" It seemed clear she did; he frowned and considered the question.

Rubiah commandeered a pair of scissors and cut off a long lock of her hair, twisting it into a bracelet of sorts. She tied it tightly around Maryam's injured finger. The doctor raised his eyebrows.

"It will get rid of the poison," she stated firmly. "I learned it at home."

"Interesting," the doctor murmured. "Does it often work?"

Rubiah shrugged, her eyes on Maryam. "I don't know," she answered vaguely, "I never had to try it before." She paused. "It's supposed to." She fervently prayed it would: she couldn't imagine her life without Maryam.

Mamat stayed with Maryam in the back room of the dispensary until past noon, never letting go of her hand. She held it with all the strength she had left, afraid she'd be lost if that anchor slipped away. Mamat's presence alone calmed her, made her believe she would live.

Later at home, sipping tea in bed with a relieved Aliza curled up next to her, Maryam tried to get past her fear. "Do you think Ali left it here?" she asked Mamat. "He seems really interested in *jampi* and things like that: he even got into a fight with Ghani about it. Maybe he knows too much about it," she considered.

Mamat sat at the foot of the bed, with Yi leaning back against him. "You just talked to him yesterday, didn't you? It seems too quick for him to get to work on this."

"How much work does it take?" Maryam asked him. "One visit to the *bomoh*, that's all."

"Someone's thought about this a lot," Mamat mused. "Yam, I'm worried."

Maryam looked over at Aliza's wide eyes. She smiled at her and at Yi, clutching his father's arm. "I'm fine now, don't worry." She patted her daughter's shoulder. "See? Nothing to be frightened of." She gave Mamat a meaningful look, which he understood immediately. It was their job to calm and comfort their children.

"Right!" he said heartily. "It isn't easy to hurt your mother!" He moved Yi away from him and waved at Aliza. "Hey, it isn't a holiday, you know! School tomorrow!" He overruled their murmured protests. "We all need a rest here, and the main thing is, everyone is alright. Why, *Mak* is going back to work tomorrow…"

Maryam nodded enthusiastically. "Of course! I'm fine now! Go, as your father says." She hugged them both close and smiled broadly as they left the room, looking nervously behind them. "I'm fine!" she repeated.

When they'd left the room, she fell back on the pillow and her smile faded. "Yam," Mamat asked in an urgent whisper, "what if it had been Aliza or Yi who picked it up? Then what? Whoever left it doesn't care who it hurts as long as it stops you from investigating."

Maryam nodded. "I know." She took a long sip of tea. "That's why we've got to find out who it is. It's personal now, Mamat, and I won't feel safe until it's over."

Chapter 17

THE NEXT MORNING, Mamat left early for the poultry market and returned with two large white geese. Geese were superlative watchdogs, loud as baying hounds and nasty as Rottweilers. No one would sneak quietly into their yard with geese on patrol. The two birds instantly tried to bite him as soon as he freed them from their wicker cages, even though he'd just offered them food. They were perfect.

Several minutes later, they began an ear-splitting racket, honking and hissing, flapping their wings and generally sounding the alarm. When Maryam looked out the kitchen door, she saw Dollah and Arifin trying to maneuver around them and approach the house. She smiled grimly: there would be no more ambushes.

She invited them up into the living room and performed the coffee ritual without thinking. Rubiah joined them, and Dollah leaned back in his chair after cigarettes were lit all around.

"How sad," he began. "I never thought a day like this would ever come. An evil *jampi*! I can't believe it!" He shook his head, and looked well and truly unhappy. "I've never imagined this kind of thing in Kelantan. In our own place.

"What's the world coming to?" he asked rhetorically. "Grown men throwing women down the steps," Maryam began to blush, "people leaving evil spells under the stairs. What next?" He looked mournful. "I'm ashamed, I really am." He took a sip of coffee and appeared to consider what to do next.

"So I've brought some of these boys here to talk to you, to help your investigation. Arifin, Din, Awang," he continued, turning his head to look directly at them as he introduced the women. "I know you've already met them," Dollah explained ruefully, "but we all want to help, don't we?" They nodded dutifully. Dollah leaned back with the expression of a man who has gone beyond the call of duty for a good cause.

Dollah had brought the men who were of an age with Ghani, the most likely to be closest to him. Also perhaps the most likely to be jealous of Ghani's looks, if Aisha's theory had any basis, but Maryam could not credit any of Aisha's perceptions at this point.

Arifin turned towards Maryam and Rubiah with a completely open expression. "Yes, *Mak Chik*. What would you like to know?"

"I understand, *Che* Arifin, you've fought with Ghani."

"Yes, in the past," he answered calmly. "We were accustomed to arguing, you know how it is, and so we kept it up. If I'd ever suspected, for even one minute, he would meet such a terrible and undeserved end, well, I never would have said one angry word to him. Never."

"When did it start?" she asked Awang. He looked surprised to be called upon, but manfully volunteered.

"You mean, Arifin? It was after Arifin was married." Arifin examined his fingers intently, and Awang studiously looked away from him. "He thought Ghani was flirting with his wife, and he didn't like it."

"Was he?"

Arifin squirmed. "I guess not." He took a deep breath and looked soulfully into Maryam's eyes. "No, let me be perfectly honest. There was nothing going on. But I let my jealousy get the better of me. I'm definitely trying to stop thinking that way. And of course," he added piously, "this tragedy has made me determined never to be that way again."

It was hard to credit this level of earnestness. Maryam tried again. "Awang, are you also from Tawang?"

He nodded, as did Din. "Did Ghani know your wives also?"

They looked nervous. "Well," Awang began, "of course, we all knew each other."

"Were you jealous of Ghani, too?" she asked gently.

The boys took deep breaths, as though this would be a long explanation. Dollah leaped into the breach. "*Kak*, you know how young men are! Hot blooded, like fighting cocks, right?" He smiled at her and Rubiah, three wise older people, amused at the foibles of the young. Maryam nodded.

"So, were you?" she insisted.

Awang shifted his seat, and then began. "Yes, I admit it. It was hard not to be." He was now on solid ground, and looked like a choirboy. "You know, I'm so sorry about that. I wish it wasn't true. But, you never know when death is staring you in the face, do you, *Mak Chik*? I wish I hadn't. I can never make it up to Ghani." He sighed repentantly.

"Was there a fight that night? Teasing that got out of hand?" She looked at them sympathetically, as their own mothers might, looking for an innocent explanation.

Din clearly felt it was his turn to take the floor. "That night there was some argument, well, not an *argument* so much as… yes, teasing as you said, *Mak Chik*, out of habit, really, nothing meant by it." He swallowed and widened his eyes. "Ghani had his knife next to him while he played, you know. Ali, do you know of Ali, *Mak Chik*?" Maryam nodded. "He was there before, and they had a real fight, yelling and pushing. He was afraid Ali would come back again: Ali might have threatened him! I can well believe that." He nodded forcefully, offering Maryam the fruit of his extended meditation on this topic.

"I'm ashamed to say I didn't reach out to help him. Could I, we, have saved him?" Din continued, his expression angelic. "I don't know, *Mak Chik*. I regret it, I really do. I should have fought with Ali and protected Ghani; we should never have let our friend be treated in that way. And maybe…" He appeared to choke up here, and Awang quickly interjected: "Maybe even *killed!*" Awang lowered his voice on the last word.

"But *nasi dah jadi bubur*: the rice has already become porridge, what is there to be done? If I could undo it, I would." All three murmured in agreement, and Dollah nodded approvingly.

"Being jealous, you mean?"

Arifin slumped his shoulders to signify loss and dejection. "All of it, *Mak Chik*," he said gravely. "My jealousy, arguing with my wife about it, arguing with Ghani. I can only make it up going forward," he said with almost religious exaltation. "And that's what I intend to do." Din and Awang reiterated his intentions in very similar words, stressing the fundamentally brotherly nature of their relationship to Ghani, as well how worthless was jealousy as a motivating emotion.

Dollah was smiling beneficently, clearly enjoying the performance, perhaps having even directed it. These boys had been coached, and coached well, but Maryam doubted one word was true. She looked over at Rubiah, and read from her expression she was thinking the same thing. They were silent for a long moment.

"I had no idea you were such wonderful actors, children. Really wonderful. Is that the end of your performance, or is there more?"

They all affected amazement: "What do you mean, *Mak Chik*? I'm no actor," Awang insisted, blushing slightly.

"Don't underestimate yourself," Rubiah told him approvingly. "You were excellent. Thank you for coming: it's a treat to start the day off with a show like that."

"What are you saying?" Dollah asked, his face a mask of virtue.

"*Abang* Dollah, this is not helping me. Perhaps it's my fault," Maryam said graciously. "I'm sure it is. But perhaps, boys, we can see you some other time? Would that be alright?" Her smile dripped sincerity: she too could play at this.

"Well, I guess." "Sure." "Of course, *Mak Chik*." They each stammered their assent, unprepared for her request. "Yes, it would." "I mean, it would be fine." "Yes."

"Good!" Maryam stood up with her best hostess smile. "I know you have so much to do. More coffee? Have some more cakes! I insist."

Dollah looked confused, and a bit put out. There was, however, nothing overt to complain about, so they ate their cakes and drank their coffee while Maryam and Rubiah made bright, brittle small talk.

"Mamat," Maryam asked him after the children were asleep, "do you think there's something strange about Dollah?"

"Strange how?" He listened with half an ear only, reading the paper as he spoke.

"I don't know exactly. I mean, I hate to think he'd be, I don't know, threatening."

"What?" Mamat was still perusing the sports page; Kelantan's soccer team had recently trounced Perak, and he could not read enough about it.

"Do you think he killed Ghani?"

Now she had his attention. "What?"

"Well, it's like this. He's been volunteering all this information, even coming here to give it to me. But it isn't the whole story: he leaves things out, he doesn't tell me things I need to know. And he's actually used me to get to Hassan."

"Isn't that a little severe?"

"Is it, Mamat? Think about it, all right? He sets me up to see Hassan, and I get thrown out on my face." She still shuddered to think about it. "Then we get the *jampi* under the stairs. Now I know Hassan would be able to do that himself, without using a *bomoh*…but so would Dollah. And he's made so much of how Hassan could have mistaken Ghani for him in the dark: well, doesn't that mean he could have mistaken Ghani for Hassan the same way? What if he wanted to kill Hassan? And it went terribly wrong? I think Dollah's trying to guide me to his own conclusion, and he's working pretty hard to do it."

Mamat stared at her. "Are you serious?"

"Never more than I am now. I'm playing for my life."

Mamat nodded, and tried to take it all in. "I always liked Dollah. I have a hard time thinking of him putting down that *jampi*, not caring who might pick it up. But I don't know. You may be right." His brow uncharacteristically furrowed, he thought further. "It's just that I..." His voice trailed off. He began again.

"It's just that I'm frightened by this, Yam. If we were to trust the wrong person, and were led down the wrong road, then we could be in real danger."

"That's what I'm saying, Mamat. A wrong move could kill us. Really." She put her head in her hands. "I hate this. I wish I'd never heard of any of these people. I've got to clear this up as soon as I can, before something else horrible happens." She rose from her chair as if to do something, but instead looked around, almost confused. She opened her mouth as if to speak, but decided against it. Mamat stood next to her and wordlessly stroked her hair, putting his forehead against hers.

Without speaking any further, they went to bed.

Chapter 18

Maryam arrived home the next afternoon to find Mamat and their village *bomoh* working around the house posts. Mamat stood up and smiled when he saw her. "You're home. I'm glad." Their *bomoh*, a wizened old man, smiled up at her as he dug a small hole in the ground.

"What are you doing?" she asked.

"Protecting us," announced Mamat proudly.

"How are you doing that?"

"Just like someone left an evil *jampi* under the stairs, we're putting protective ones all around the house." He put up his hand as she started to speak. "Yam, don't argue with me. Someone's tried to kill my family. I think whoever it was might try again. I'm not taking any chances: as you said, it's personal now.

"I even have something for you to wear." He held up a small yellow cotton cloth, covered in Thai letters written in black ink, interspersed with spidery designs and the outline of a woman.

"Keep it on you all the time," the *bomoh* advised her, burying a similar cloth and covering it carefully. "It will help you resist black magic used against you."

Maryam nodded and smiled. Like most of her neighbours, she believed in the supernatural, but not so devoutly as to wear protective spells. Still, she'd had a narrow escape and was lucky to be alive, and this was not the best time to do without protection. She tucked it into the folds in her sarong and went in to prepare dinner.

"We found Faouda's husband," Osman told Maryam, sitting in her living room later that evening. Dinner was over and Aliza and Yi were sprawled on the floor watching "Rawhide" on television, while Osman's plate was heaped with a hearty dinner.

His announcement re-energized her. "Who is he? Where is he?"

Osman dug into his meal. Maryam reckoned he must be hungry: God only knew what he ate when he was on his own. Cold curry wrapped in banana leaf, most likely. She waited until he had swallowed, drumming her fingers on the table nervously.

"I got the information from the registrar's office," he said proudly, "and then from the Kuala Krai police."

"Excellent work," she assured him. "It's very impressive."

"Well," he was obviously pleased with himself and with her praise, "his name is Johan bin Awang—why is everyone here named Awang?—and he lives in Kuala Krai. Been married," he read from a paper he'd taken out of his pocket, "divorced, no kids." Faouda had told her the truth about that at least. "Truck driver," Osman continued, "Works for a lumber company and does long distance hauls, mostly to the West Coast through Thailand. No police record, no trouble. Malay," he finished reading the identity card information.

"Of course, he's Malay; honestly," Maryam chided him. This was Kelantan, after all. "And they were married on that Friday?"

He nodded. "Yeah, they were, in Kota Bharu like she said."

"Do we know where they stayed in Kota Bharu?"

Osman shrugged. "Not yet, but when we talk to him I'm sure we'll find out."

Maryam nodded. "Are you going to bring him up here to talk to him? I'm sick of Kuala Krai. Don't make us go down there again."

"Too hot?" Osman teased her.

"Too hot, too far, too much jungle. Can we?"

He shifted uncomfortably in his chair. "I think it would be better, *Mak Chik*, if we spoke to him in Kuala Krai. Not in his house," he added hastily, reading her expression. "At the police station. Nice and cool, and you don't have to find him. I just can't justify bringing him all the way up here..."

Maryam sighed and nodded regretfully. "I know. You're right. I wish you weren't, but you are," she reflected honestly. She summoned up a huge smile. "You're so professional! Thank you. Now come, you must have some more to eat. I can't even imagine what you've been eating since you've been here." She swooped down on his now empty plate and walked into the kitchen to fill it once more.

The next morning Maryam watered the flowers set in pots around her newly protected yard. It didn't look any different, but Mamat was right, it *felt* different. As she stood back to admire her garden, Dollah arrived, smiling warmly and apologizing for disturbing her. "I felt I should speak with you, *Kak*."

Maryam invited him in and started coffee. She agreed: he should speak with her and apologize for leading her into the middle of his brawl with Hassan while neglecting to mention any relevant facts about his musicians. In fact, Maryam believed Dollah had done as much as possible to mislead her without outright lying, and had put her life in danger as a result.

"So, *Abang* Dollah, what brings you here?" Maryam asked.

Dollah looked a bit shamefaced, and lifted his eyes to Mamat as if asking for help. Mamat watched him steadily and offered nothing. "It's a bit awkward, *Kak* Maryam." She waited. He sighed and continued.

"I see this has all become more complicated than I thought it would be. You know, I heard about what happened." Maryam looked at him enquiringly. He cleared his throat. "With Hassan.

He had no business treating you so rudely. It just goes to show how *kurang ajar,* badly brought up, he really is."

Maryam's cheeks burned as she recollected landing in the dust at the bottom of his stairs, lying in a heap with her face in the dirt.

"I'm sorry, *Kak.* I had no idea he would act this way. You can see why I feel this way about him."

"Why didn't you tell me you two were feuding?"

Dollah shifted uncomfortably. "I didn't think it mattered."

Maryam leaned in, willing herself to stay calm. "He was only there at your performance because of it. Of course, once I asked about it, I'd be involved. You knew that would happen."

Dollah hung his head. "I didn't think…"

"And what exactly do you do when you go to each other's performances? You don't make any trouble. What is it?"

"Nothing much."

She sighed impatiently. "*Abang* Dollah, you put me in a very difficult situation. Why are you here if you only want to hint, not talk?"

"We watch each other, and see what other *dalang* are doing. Get ideas, maybe." Dollah paused. "You know, we use *jampi* to open the performance, and to attract the audience. So when we fight, we use them to drive away the audience, to interrupt the performance. Of course," he grew animated, as he always did when discussing *Wayang Siam,* "*jampi* won't make a bad *dalang* good, but it might make a good *dalang* just a little bit better. So a rival *dalang,* he might try to make a very good *dalang* a little worse, and have fewer people watch. You understand."

Maryam felt comprehension dawning. "Are you telling me that Hassan came with spells to drive people away, maybe to hurt you?"

Dollah nodded.

"So," she continued, "Hassan knows a lot about *jampi.* And so do you."

"Well, yes." He admitted. "It's part of being a *dalang.*"

"And either one of you," she was remorseless, "would be able to concoct the spell under my house. You both know enough to do it."

"What was that?" Dollah appeared to be horrified.

"There was a wax doll under my stairs, with an *ikan keli* spine stuck right through it. And a written spell, and nails in it, and it was wrapped in a white shroud."

"I'm shocked! This is terrible."

"I almost died!" she added. "And what if my kids had found it instead? Do you have any idea what could have happened? Did anyone consider that before leaving that here, in my house?"

"What a horror! Oh my God! I can't tell you how appalled I am to hear this."

Maryam flicked the ash of her cigarette over the railing. "Are you really that surprised, *Abang*?"

Dollah was very still. "Why do you ask that, *Kak*?"

Maryam took a deep breath. "I think you knew about the spell. That's why you came here: to make sure I knew Hassan could easily have left it here. I suppose you thought I'd go back to see him again. That's what I think."

Dollah was silent. Her straightforward accusations were an affront to Malay courtesy, and he had rarely seen an adult act in such a way. She'd been provoked, however, and he could understand why she'd lost patience. Understand it, yes, but it still astounded him to see a woman act that way.

"*Kak*, these are serious things you're saying about me."

"Yes they are, but are they true? This is the way I see it: there's a lot you could have told me, but didn't." She ticked them off on her fingers. "Why did you let me find this out on my own and put myself in danger when you could have told me right at the start?"

Dollah was silent, thinking so hard Maryam could almost hear it. "It didn't work quite the way I planned, *Kak*."

"How did you plan it?"

"I just wanted to protect you." Maryam snorted. "Really! It was my only intention."

"You were protecting me by directing me towards Hassan?"

"Well, not exactly. But you see, Hassan could easily have done this. In fact, I think he did."

"Really?" she said drily.

He nodded energetically. "Now, listen to me. He might have mistaken Ghani for me, or have fought with him and killed him before he realized what was happening. I know what you're thinking: how could he mistake a kid fifteen years younger and six inches taller for me? But in the dark, sometimes you see only what you want to. He could easily have left the spell under your stairs. He knows how, he wouldn't have to work with a *bomoh*, and he knows where you live. See?"

"You don't need a *bomoh*, and you know where I live, too."

"You're right," he nodded. "But why would I kill Ghani? I loved that kid. I've got no reason to hurt him."

Maryam grudgingly granted him that much.

"Why didn't you warn me about Hassan?" she demanded. "If I knew, would I have shown up there and walked right up to his door like that? He thought that's what I was doing, and he certainly punished me for it." She paused, tamping down her rising anger. "You misled me. You didn't lie to me, but you didn't tell me what I needed to know either."

"You're right, *Kak*. Forgive me, please."

Maryam thought he would continue to argue, but an outright apology brought her up short. "Well, I mean, of course," she stammered, unready for it. "But will you help me now? I can't continue not knowing whether to trust you or not." She looked at him intently, searching for a clue that would let her know if he were lying.

"You can trust me," Dollah said with feeling, but exactly what sort of feeling, Maryam wasn't really sure.

Chapter 19

MARYAM CONSIDERED THE PRIMARY victim of Ghani's behavior: Aisha. Whether she went mad from guilt or grief or both, she was the key figure. The *dalang*'s feud led to a seemingly infinite series of dead ends, and Maryam hoped by taking the story back to its simplest beginning, she could make sense of it. It was worth attempting to wring some sense out of Aisha. Perhaps if Maryam ignored all extraneous issues, she could impose clarity on what now seemed utterly opaque. Maryam hopped into a taxi and headed back for Tawang.

Circumstances appeared to have deteriorated since her last visit. As she approached the house, she spotted Azizah hanging the wash in the back, with her two small grandchildren asleep on the porch. Maryam hailed her.

"Hello, *Kak*! How are things going?"

Azizah turned to look at her, with a wooden laundry peg between her teeth. She, too, looked pale and worn out. She nodded at Maryam, and finished hanging the sheet. "Haven't seen you in a few days," she said noncommittally.

"I know," Maryam smiled pleasantly. "I hope Aisha is well."

Azizah shook her head sadly. "Worse really."

"No!"

She nodded. "Yes, I'm sorry to say. She hardly speaks anymore. Just stays in bed."

"She doesn't want to take care of the kids?" Maryam was astonished.

Azizah looked at her mournfully. "Doesn't even want to see them. We've had the *bomoh* here I don't know how many times…" She bent to pick up another piece of washing and spread it out on the line. "I'm at my wit's end, I can tell you."

"How awful! She just doesn't respond?"

She shook her head and said nothing, intent on her task.

"Does she speak to anyone?" Maryam pursued.

"No," Azizah sighed. "I'm afraid; what if she stays this way?" Tears began spilling out her eyes. "My poor girl." She tried to control herself, to keep herself from crying. She leaned against the wet sheet she'd just hung on the line.

"*Kak,*" Maryam asked softly, "May I talk to her?"

"You can try," Azizah wiped her eyes. "I don't know if you'll get very much."

Maryam nodded. "You may well be right. But I'd still like to try."

Azizah nodded. "Go ahead. She's in the living room."

Maryam walked into the living room from the dazzling sunlight outside. She could make out a couch and coffee table, as well as a larger table and chairs, but didn't see Aisha anywhere. She walked in carefully, craning her neck to look into each corner. She saw a bundle under the window, which gradually resolved itself into a human shape curled on a sleeping mat. It was Aisha, lying on the floor, eyes wide open. Maryam tiptoed over to sit down next to her. Aisha reacted not at all.

"Aisha," Maryam called softly. The girl did not blink or move. Her eyes remained fixed on a point in the distance and she lay on her side, her hands tucked under her cheek, her legs brought up towards her chest. "Aisha, it's me, *Mak Chik* Maryam. Do you remember me?" Aisha was motionless, her breathing even, her mouth closed.

"Aisha, please!" Maryam pleaded. "Please speak, just for your mother. She's out of her mind with worry. We all are," she added in a whisper. Maryam slipped her own hand under Aisha's head, and lifted it up just a bit, to see if Aisha would move her eyes. They seemed to flicker, but did not focus on Maryam.

Maryam was perplexed: when she met Aisha just a few days after Ghani's death, she seemed in control, packing up her house to move to her parents' place. The madness seemed to come upon her only after she came home. Common sense told her a complete breakdown like this would have begun almost immediately after she discovered Ghani's death: not gradually, days after the worst was over. It was entirely possible that reactions could be delayed, but something about this bothered her.

She held Aisha's chin in her hand and looked deeply into her eyes. They were opened, but unseeing: the pupils were large, covering almost all of the brown. She put her head down again gently, and patted her hair.

"*Kak* Azizah," she asked as she left the house, "who's been feeding Aisha?"

"Feeding her?" Azizah thought about the question. "Well, I do, of course."

"Anyone else?"

"Not usually. Sometimes Ali will help out. You know, he and Aisha are very close. He's so worried, he can hardly sleep. I'm trying to keep the kids from noticing it, but I don't know how much longer I'll be able to do it."

Maryam nodded. "Is Ali here?"

"No, he's working."

"Do you think he might be able to come see me?"

Azizah shrugged. "Why?" She cocked her head at Maryam. "What would Ali know?"

"Maybe nothing," Maryam comforted her. "Maybe nothing at all. But if you don't mind, I'd like to talk to him."

She nodded, but gave Maryam a sharp look. Maryam took her leave, suddenly anxious to return to Kampong Penambang.

Arriving with relief at her own *kampong*, she walked right past her house, giving instructions to Aliza to begin dinner, and sought out *Pak* Awang, the *bomoh* she'd last seen placing protective spells around her house. She found him on the porch of his house, drinking coffee and enjoying the first hint of coolness in the late afternoon.

"*Chik* Yam!" he called out to her. "How nice to see you. I hope everything is alright?" He seemed concerned.

"Oh, fine, fine," she assured him. "No problem with our *jampi, Pak Chik.*"

He smiled, proud of his work. "Good, I'm glad."

She sat on one of the lower steps. "I've just been thinking… well, you know, could you give anything to someone to make them quiet?"

"Quiet?"

"Like they were asleep, but not."

He looked at her sternly. "That's a very serious thing, *Chik* Yam. Are you thinking of anything like that?"

"Not me, no. But I've just seen someone, and I have a feeling it isn't right."

"I'm not sure what you mean."

She sighed. "It's difficult to say."

"Well, you've got to tell me something. How can I answer otherwise?"

She nodded. "I know, I'll try. It's like this. There's a girl, and her husband dies. He's murdered really. And I saw her very soon after, one or two days, and she was fine. Well, sad, of course, but normal; you know." She lit a cigarette, one of her own home-rolled, and offered one to *Pak Chik* Awang. He took it silently, listening carefully. "Then I saw her a few days later, and she was strange. Walking around the house with no direction, not really paying attention when people talked to her, not making much sense when she was talking. In her own world, I'd say.

"I was just there today, *Pak Chik*, and came straight over here from there. Now she's lying on the floor in her house, curled up on a mat, staring at the wall. She doesn't speak when spoken to, she doesn't focus. I picked up her head, and looked into her eyes, but she didn't react at all.

"I did notice something, though. The blacks of her eyes are wide: you can hardly see any brown, and her eyes are opened very wide." *Pak Chik* Awang nodded. "Now *Pak Chik*," Maryam continued, "is she mad? Or, could it be she's drugged? What would cause something like that?"

Pak Chik Awang thought for a long while. "Is she eating?" he finally asked.

Maryam nodded. "I think so anyway. Her mother says she is. I asked her mother, 'Who feeds her?' Her mother said she did, and sometimes her brother helps."

"Would either of them want to harm her?"

Maryam shook her head. "I don't think so, that's why I'm so puzzled. She and her brother are really close. Her mother—well, of course her mother loves her. She's terribly concerned. And this girl's children are now there, too. Her family couldn't have any reason to harm her. I think they want to care for her."

"You're sure?"

"Yes, I am."

"It's strange." He thought for a while more. "Of course, it's possible."

"What is?"

He held up his hand, directing her to desist. "Someone could be giving her small amounts of a poison to keep her silent. Even something like opium, if they could find it. I don't know there's much around here. I haven't seen it. There are others though." He stroked his cheek. "Yes, I believe with a small dose she could be put in a state like this. Maybe *kecubong*. They could get it from a jungle area, or buy it, I suppose."

"Would it kill her?"

"It depends how much she was given. If it were a small enough dose, probably not."

"Would she be able to recover if she wasn't fed it any longer?"

He shrugged. "She could, if nothing's been harmed. It's a dangerous game to play, especially if you're planning to have her recover rather than die. You know, even if they didn't intend to kill her, they still could by mistake. Once you start giving someone poison, all kinds of things can happen. Would her family do that?"

"That's just it, *Pak Chik*. I don't think so: I can't see why they would. But it doesn't make sense to me that she was normal right after her husband's death and only later began to sink into this faint. If she were going mad from grief, as her mother says, shouldn't it have started right away?"

"I would think so," he answered slowly, still thinking. "I really do think so." He was silent for a minute or two. "Could anyone else have given her anything?" he asked. "I'm thinking now, maybe someone bringing something for her. Could that be possible? If not, then the only people who could poison her would be those feeding her every day."

"Could it be something else, *Pak Chik*? Aside from poison, something natural?"

Pak Chik Awang thought. "I suppose anything's possible. An evil *jampi*: it could be that. It's hard to tell."

"Would you look at her for me, *Pak Chik*?" Maryam begged him. "Could you come with me to Tawang?"

"You said they'd brought in a *bomoh* already."

She nodded. "I'm sure that's one of the first things her mother did."

"Well, of course," the *bomoh* agreed. "I can't just take over from another, you know. It wouldn't be right."

"Could you look together?"

He considered it. "I suppose I could, *Chik* Yam, if you spoke to the mother about it. Why don't you do that," he urged her, "and if she agrees, we can do it right away. That poor child."

Maryam needed no more encouragement, and raced back to Kampong Tawang immediately, even though showing up at *Mahgrib*, the twilight prayer, was definitely not done. After all, it was not only prayer time, but dinner time as well, and an unannounced visitor arriving just then was assumed to be looking for food. Maryam knew it was rude, and feared it might be misinterpreted. But she wasn't hungry, so she would decline any invitations to eat, and was sure that her mission would trump missing prayer. There was no time to lose.

She took her taxi almost to the bottom of the steps, and called loudly to Azizah. She came to the door, wiping her hands on a towel, clearly mystified to see Maryam standing there.

She frowned worriedly. "*Kak*, is something the matter?"

"I'm afraid for Aisha."

"So am I," her mother answered, still unsure why Maryam was standing at her steps, wringing her hands.

"May I come up?"

"Of course, of course, excuse me," Azizah stood aside on the porch.

"Let me tell you what I've been thinking." Maryam explained what she feared, and her conversation with *Pak Chik* Awang. Azizah nodded, saying nothing. "I know you feel the same," Maryam concluded.

Aisha's mother looked devastated. "What are you saying?"

"*Mak Chik*," Maryam said urgently, "Have you thought Aisha may have been poisoned? That's why she's so...quiet. I don't mean just *jampi*: maybe *kecubong*, or even opium! Something to make sure she doesn't talk. Someone who thinks she knows something or she's seen something. Tell me," she put her hand on Azizah's shoulder, "has anyone been over, bringing any presents for Aisha? Any fruits or candy, just for her? Please *Mak Chik*, this could save her life."

Her mother started crying, burying her head in her hands and rocking back and forth. "My little girl!" She cried. "I can't lose my little girl."

"We've got to act," Maryam was impatient, nearly shaking the weeping woman. "Come now, *Kak*, tell me!"

Azizah tried to calm herself and think clearly. "*Abang* Dollah, of course. He knows Aisha well, and he brought some cakes for her. Her favourite, that his wife baked."

"When was that?"

"The day she moved in here. He's been by a few times to cheer her up."

The women looked at each other. "Anyone else?" Maryam asked.

She thought. "Well, of course, her friends here. The other boys who play in the orchestra and their wives. Fruits and stuff like that."

"I'd like to bring my *bomoh* here: he might be able to tell what's wrong with her. If she's been poisoned."

Azizah began weeping afresh. "Yes, yes! Let him come. I just want to save my child!"

Maryam once again rushed into the taxi, and raced back to Kampong Penambang. She feared to lose any time and felt Aisha might be sinking quickly. It was night by now, but she didn't allow politeness to deflect her.

"*Pak Chik* Awang!" she called, even before she had reached his steps. "*Pak Chik*! Please!"

He came out of his house and padded quickly down the stairs. "Well?"

"Her mother asks you come and see her," Maryam was panting now, both from running and anxiety. "Can you come now? Please? I'm very frightened for her."

Pak Chik Awang grabbed his bag, and clattered back down the steps. "Let's go!" he ordered. Once again, Maryam was in the taxi hurtling toward Tawang, slowing down to avoid the ruts, which made Maryam grit her teeth in impatience. She fairly bounced on the back seat, willing the driver to go faster. Aisha's parents were waiting for her on the main road, to more quickly take her to the house. The father was silent, his jaw set and clenched, while her mother sobbed openly as she pulled Maryam by the hand to the house. They nearly pushed the old *bomoh* up the stairs and into the living room, while the family gathered silently to watch him with hopeful eyes.

Pak Chik Awang knelt next to Aisha, who hadn't moved since Maryam saw her last. He pulled her into a sitting position, waving her mother to sit behind her, supporting her. He tipped back her chin, stared into her eyes and tried desperately to have her focus on him: calling her name, even tugging gently on her hair. He looked inside her mouth and at the tips of her fingers.

He sat back on his haunches and regarded her for a long moment, while Aisha lay limp against her distraught mother. He shook his head and looked up at her father. "She needs to go to the hospital—or to a doctor," he said. "I can do a few things to keep her safe, but I don't have the medicines the doctors will have. She should be taken right away."

Aisha's mother fainted behind her, falling back against the wall. Her brother picked up Aisha's limp body, and slid into the taxi with Maryam and *Pak Chik* Awang. "To the General Hospital," Maryam ordered. "Hurry!" She watched the roads streak by in a blur. This time there was no slowing for potholes, and the car seemed to take flight over the larger ones and land with a bone-crushing thud.

They stopped abruptly in front of Kota Bharu's sprawling General Hospital. It had more of an atmosphere of a county fair: the road leading to the entrance was packed with hawkers selling food and snacks, soap, shampoo and towels. As Ali carried his sister behind *Pak Chik* Awang, the assembled crowd murmured their concern, whispering their own diagnoses and shaking their heads that such a young girl should come to this.

"Go tell them," *Pak Chik* Awang gave Ali a push toward the admitting nurse. Nothing in the Emergency Room seemed to count as an emergency: prospective patients had set up camp in the room and resigned themselves to never getting closer to an actual doctor than they were now. Whole families sat on the floor around their sick relatives, plying them with tea and Panadol while they ate their dinner.

Ali leaned over the nurse's desk in a way that Aisha was almost laid out full length upon it. "My sister!" he cried. "She's been poisoned! Help me!"

The nurse looked up at him as though he were an apparition come to haunt her. "There are forms," she lifted a languid wrist towards a table at the other end of the room. She regarded Aisha with distaste. "You can wait…"

Maryam barged in around Ali. "This girl is dying," she boomed, leaning in toward the nurse. "Do you want to let her die here? How can you be so heartless?" The other encampments quieted down to hear the discussion. The nurse suddenly appeared uncomfortable. "Now *Mak Chik*," she said, nervously turning her head. "We have rules."

"Rules! She's dying, don't you understand?" Maryam saw a pair of doctors walking behind the nurse. "Doctor," she shrieked, surprising herself with the pitch and volume of her scream. "Help me!"

The doctors turned to her. Patients did not shriek in the hospital waiting room. Patients and their families remained patient, gave themselves up to fate and waited their turn. They did not look as though they might jump the nurse and hold the doctors hostage.

"What's the trouble?" one asked.

"She's dying," Maryam continued at top volume. Ali watched her, both admiring and aghast. "She's been poisoned. Help her! Please!"

A doctor moved the now clearly sulking nurse out of the way and began to look over Aisha's lifeless form. "Do you know what it is?" he asked.

"I think *kecubong*," Maryam answered, decidedly more quiet now that someone was paying attention. She gave the nurse a triumphant look. "She's been getting worse every day."

"Take her in," the doctor said to Ali, who scooped her up and followed the doctor to the exam room. Maryam sat down with *Pak Chik* Awang in the waiting room, taking deep breaths to calm herself.

Pak Chik Awang looked amused. "I didn't know you could scream like that."

"Neither did I," Maryam admitted. "But it worked," she added with a touch of pride.

Aisha's parents burst into the room moments later, and Maryam pointed them to the room where she lay.

"What did you think?" Maryam asked the *bomoh*. "Did you think poison?"

"I did. Did you see her eyes?" he asked. "*Kecubong*, maybe mixed with opium. Someone wants her more than just quiet, *Chik* Yam. I think they wanted to make it look like she was falling into madness and would then die of it, but her death was their objective. I'd put money on it."

"Where would you get these poisons?"

Pak Chik Awang shrugged. "You can always get it if you're really looking for it."

"Opium?" Maryam was doubtful.

He nodded. "Not in Kelantan, but you could in Thailand. And *kecubong*...well, if you didn't buy it, you could find it in the jungle. It grows there."

Maryam shivered. Aisha must have seen something, must know something. Maybe she didn't even know what she'd seen, or she knew, but wanted to keep quiet. Maryam sat quietly, hoping for good news.

Chapter 20

JOHAN, FAOUDA'S NEW HUSBAND, was not pleased to find himself in the Kuala Krai police station. He slumped scowling in a chair, complaining loudly about wasting his whole day at work, if not more, for what he considered police bullshit.

Osman had ushered him into a small room equipped with a table and four scruffy chairs. He sat away from the table, willing himself to fade into the walls. Johan swung his legs and kicked his chair rhythmically. It was incredibly annoying.

"Who are you? I'm thirsty."

"I'm *Mak Chik* Maryam…"

"You're the one! My wife told me about you." He leaned forward on the table, stretching his arms in front of him. "Tell me, what's your problem?" he continued. "Why are you doing this?"

"I'm working to find out who killed Ghani," she answered equably.

"Well, I didn't," he announced. "And I don't know who did. *And* I don't care, either. Get me something to drink," he added sullenly. He turned to Osman, who held his hand up as if to ward him off. "Talk to *Mak Chik* Maryam now," he said, indicating her chair with his chin, and Johan slumped back down into his chair.

140

Maryam turned to Osman and mouthed, "Drinks?" He opened the door and asked a policeman to get some cold drinks. "So," she began, looking Johan over. She didn't much like what she saw. His hair was tousled and greasy, and he wore a grimy white T-shirt and jeans. His face was wide and square, with small eyes and a wide mouth. As one who hoped to soon become a grandmother, Maryam could not help speculating on what his and Faouda's children might look like: the eyes were going to be tiny and the face wide. It didn't sound like a recipe for beauty. She forced herself back to the present. "I hear you went to Kota Bharu to get married."

He scratched his chest extravagantly and yawned. "Is there a law against it?"

"No."

"Then why are you asking me?"

"I just want to know where you were while you were up there."

"Sightseeing," he smirked. She longed to smack him.

"How long have you known Faouda?"

"A while. Look, where's my drink?"

"It's coming. I get the feeling you'd rather not talk to me."

"You got that right."

"Would you prefer to talk to *Chik* Osman? He's the Chief of Police in Kota Bharu."

Johan cast a contemptuous eye on Osman. "No, I'd prefer not to talk to anybody."

"That might not be possible."

"Try."

Maryam rose. "Suit yourself," she muttered softly. She left the office and Osman followed her. "I can't do anything with him. Do you see how snotty he is?"

"Can I help you?" one of the older policemen asked.

"He's impossible," she told him, rolling her eyes.

"May I, *Chik* Osman?" he asked politely. "I'll take care of it. Stay here for a moment."

"Thanks," Maryam said, standing at his desk while Johan was being convinced. There was a sudden report, like a pistol shot, which startled Maryam and sent her jumping into the furniture. "What was that?"

The policeman came out of the room and stood gesturing for her to enter. "He's all yours now, *Mak Chik*. I believe he may be more cooperative." He smiled at her and then at Osman and sat back at his desk.

They went in to find Johan with a bright red cheek and a small trickle of blood running down his chin. He was patting it clean with the hem of his T-shirt.

"I guess I'm supposed to be more polite."

"It would help," Maryam replied. "Do you want to talk now?"

"OK." He settled back into scowling, but at least he now had a reason for that, Maryam thought. She had little sympathy for him. The side of his face was beginning to swell. Osman took in Johan's face and walked out of the office: he was speaking to someone there, but while she could hear the sound of his voice, the words were indistinct.

"I'll start again," she began. "When did you come up to Kota Bharu?"

"I dunno. Thursday, maybe."

"And when did you find Faouda?"

"Friday morning, at the taxi station."

He and Faouda had coordinated their stories at any rate. "Where did you stay that night, before you found her?"

"At a hotel in Kota Bharu."

She waited.

"The Hotel Tokyo," he finally specified. "It's on Jalan Temenggong, on the second floor. That's where we stayed the whole time we were there."

"And you left on Monday morning, early?"

He nodded. "Had to get back to work."

Maryam felt she was getting nowhere with him. She tried to order her thoughts to make them more effective.

"When did you find out Faouda married Ghani?"

"Right after it happened, I guess."

"Did you want to marry her?"

Their drinks had arrived. Johan gulped his while Maryam continued her questioning, trying to keep her momentum. "Well, did you?"

"I did, and she knew it." He gingerly wiped his mouth. "I asked her already. I thought she'd said yes."

"And then?"

"And then I heard she married this musician guy, so I went to see her. 'What's this about?' I asked her. 'I thought we were getting married.'"

"Had you asked her before she was divorced from, I forget his name…?"

"Yahya? The older guy? Well, nothing happened."

"Of course not, but did you?"

He nodded. "I told her, 'Faouda, get out of this marriage. It isn't going to work. He's an older guy with kids your age. He doesn't want children, and besides, give his wife a couple of months and she'll have you run out of town.'" He crossed his arms.

Osman slipped back into the room and sat in his chair against the wall. He watched them both like a spectator at a tennis game.

"Good advice," Maryam told him.

"It sure was. Besides, I didn't like her living with him. It wasn't right," he scrunched up his eyes. "I mean, anyone could see it wasn't going to work, so why drag it out, right? I was taking a load of lumber to Alor Setar, the West Coast, so I was gone—maybe a week, maybe a little more. When I come back, guess what? She's divorced and she's married! I was stunned, no kidding. What happened?"

"What did she tell you?"

"What was there to tell? She met Ghani, she says they're in love. They got married. She's the second wife.

"'For God's sake, Faouda,' I tell her, 'Another second wife? And now he lives up near Kota Bharu? When are you ever going to see him?'

"'Don't worry about that,' she says, all pleased with herself. 'He's crazy about me. He'll be here all the time. He can't get enough.'

"Wrong! I knew right away, 'cause I'm a guy and I know how guys think, he'd already gotten all he wanted. She's very trusting that way." He nodded to emphasize just how naïve Faouda really was and took another long pull at his tea.

"So to prove her point, she goes up to Kota Bharu to be with him. And naturally, it doesn't turn out the way she plans. I knew it," he took another swig of his *teh beng*, sweet iced tea loaded, as were almost all beverages in Kelantan, with sweetened condensed milk, "so I went up to Kota Bharu right after her. I thought, I'll be there when she gets divorced and we'll get married right away. And I was right! It happened just like I told her it would. She shows up, the wife pitches a fit, Faouda's divorced. It took hours, I tell you, just hours before she was out on her ear.

"I found her at the taxi station, sort of drifting, and was she surprised to see me! She throws herself at me, right in the middle of the station, all these people around and says, 'You were right! I can't believe I was so stupid. Can you ever forgive me?'"

Maryam thought it sounded like a soap opera, but it clearly worked on Johan; he positively glowed.

"I took her to a coffee shop, let her clean up her makeup and stuff, and said, 'It's time for us to get married.' 'Oh, yes!' she says. 'Right now!' So we went over to the *khadi*, but it's Friday and we can't do anything. It's closed. So, I thought, we're so near Sungei Golok, we can cross into Thailand and find a *khadi* there! Not so strict, you understand."

He waited for her to acknowledge what he said. "We just wandered down an alley and found one. He was having his lunch, but when we showed up wanting to get married and happy to pay, he got right on with it. No waiting there, I tell you! I paid him, and we were married! Just like that. Great, isn't it?"

He nodded enthusiastically. "It's legal." He gave her a sober look, daring her to say it wasn't. Maryam sat silently; everyone knew anything and everything was for sale in Sungei Golok, a wide-open border town just across the river from Kelantan. Why not marriage?

"So we go back to the hotel, which we can, because we're married." He gave Maryam a dirty look. "And that's it. Now we're back in Kuala Krai, and I'm looking for a house for us to live in. So there it is."

He leaned back in his chair and gave himself over to a well-deserved drink.

Maryam smiled at him. "Well, it was certainly exciting. Precipitous, even."

"It's true, what are you talking about?" he said, his eyes narrowing.

"Oh yes, I don't doubt it for a moment," she soothed him. "But," she added as innocently as possible, widening her eyes until they threatened to tear, "doesn't Faouda need to wait before she remarries? I don't think a woman can remarry that fast, even if it's alright in Sungei Golok."

Johan glowered silently.

"Religious law," Maryam prompted him. "What is it, three months until she can marry again?"

He grunted contemptuously. "No matter," he waved his hand dismissively, "We knew she wasn't pregnant."

"How?" Maryam was genuinely interested.

"She just knew. She told me."

Maryam sighed with disappointment; of course, his answer would be completely meaningless. "It isn't a legal marriage," she opined firmly. "If the *khadi* in Kelantan found out…"

"Well, he won't," Johan growled. "Come on, *Mak Chik*, you and I aren't here to argue religion. We're married, and that's an end to it."

"Someone's bound to figure it out, you know. And then you won't be married anymore."

He mumbled something uncomplimentary into his tea.

"Never mind," Maryam continued briskly. "You're right: this is between you and the *khadi*." In her own opinion, however, it was an important test of character which both Johan and Faouda failed abysmally. "Anyway, did you see Ghani while you were up there?"

"Why should I?"

"I don't know. Did you?"

"No."

"You're sure?"

"Yes."

"But, Johan," Maryam protested, "people saw you at the *Wayang Siam*. So you must have. This was when…? I guess the night before you left for Kuala Krai."

He sat and looked at her. "I wasn't there," he said stubbornly.

"Alright," she said. "You ought to speak with Police Chief Osman." She stood up to leave. He looked up at her, squinting.

"OK, OK, sit down." He tightened his lips. "She wanted to see him and to show him she was already married again and didn't care. It's fine with me, I don't care. She just wants to stick her finger in his eye. Good for her. So we went to the performance."

"Were you there at the end?"

"It was pretty late," he said evasively.

"Was the performance over?"

"It was winding down."

Maryam knew full well *Wayang Siam* performances did not wind down. They were either on, or it was over. "So it was already finished."

"Maybe."

"Did she go over to talk to him?"

He nodded.

"Did you go with her?"

"No, I stayed a little bit away. Let her talk to him, I thought."

"You're not a jealous guy, are you?"

"No need to be."

"Did you see anyone else talking to him?"

He shifted in his seat. "Tell the truth, *Mak Chik*, I did. When we went to see him, he was talking to his wife. He seemed angry, and she was crying and grabbing at his shirt. I couldn't hear them, but then, you didn't have to hear them to see what was going on. I pulled Faouda away. 'This is a bad time,' I told her, 'don't talk to him right after he's had a fight with his wife. Let's get out of here and we'll come back when it's all calmed down.'"

"So, what did you do?"

"We walked down the road toward Chinatown. There're always a few stalls open there no matter how late it is."

"How late was it?"

"By then? I don't know. One, maybe? Anyway, we had coffee and then walked back, and the wife was gone and everything. Faouda goes to the back and calls him, real quiet, and he comes to the door. She tells him she's married and she doesn't care about him, and he says, 'Good!' Then we left."

Maryam considered this. "That's all?"

He tried to look innocent. "That's all. Nothing else. We went back to the hotel, slept for a few hours and then got up early to go home."

There was something more, she was sure, but she wouldn't be prying it out of him now; it might take a few tries before he finally told everything he knew. She gathered her things, rose stiffly and thanked him. Osman rose and held the door for her. There was always another time.

Chapter 21

IT WAS CLEAR SOMETHING was very wrong. The yard in front of Aisha's family home was filled with people milling around: men in prayer caps, women delivering dishes to the back door. It was a hushed crowd, even downcast. The atmosphere was ominous and Maryam expected the worst. She approached an older woman leaving the kitchen. "*Kak*, what's happened?" she asked.

The woman adjusted her headscarf lower over her forehead and sighed. "So much death here. Their daughter just died at the hospital. Aisha."

"Aisha!"

The woman nodded. "I know. So young, and leaving two little children. Those poor things: they've lost both their father and their mother so quickly." She closed her eyes for a moment, as if to hold back tears.

Maryam stood rooted to the ground, looking up into the house. She'd feared this as soon as she arrived and saw the neighbours gathered, but didn't want to believe it. "Is the family inside?"

The woman nodded. "Such a pity. I don't know how they bear it."

Maryam and Rubiah walked up the steps and looked in. The family was putting out large trays of food to feed their guests. No doubt prayers would begin soon. Aisha's mother and father were sunk into grief, their heads down. The local *imam* sat with them, offering comfort, while their families gathered around, surrounding them with concern. Aisha's brothers and sisters sat quietly, occasionally murmuring to each other. Neighbours were working in the kitchen, bringing out trays of food. Everyone looked stunned.

Maryam caught Ali's eye and gestured to him to come outside. He looked utterly drained and walked onto the porch reluctantly.

"I'm so sorry," Maryam began.

"Yes," he replied. "We were going to say something to you after prayers, to thank you for taking Aisha to the hospital. Maybe if we'd done it sooner? I don't know. Why, *Mak Chik*?" He looked as though he would cry.

She shook her head. "We will find whoever did this, Ali." She craned her neck to look inside. "Where are the children?"

He looked confused. "Inside, I guess."

"Your mother will take them." It wasn't a question. Who else could care for them?

Ali shook his head. "No, *Mak Chik*, I will." Maryam looked astonished. He gave her a ghost of a smile. "I'm getting married soon. My wife and I will raise them as our own. She's already agreed. It'll be nice," he said vaguely, "to start out with little children already. A piece of my sister," he added, his voice clogged with tears. "I couldn't save her but I can raise her children. She would have wanted me to." He could no longer stop himself from crying. "I can't believe my sister is gone!"

"She would be so grateful to you," Maryam said with heartfelt admiration. "You're really helping her now." She patted Ali's arm and walked down the stairs. Among the men in the yard, she spotted Dollah and all of his musicians, looking solemn and subdued, and decided against even greeting them. "It's time to leave," she told Rubiah and Mamat. "We can't ask anything now."

As they walked from the village, she said softly, "I was too late to save her. I should have realized it as soon as she seemed ill."

"It isn't your fault," Rubiah held her arm. "The family called their *bomoh*. No one suspected it."

"No," Maryam insisted. "I'm supposed to be investigating this." She looked at the ground while Mamat and Rubiah exchanged glances over her bowed head. "I've taken too long. And while I've been taking my time, Aisha's been dying." She looked sideways at Rubiah. "I hope it isn't Ali. I don't think it's him."

Rubiah said nothing: she wasn't so sure.

Maryam pursued it further. "That family's suffered enough. If it had been Ali, and it wasn't," she reminded Rubiah, "then I would look the other way."

Rubiah gasped. "No you wouldn't…"

"I would," she insisted. "He doesn't deserve to be punished. I mean, he wouldn't."

"I'm surprised at you! We're after the truth here. I'll look for the truth no matter where it leads."

Maryam shrugged. "You can do what you like. Anyway, it doesn't matter, because I don't think he did it." Maryam closed her mouth firmly. Perhaps this was not strictly according to the detective's code (if there was such a thing), but it would be a higher justice served, a cosmic justice. Anyway, this was an academic discussion concerning an innocent man. She held her head high, her eyes straight.

Rubiah gave her a hard look, but held her tongue.

Chapter 22

WHEN OSMAN SENT WORD he had brought Hassan in for questioning at the station in Kota Bharu, she was profoundly uneasy. Osman was well within his rights to take in suspects at his discretion, particularly in the face of such a serious crime. Judging from Johan, however, it made them cranky—and perhaps resentful. She wondered if questioning them at home would be a better way of overcoming their reluctance, but maybe the official atmosphere of the police station actually encouraged them to talk. In their own homes, it might seem too much like an unwelcome social call.

Rubiah came with her to the station, both of them more resigned than eager for the discussion. Hassan was holding court, regaling the staff with stories of his conquests in far-off villages. The men were both delighted and disbelieving: nothing like that ever happened to them. "It's a *dalang*'s life, you know," Hassan was finishing smugly. "It can be hard, but there are some advantages." He winked, and the men were completely won over.

They all rose when Maryam and Rubiah came in and escorted them to an empty office. Osman stayed away this time, having spoken to Hassan on his own before Maryam arrived. Hassan sauntered in a few moments later to join them, apparently having already ordered coffee. "Well, *Kak*," he greeted her with a wide smile, displaying his three gold teeth glinting in reflected sunshine. "It's nice to see you again." He looked closely at her. "Have you fallen again? You don't look so good."

Maryam was silent.

"When you fell down the steps," he continued, his grin even wider, if that were possible, "I was afraid you might have hurt yourself. A bad fall, I thought. But now I think you might look even worse! You've really got to be more careful, *Kak*. I'm worried about you, I don't mind telling you." He sat down and crossed his legs, a man without a care in the world. "And you *Kak*? How are you today?" he asked Rubiah.

She, too, remained silent.

"No one talking today?" He took out a cigarette. "You had me brought here just to look at me? Well, go ahead. Me, I never understood why women found me attractive; too short and small, I'd say, but what do I know? Maybe it's because I'm wiry. Do you think that's it?" He paused, and shrugged. "OK, I can look at you, too."

He lit a cigarette and blew out his first lungful of smoke at the ceiling. "Want one?" He offered his cigarettes all around. They didn't take any. He shrugged and put the packet on the table. "When you come back down to earth, ladies, you might need a smoke. There it is." He smiled again and waited.

"*Abang* Hassan," Maryam began deliberately, "did you place a *jampi* under my house?"

"No! What a question. Why would I do something like that?" He seemed to dare her to find out anything from him. "Do you think I hate you, *Kak*? Not at all."

"You're in some kind of a fight with Dollah, though."

"All *dalang* compete with each other," he said easily. "It's part of the job. Why would you be involved in any of it?"

"I thought it possible that Ghani was in the middle of it without realizing, and that maybe he was mistaken for one of you."

"What do you mean?"

"You know: that you thought he was Dollah, or Dollah thought he was you."

He appeared to think this over. "I don't think so. Are you saying you think I was trying to kill Dollah? That's quite a leap."

"I'm just asking."

"Well, you've had your answer."

She nodded. "I do. And do you know what I think, *Abang* Hassan? I think maybe you did mistake Ghani for Dollah in the dark. Maybe you even tried to kill me, too, after you threw me out of your house and laughed at me while I lay in the dirt."

"I did no such thing, *Kak*. Quite the contrary, I was concerned about you. No really," he assured her, when Maryam grimaced. "When I thought about it later, I thought, 'It's possible Dollah hasn't told her everything. She could have innocently walked into this.' That's what I thought, and maybe I'm right." He regarded her shrewdly.

"Maybe *Abang*, maybe. I'd certainly like to believe that of you. I'd think you were a much nicer person."

He smiled again. "Maybe I am."

"Maybe," Rubiah agreed. "Do you have…what shall I call it? A feud with Dollah?"

"No more so than other *dalang*. Look, *Kak*, I have no reason to kill Dollah or even hurt him, and certainly none to kill a musician. What do I have to do with Dollah's musicians?"

"I know!" Maryam took over again. "It doesn't make sense to me either. But here's my problem." She leaned closer to him, over the table. "You said you weren't at the performance, but you were. People saw you. And you lied. So, I ask, why did you lie? Because once you were seen there, we could imagine a line connecting you to Ghani's death." She paused for a short moment, out of breath from anxiety. She could hear the blood pounding in her ears. "You wouldn't have needed to go to a *bomoh* to get the *jampi* done either: you could do it yourself. You know how. And that could easily have killed me, or hurt me, and that would be the end of the investigation. Now, do you think you could tell me the truth?"

Maryam sat down and concentrated on slowing down her breathing. Rubiah looked at her in amazement. "You're crazy." Hassan tried for the same tone of insouciance he'd had when he'd walked into the room, but couldn't recreate it. There were spots of red in his cheeks now, and his temper was getting the best of him. "What *jampi*? What are you talking about?"

Now Maryam allowed herself one of Hassan's cigarettes. She passed one to Rubiah and they both lit up. She felt the tide had turned now: she and Rubiah were calming down and Hassan was more agitated.

"It's obvious," Maryam continued. "Doesn't it fit?" She leaned forward towards him. "You're at the performance where Ghani dies. You throw me out of your house and complain to the police that I'm attacking you. You even place a *jampi* under the stairs to my house, and *Abang*, you know all about *jampi*. What does it sound like to you?" She had to admit she couldn't fit Aisha into the picture.

"It sounds like you've lost your mind," he snapped. "This is too much for you. Go back to the market, stay out of this. You're in too deep for your own good."

"Are you threatening me?" Maryam asked, now angry herself.

"No. I'm just telling you the truth, and you need to be told it. Just stay out of this or you'll be sorry you ever got involved."

"I'm already sorry."

"I didn't kill anyone."

"You would say that, wouldn't you? I didn't expect you to confess, *Abang*. I'd just like you to consider the truth."

They were interrupted by an uncertain knock at the door, and it was Rahman, with coffee and curry puffs. He placed them on the table and scuttled out of the room.

"Why would I know a musician anyway?" Hassan continued, reaching for coffee and a curry puff and contriving to eat, drink, smoke and talk at the same time. "I'm the best *dalang* in Kelantan. I talk to other *dalang*, not their drummers."

"Did you see anyone else around?" Maryam asked patiently.

"There were plenty of people around," he answered grudgingly. "Dollah was around," he said pointedly. "This musician's wife was around, his second wife was around. They all had reasons to hate him. I have none, you see."

Maryam had considered Hassan capable of any mayhem if he put his mind to it, but he had no reason to attack Ghani. Unless, of course, he'd mistaken him for Dollah.

"Why were you at the performance?"

"To watch Dollah play." He was suddenly wary. "To see how he was doing."

"And…?" she prodded.

"And to try to get in his way. To leave a *jampi* under the stage so he wouldn't perform as well. To drive the audience away instead of drawing them in. All *dalang* do this, you know. You ask Dollah if he doesn't do it to me, maybe even to others! It isn't murder."

"If they end up dead it is."

"Why don't you look for people who wanted this guy dead? One of his wives, for instance."

"Well, the first wife is dead."

"Then it's the second wife," he stated confidently. "It's always the wife, isn't it? They start hating each other and end up hating the husband." He shook his head and leaned back, satisfied he had solved the case for them.

"He didn't die because of some *dalang*'s argument," Hassan added, as though he were musing only to himself. He took another sip of coffee.

Maryam agreed, but remained suspicious of him. "You know, *Abang*," she began in a conciliatory way, "I think you're right. I do," she emphasized. "I don't think you really killed Ghani. But I do think you left the *jampi* under my house."

"I did not! Why would I?"

"Why would you throw me down the steps in front of your house? Why were you so anxious to get rid of me?"

Hassan thought for a moment, as if gauging how far he could go before being caught in a lie. "I wasn't really." He paused, but neither Maryam nor Rubiah seemed impressed. "It's just none of your business," he said finally. "I didn't want you involved, and I was right, wasn't I?" He was now picking up steam.

"Look what's happened to me because of you!" He got out of his seat and began pacing. "This is none of your affair. I don't know Ghani, I didn't kill him, I don't think I'd recognize him if he walked in here. And you know that." Hassan glared at her. They sat silently for a long minute or two.

"Let me tell you," he came forward on his chair, "If it was Dollah who was found killed, then you'd at least have a right to talk to me. Not," he added carefully, "that I would ever do anything like that. But this kid? You need to talk to someone else."

She sat in Osman's office, now morose and clearly upset. "Well?" he asked, interested.

She shook her head. "I just don't think he did it. It doesn't make sense, does it?"

"Not really. I know he's been nasty to you, and to me too, but that's not a crime."

She tapped her fingers on the table. "I know. And Aisha's death bothers me."

"Of course; such a senseless loss of life."

"No," she shook her head. "No, it's because I can't fit her death in here at all. Why would any of the people who might have killed Ghani kill her? I don't see it."

"Maybe she knew something," Osman suggested. "Or saw something we haven't found out about yet."

"Maybe I'm on the wrong track altogether," she said distractedly.

"You feel that way because your last conversation was so unpleasant. You'll see, it will come to you later."

She looked squarely at him. Was he speaking from experience? "I suppose so. You know, some of the other people are so much more likely." She wondered whether she should list all her favorite suspects, pretty much covering everyone involved in any way.

"Dollah could have done it."

"Do you think we should talk to him?"

She shook her head. "You can't do that. People will say I destroyed *Wayang Siam* in Kelantan all on my own."

Osman stared off to space for a short time. "Leave this to me."

She nodded absently and stood up slowly. She was suddenly tired, unwilling to concentrate on murder. "I'll keep looking. All the suspects look promising," she said, spouting unthinking clichés in order to take her leave.

When she was gone, Osman leaned back in his chair. He had Hassan taken back to Kampong Laut. Hassan favoured Osman with a sulphurous look as he left, and Osman had to remind himself once again that being infuriating wasn't yet a crime.

Chapter 23

THE KIDS WERE OUT; Mamat was probably at the market helping Ashikin get some stock loaded. Maryam stepped out of her clothes and into her bathing sarong: a good bath was just what she needed. She stood in the little shed they'd built over a well in the back and began splashing bucketfuls of cool clear water over her head.

She washed her hair, washed herself, and then began the entire process over again, in an attempt to feel cleaner, maybe even purer. Now soaking wet, she put a towel around her hair and turned back towards the house.

Suddenly the geese burst into hysterical honking and scrambling. She peeked around the side of the house, and there he was, Johan. Just as she remembered him: big and square-faced and greasy-haired. "What are you doing here?" she demanded. "Have you no manners? Get out of here. Walking in on someone bathing, I've never heard of such a thing. Out! Get out of here." She walked the few steps towards the house.

He was right there next to her, ignoring the geese attacking his ankles. He stood before her calmly. "*Mak Chik*, I've been thinking about this since the last time I saw you. I owe you this." He swung his arm and punched her as hard as he could in the face. She fell flat on the ground, the pain exploding in her cheek, her jaw on fire. She tried to take a breath to scream, but couldn't make a sound. "That's what they did to me, the police," he hissed at her, bending over her. "If you tell them, I'll come back and kill your kids." And then he was gone.

She lay on the ground for a few moments, in a tangled heap of sarong and towel, feeling blood running down her cheek, mixing with tears. She crawled up, and sat still on the dirt of her yard, surrounded by circling geese. She was dazed, and could feel her cheek swelling. She carefully felt her teeth, to see if any were knocked out, but they were all accounted for.

I must get up, she kept telling herself, but the effort involved seemed far too much for her. I can't just sit here and wait for the kids to find me, she thought. She began crawling back towards the well. I'll just wash up, she encouraged herself; I'll just get myself back into shape. It will be fine. I won't tell the police. On that she was completely clear. She would not put her children at risk.

She dragged herself up by the low wall of the well, and slowly, painfully, began rewashing herself: her hair, her body, her injured face. Her face hurt just to touch it, her newly washed hair was now caked in mud. She'd never felt so dirty. Her shoulders ached when she tried to pull up the bucket. She bent over and wept with frustration.

Mamat's motorcycle pulled around the side of the house, accompanied by shrieking geese. She couldn't remember hearing a sound which made her happier. He heard the splashing of water and looked around the back, taking in her filthy sarong and dirty towel and the odd way she leaned over the well.

"What happened to you?"

She turned to look at him—crying, with her face swelling larger each moment, her cheek cut, her upper lip already ballooned. He rushed toward her.

"What happened? Tell me."

She found it difficult to talk. "Johan. He came here. He hit me, like the police hit him. Then he said if I told them, he'd kill our kids."

Mamat grabbed clean towels and sarong and helped Maryam wash off. He half carried her into the house, put her into bed, wrapped ice on her cheek and filled her with Panadol. She cried softly.

"I'll protect you," he told her softly. She nodded, no longer wishing to speak. "I think we should tell the police."

"No!" she cried. "He'll kill the children. I won't take that chance!" Her words weren't too clear, but Mamat got the gist. He couldn't bear to look at her this way. "He's killed at least once," he told Maryam, "he might kill again."

She regarded him silently with tears in her eyes; her lip was now too swollen for her to enunciate, and it hurt to move her mouth. But she was terrified, Mamat saw that.

"Not now, *sayang*. Now you just rest. Don't even try to talk." He sat with her until she fell asleep, ashamed that he'd failed to protect her.

Chapter 24

"SOMEONE'S TRYING TO KILL ME," Maryam told Mamat with great resignation.

Mamat had been thinking about little else since he found Maryam on the ground behind the house. "I won't let it happen," he soothed her. They sat together on their porch at sundown, caring for Mamat's birds. He raised *merbok*, doves famed for their beautiful singing, and he kept them in elaborate cages hung over the porch. He took them out in the evenings to feed by hand, pet them and generally spoil them, and both he and Maryam took a great interest in the birds. He hoped she would find it calming, holding them in her lap, smoothening their feathers and listening to their gentle cooing.

She held them indifferently, petting them without paying attention, too sunk in her reverie to care. "I feel it coming, but don't know what I can do to stop it," she told Mamat. "I think I'm going to die."

Mamat felt his stomach drop as she said it. "Don't be ridiculous," he scoffed. "You're fine. Don't even say things like that."

"I'm serious," her head lowered as though speaking to the bird in her hands. "Someone's killed Ghani. Now Aisha's also gone. I've never been punched in the face, ever. I've never felt

anything like that in my life. I'm next, Mamat. I'm telling you."
She paused. "And there's nothing I can do about it. It's my fate."

"Stop talking like that." He was becoming agitated, and
the birds he held felt it. They began fluttering their wings and
crying out to each other. He put them back in their cages; it
wasn't fair to upset them like this. He walked nervously under
them, watching Maryam sit quietly on the steps, leaning her
head against a house post. He sat down next to her again and
put his arm around his shoulder. "It isn't as bad as all that," he
tried convincing them both. "I'm right here," he assured her. "I'll
take care of you."

She turned to him. "Everyone hates me. Dollah hates me,
Hassan hates me, Johan hates me. I'm sure Faouda hates me, too.
And Mamat, any one of them could have poisoned Aisha. I'm
next," she repeated morosely. "Just look at me," she reminded
him. "In the past couple of weeks I've been face down in the
dirt, I've been attacked by *jampi* in my own home…I feel like
I'm halfway to dead already." She put her hands in her face and
sighed, almost a sob.

Mamat could not bear seeing her drained of courage. It was
what made her what she was: her willingness to get things done
and not fear the consequences. As her husband, he should have
kept her safe. The fault was his. "Come on, get up," he ordered
her, standing himself and yanking her hand. She needed action
to regain her balance, and he'd been too passive. They would
seize the initiative. "We've got to find out who did it before they
can get to you. Come on. It's urgent, Yam."

Aliza had called for her Aunt Rubiah, who immediately
bustled over, determined to bring Maryam out of her funk.
She'd never seen her so low. She sat down next to her, offering
a few cakes she'd grabbed on her way out of the house. "Yam,
think! You aren't going to sit on your porch and wait for an
attack!" She slapped a cake into Maryam's hand and gestured
with her chin, ordering her to eat it. "It's time to go on the offen-
sive!" She declared. "You have the answer, you just can't," she
hesitated, unsure of the correct word, "uncover it."

Maryam raised her eyebrows without energy, adjusting a handful of ice wrapped in a cloth against her jaw. It was still swollen and purple, and she chewed the soft cake cautiously. "Osman said," she said indistinctly, "we had to investigate according to the rules. We couldn't beat people to make them talk to us."

Mamat and Rubiah had to lean close to try to understand. "But now, I wouldn't want to tell anyone anything. No matter who asked me," she added. Maryam shifted in her seat, and ran her hands over her face. "Wait, I need to rest for a moment." She readjusted the ice pack and closed her eyes.

Rubiah drank half a cup of coffee, and then, with a meaningful look at Mamat, prodded Maryam again. "Well?" she ordered.

"I'm going back to the very beginning." Rubiah nodded approvingly. "It's gotten too complicated," Maryam continued. "There's too much piled on top of the first crime."

It took Rubiah a moment to interpret what Maryam had said. "Right," Rubiah answered. "Go ahead. I'm listening."

"You know, this may be stupid," she gave Rubiah a stern look, as though Rubiah had agreed too quickly, "but something's been sticking in my mind." She looked around at Mamat and Rubiah, and they saw a little of her spirit return. She had bruises all over her body, and her jaw clearly hurt, but as long as she could concentrate on what to do, and order people around, she could come out of the depression into which she'd sunk. She was to be greatly encouraged in anything which would make her feel in control.

"You know the saying about being a second wife? *Cuka diminum pagi hari*: vinegar drunk early in the morning."

Rubiah nodded.

"The drink part."

Rubiah was baffled.

"Poison in the drink! You know, the proverb means it's drinking bitterness," she explained, slowly, as though to the simple-minded. "Rubiah, you know what people say. They say poison is the favorite weapon of second wives getting rid of their rivals."

"That's true," Rubiah nodded.

"So, that's what our proverbs are telling us! It's like poison drunk early in the morning, adding another wife, I mean." She thought for a moment. "How would a second wife poison the first? In her drink.

"What if," Maryam narrowed her eyes and looked at the wall, listening to an inner voice, "Aisha was poisoned by the second wife? Maybe it had nothing to do with Ghani's murder; maybe Faouda just wanted to get rid of her so she'd have Ghani all to herself.

"I wonder," she said softly, "maybe she had it all ready to get rid of—what's her name?—the wife we saw in Kuala Krai."

"Um, wait. Maimunah!" Rubiah was pleased with her memory.

"Right. But then she decided she didn't care anymore. But she had the poison all prepared." She shook her head disapprovingly.

"She didn't have any time," Mamat said, though he liked the theory. It was straightforward and easily explained. "She only met Aisha once for a couple of hours. I just don't see how she could have…" He trailed off.

"Rubiah, remember when we went to see Aisha? Even though her husband had just been killed and she was living at her parents' house, she still apologized for not giving us anything to eat." She turned to Mamat. "She was still so polite. She would have given Faouda something to drink when she turned up.

"And Faouda poisoned her right there." She breathed in abruptly, and put her hand to her mouth. "Do you remember?" she asked Rubiah urgently. "When we first met Aisha, she made us coffee, didn't she?"

Rubiah nodded, knowing now where this was leading.

"I think it was in the tea. We came so close to disaster! Oh my God!"

She stood up now, aflame with her conclusions. She took one of Mamat's cigarettes and slowly, stiffly, began limping around the living room. "Where do you find *kecubong*?" She took a deep drag. "It's a jungle plant. And where's the jungle?"

Rubiah gasped. "Kuala Krai! Oh my God! Maryam!" she jumped to her feet and hugged her.

Mamat took the opportunity to order Aliza to make some coffee. It was impossible to think with insufficient caffeine. The brain needed energy.

"Could someone have added opium to her food afterward? Dollah, for one. I mean, he goes to Thailand too. I'm just thinking," he apologized.

The two women stared at Mamat. Who would have thought? "Mamat," Maryam said slowly, "I do believe you're right. Her mother said they'd both brought over food."

Mamat cast down his eyes, accepting their praise. The three sat silently, drinking their coffee. Maryam's jaw was throbbing, and she couldn't speak any longer. Rubiah looked at her expectantly, but Maryam waved her away, and shook her head.

"We should ask Aisha's mother about the food," Rubiah then decided. "Though I hate to bother her, all she's been through."

"Her mind won't be on it," Mamat pointed out. "You can't ask her to concentrate at a time like this."

"We can go over tomorrow," Rubiah countered. "Or go to the hospital. Maybe the doctors can tell us something."

Maryam wondered whether the doctors would tell her anything. If not, Osman could request the information. They'd be duty bound to tell him; after all, he was the Chief of Police.

Chapter 25

OSMAN LEANED ACROSS THE DESK, his eyes alight. Maryam had applied her makeup with great care, covering the bruise on her face, and Osman did not seem to notice it. She sat back in her chair, drinking thick iced tea and picking through an assortment of cakes, taking a well-deserved breather before finishing her explanation.

"So that's how I figured it out. Our own Malay proverbs, they give you so much wisdom if you only listen to them." She nodded judiciously. "I never realized how much they really tell you about the world."

Osman nodded. "We should go down to Kuala Krai and talk to Faouda."

"Of course," Maryam agreed, reluctantly. "I mean," she said almost humbly, "it's a great theory, but we've got to prove it. And it still doesn't solve who killed Ghani."

"But with Aisha, it could be just Faouda, right? Someone else didn't necessarily slip her some opium." Osman still resisted the idea of two poisoners: he preferred to keep it simple.

"I think the most likely people would be Dollah and his troupe: Aisha's mother said they all brought food over for her, and they do travel to Thailand all the time. Hassan does also," she added, "but I haven't heard of him bringing anything to Aisha's house. He really doesn't know her," she added regretfully.

She much preferred Hassan as a suspect over anyone else, with the possible exception of Johan. Unfortunately, she couldn't connect him to Aisha no matter how convenient it would be.

She had not mentioned Johan's assault, and had no intention of doing so, but couldn't resist bringing him to Osman's attention. "When we go to see Faouda," she advised him, "we should talk to Johan as well."

"Why?" He wasn't objecting, merely requesting clarification.

Maryam tried to stay casual. "He's been in Thailand too, you know. And I always thought he might have killed Ghani, out of jealousy maybe." She prayed he would agree without demanding further explanation.

He did. "Very good idea, *Mak Chik*. He has motive and opportunity, don't you think?"

"Without doubt," Maryam answered firmly. She hoped Osman noticed only her confidence, and not the fear underlying it. She dreaded facing Johan again: he might really kill her this time.

Osman was beaming, relief and anticipation emanating from him in equal quantities. He ordered his staff around with authority, arranging to speak to his suspects in Kuala Krai. He assumed Maryam would come with him, but she didn't want to lessen his glory in any way. Besides, she'd seen enough of Kuala Krai to last several lifetimes. He insisted. "I'll need you there to help with the questioning," he advised. "Please." She acquiesced with as much grace as she could muster, and then hoped for the monsoon to wash out the roads.

Osman bounded up the stairs to the Kuala Krai police station in great good humor. He pictured himself the young, vital chief of the Kota Bharu police: the man who'd cracked the case, a debonair yet intrepid figure from the big city. He was greeted by his colleagues with cries of congratulations, and warm slaps on the back, and plied with questions about how he did it.

"It was mostly theoretical work," he instructed them modestly. "We had very little in the way of hard evidence to go on." They nodded attentively. "It was psychology," he added. "You know, as a policeman, you've really got to understand the criminal mind and how it works. And of course, the local culture. Otherwise, how can you understand what they're doing?"

Osman wondered briefly if in his expansiveness he had gone too far. But his audience still seemed enthralled. "In this case, I had to think about how a second wife might feel. It wasn't easy, I'm not even a woman." They laughed, and Osman was quietly rapturous. "But with psychology, you can put yourself in someone else's place and anticipate their next move."

Maryam watched him with both amusement and pride. It's as though he's my son, she thought to herself: young and sometimes stupid, but I can see at last he's growing up.

Moments later, Osman and Maryam were ushered into the small interrogation room to meet with Faouda. She sat stonily in her seat, watching Osman from under beetling eyebrows. "Who are you?" she asked.

"I'm the police chief from Kota Bharu."

"What do you want?"

"I wanted to talk to you about Aisha's death."

"Aisha's dead?"

Osman thought her face had lost a little colour. "She died a few days ago. Poisoned."

"Really?" She'd recovered her poise and her colour, and affected to be utterly disinterested in the information.

"You're in a difficult situation, Faouda."

"Me? Why?"

"Well…" Osman floundered. The language defeated him. He worried if they ever got beyond monosyllables, he might not even understand her answers.

Maryam smoothly took over. "You were her husband's second wife."

"For a week, maybe."

"Second wives have very difficult relationships with first wives."

"I wouldn't know," she replied airily. "I was only a second wife for such a short time," she pointed out. "It's not like I had a whole life there, or had kids, or anything like that. It was just for fun."

"For fun?" Maryam was appalled. "You wreck people's lives for fun?"

Faouda glared at her, and then silently accepted the cigarettes and tea served by a junior policeman. She leaned back, hanging her arm over the back of the chair. She said nothing, but her lower lip began to stick out. Maryam was tempted to slap her: Faouda and her husband aroused her desire to do so each time she'd seen them, and she wondered if everyone they met felt the same. She thought it likely. They were an unpleasant pair: sullen, selfish and snotty. Maryam remembered her own experience being hit, and knew it would be counterproductive, though extremely satisfying—to wipe the insolence from Faouda's face.

"You planned to get rid of Aisha before you met her. You've caused a lot of misery. But as I was saying to my cousin Rubiah," she took a ladylike sip of tea and flicked her ashes into a waiting dish, "taking a second wife is always a disaster for everyone. I don't really blame you; after all, you never forced Ghani to marry you. But after all this is over, Ghani's dead, Aisha's dead, and it's all because of you." She stayed quiet, as though deep in thought.

"I didn't kill anyone," Faouda said nastily. "I certainly didn't kill Ghani. Or Aisha," she made sure to add. She looked increasingly sulkier.

"I think even if you didn't kill Ghani, he still died because he married you."

"That's what you think."

"I know it." Maryam drank her tea again. "If you'd stayed in Kuala Krai, Ghani and Aisha would still be alive, and you'd be *legally* married to Johan. Why did you come here?"

Faouda was becoming irritated. "Ghani asked me to marry him. This isn't my fault alone, you know."

"Well, Ghani's dead now, so it's hard to blame him. And besides, he's a man! You know they don't think. If we women don't think, well, it all goes to hell." She paused. "Like it did."

"You know," Faouda sounded increasingly aggrieved, "I don't like the way people are blaming me for what happened. I got hurt, too, you know. You forget, *Mak Chik*: I got thrown out of Ghani's house, and his grandmother's house. I got divorced the day after I got up here. What about me?"

"What about you?" Maryam snapped. "Are you dead, too?" Faouda just answered with a sneer.

"Be grown-up for once: If you hadn't come up to Kota Bharu to kill your rival—yes, your rival—" Maryam insisted as she saw Faouda's face contort into a smirk, "Aisha would be here still, taking care of her children. If you hadn't come up here, Ghani would still be alive. Don't you have any shame at all?" Maryam's frustration was growing by the moment: she really wanted to shake this girl. "You came here with your poison and gave it to Aisha the first and only night you were here at her house."

"I never." Faouda insisted flatly. "Never." She folded her arms across her chest.

"Stop wasting my time. I hate it when you lie to me."

"I'm not!" Faouda tried to conjure up an expression of injured innocence, but failed. "Why are you here, anyway?"

"Because you killed Aisha. You'll be tried for it, of course."

Faouda leapt from her seat, knocking over the wooden chair. The noise brought Osman to his feet. "What are you doing?" he demanded of Faouda.

Maryam waved him away. "We're fine, thank you. A small accident."

Faouda stood next to her fallen chair, her hands shaking. "This isn't right!"

"Why? Did you think you could kill someone and never be caught? Did you think after you've killed someone, we should speak carefully and politely to you?" Maryam leaned over the table. "Just for my own curiosity, had you already planned to kill *Mak Chik* Maimunah?"

"Oh, please," Faouda scoffed. "I never wanted to kill Maimunah. I never wanted to kill anybody. And I never did." She picked up her overturned chair and sat down with a flourish. She crossed her arms and looked pugnacious while Maryam regarded her with increasing distaste.

"I know you used *kecubong*," Maryam told her flatly.

"What?"

"You got it yourself in the jungle there, didn't you? Hard to find up here, but in Kuala Krai it's everywhere. Put it in her tea, did you?" This was a long shot, but Maryam thought it the most likely method.

Faouda's head snapped up to watch Maryam. She stayed silent.

Maryam kept her eyes on her sarong, slowly tracing out the design on her thigh, ignoring Faouda for the time being. After she felt the silence heavy enough, she turned to Faouda with a thin smile. "I think the police will just go ahead with this. After all, we know about the tea, and we know Aisha died of *kecubong* poisoning. It's clear enough." Maryam stood slowly. "Goodbye, Faouda. Good luck. I'm sure the judge will be that much angrier with you to hear you never admitted what you've done."

"What does that mean?" Faouda looked more frightened now, less nonchalant.

"It means you're a killer without a conscience, and you think you can get away with it. You can't. You've already been caught." She turned towards the door, feeling worn out by Faouda. Osman held the door for her.

"What do you think?" he asked Maryam as they sat down in another office. "I think she's getting nervous," he continued without waiting for Maryam's opinion. "She can see we've figured it out."

"Do you think so? She seemed determined to stick to her story. But I can't help but believe she killed Aisha. It just makes so much sense to me. Ghani, I don't know."

Osman exited the office, leaving Maryam to think without interruption. She was finishing her cigarette when Faouda was pushed through the door, looking somewhat more disheveled than she'd been only minutes before. Perhaps she'd been running her hands through her hair: it was standing up in clumps all over her head.

"What is it now?" Maryam asked tiredly.

"I thought you wanted to ask me questions," Faouda fought to regain her desirability in Maryam's eyes. "You were dying to talk to me."

"That was then. Now I'm sick of you," Maryam answered bluntly, indeed, rudely. "If you want to talk, go ahead."

"Will it help me?"

"Help you what?"

"With the judge," Faouda said impatiently. "If I talk to you, will it help my case?"

"I guess so," Maryam said with little enthusiasm.

"We need to make sure," Faouda ordered. "I want to know for certain."

Maryam got up slowly, as though her knees hurt her. It wasn't her knees, though: she was mentally pained by Faouda's manoeuvrings. She'd been so anxious to get a confession just a few moments ago, and now, after she'd thought about it for a few minutes, she no longer cared. Convinced of her guilt, Maryam was now prepared to let the police talk to her, or the judge, or anyone other than Maryam herself.

"Where are you going?"

"I'm going home." She turned to Faouda. "I can't play your games anymore. Call someone else."

"But *Mak Chik*," Faouda rose to follow her to the door, "I want to talk to you now, I'm ready."

"Then talk. Or I'm leaving."

Faouda pouted for a moment, and seeing it did no good at all, sat down looking more cooperative. "I'm ready. Will you tell them...?"

Maryam's expression stopped her in mid-sentence. She picked up a cigarette instead and waited for Maryam to sit down.

"OK," Faouda began, a wary eye on Maryam. "You're right."

"Wait!" Maryam ordered. She went to the door and called for Osman. "I want him to hear this too."

Faouda looked as though she might argue, but then thought better of it, and subsided into silence until Osman was settled. "OK," she began again, "You were right, *Mak Chik*. I did think to make Aisha sick. Not to kill her, mind. It wasn't me who killed her, but I did make her sick."

"Go on," Maryam ordered her.

"I had some...stuff. You know," Faouda started.

"*Kecubong*?"

She nodded. "Yeah. I had it when I came up here."

"How long had you had it?" Maryam asked.

Faouda saw where she was leading, but saw no way to avoid it. "Well, I had it for a while." Maryam raised her eyebrow. "OK. I prepared it when I was still married to Yahya. You don't know how tough it is to be a second wife," she burst out. "The first wife always looks down on you. I was sick of it: she looked at me like I was dirt.

"And then, you know, this Yahya wasn't all that generous. How was I going to live when he was giving all his money to her? He really wanted to marry me," she directed this confidence to Osman, who was scribbling furiously. "But when he did, after a while he didn't want to give me enough money to live on. God forbid I had a baby! Who knows what would have happened then?"

"Where did you get it?"

"The *kecubong*? It grows in the jungle, you know. It's not that hard to find."

"I'm surprised there's anyone in Kuala Krai left alive."

Faouda gave her a sour look. "Yeah. Well, I got it. But then I started thinking, 'What's the point?' I couldn't see staying with him forever."

"Is that when you met Johan?"

She nodded and looked uncomfortable.

"So?"

"So I decided not to do anything. I wanted a divorce from Yahya and I knew it wouldn't be any trouble. He was tired of having two wives by then. I could see that. So I never used it. But I still had it."

"And then you met Ghani," Maryam prodded her.

She nodded. "We fell in love so quickly. We got married right away, just carried away by being in love." Maryam tried not to gag. "Now, I thought I'd want to stay with Ghani forever. I really believed it then." It was hard for Maryam to remember that this was really not so long ago: Faouda spoke as though eons had already passed.

"So when I went up to Kota Bharu, I brought my powder with me. I wasn't going to kill her, honest." She opened her eyes as wide as she could and looked into Osman's face. He didn't react. "I thought…" She took a deep breath. "I thought if she just got sick, you know, she'd go back to her parents or something and Ghani would forget about her. It happens, you know. I've heard about things like that working out."

Maryam shrugged. "She gave you a cup of tea when you showed up at her house, didn't she?"

"She did. She had one too. She wanted to choke me, but she was really very polite. Wonderful manners," she offered a grudging compliment. "So while she was preparing something, I put it in her tea. She didn't taste it."

"All of it?" Maryam was suddenly struck by a thought. "Did you put all of it in her tea?"

"No." Faouda clamped her mouth shut.

"What did you do with the rest of it?"

"I threw it away."

Maryam shook her head. "No, you didn't. What did you do with it?"

Faouda hung her head. "I put it in the box of tea she had."

"Where was she that you could get to the box of tea?"

Faouda looked ashamed. "Getting cakes."

"Getting cakes for you!" Maryam was astounded.

"Really," Faouda shook her head. "I couldn't believe it either! She was so polite."

Chapter 26

THE DOCTOR MET THEM in his dilapidated office at Kota Bharu General Hospital. His small office featured a depressing colour scheme of dirty cream and faded green and was furnished with a battered desk covered with files and four equally battered chairs. The doctor waved for them to sit, and took his own seat behind the desk. He brought a grimy ash tray out from his top drawer and set it at the summit of the sturdiest pile. He offered cigarettes all around, assured them the tea lady was on her way, and settled down to business.

He was an older man, with a lined face and bright eyes, his grey hair bearing the marks of his hands running through it. He looked rumpled but kindly, and when he smiled, Maryam could easily see why people trusted him with their lives.

"Aisha binte Ramli, you say," he asked them, shuffling though files perched on the window sill behind him. It took him a while to find the file, and he opened it in front of him, taking care not to drop ashes on it. Maryam and Osman waited patiently.

"A sad case," he commented. "Poisoning. I hate that."

Maryam agreed. "What kind of poisoning, *Tuan* Doctor?"

He looked again. "*Kecubong*. Kind of strange. It looks as though it had been going on a while. I mean, she'd been taking the poison over a period of days or weeks, not all at once."

"Was she given opium as well?"

"Why do you ask?"

"The *bomoh* in my village..." Maryam suddenly wondered whether doctors cared to hear what *bomoh* thought, but it was too late. "He said he thought there might be opium mixed in."

The doctor nodded. "It's hard to tell. The *kecubong* was obvious. You could see it in tests. We weren't looking for opium right away, and the family forbade an autopsy. They took her body right away. So, you can see, there isn't any way for me to confirm that."

They nodded. "But if it was *kecubong* only, Doctor, would it have led to the same outcome?" She put it as delicately as she knew how.

He thought for a moment. "Probably. Let me put it this way: if there was opium involved, it would be consistent with the symptoms, but I can't prove there was. I can prove *kecubong*."

Maryam looked over at Osman. He cleared his throat, not having prepared to speak during this meeting. "If it goes to trial, Doctor, would you be prepared to testify to that?"

The doctor nodded. "Yes, of course I would. Poor thing. She was so young. She left young children, too, I see. What will happen to them?"

"Her brother's taking them," Maryam told him, feeling very proud of Ali. "He's getting married and they're taking the kids as their own."

"Wonderful." He stood up. "Is there anything else?"

"No, thank you so much, *Tuan* Doctor," Maryam said gratefully. "You've been such a help to us."

"Thank you, Doctor," Osman extended his hand. "We will be in touch for the trial."

The doctor smiled and walked them to the door. He walked away down the corridor, running his hands through his already disheveled hair, his mind focused on his work ahead.

Chapter 27

IT WAS LATE AFTERNOON. The air became cooler as shadows covered more of the ground. Maryam and Rubiah revisited Ali in his parents' home. Grief now hung heavy on the house.

Azizah greeted them spiritlessly, and called to Ali to speak to them. He came onto the porch in a clean sarong and T-shirt, his hair still wet from a recent bath. "*Mak Chik*," he greeted them, inviting them to sit in the shade of the porch.

He waited for them to start. In the silence, his sister came quietly with coffee and cakes and served them with a polite smile. Maryam and Rubiah exchanged glances—was no one speaking here anymore? Ali seemed to rouse himself: had he seen their looks? He waved his hand over the cups and plates. "Please," he said.

"Ali," Maryam began, "I'm so sorry. I really am." She took a deep breath. "I really think you're wonderful for taking Aisha's children. You're a wonderful brother."

Ali waved again, dismissing Maryam's praise.

"I think we've found who killed your sister."

Ali's head jerked up, and he nearly leapt to his feet. "Who is it, *Mak Chik*?" he asked intently. "Tell me, please!"

"Faouda," Maryam said softly.

"Faouda!" Ali shouted, bringing his mother to the door.

"What happened?" she asked. Her face was etched with grief, and Maryam worried about causing her more hurt.

"It was Faouda who killed Aisha," Ali told her, breathless with excitement. "I knew she did it." He pounded his thigh.

"Faouda?" Azizah asked, looking as though she would cry. "She killed my daughter?" She buried her face in her hands.

Ali stood to comfort her. "Is she going to jail, *Mak Chik?*" he asked. "She's going to be prosecuted, isn't she?"

Maryam nodded. "She's already in jail, and she'll be tried for murder."

"Convicted, too," Rubiah added. "You can bet on it."

Azizah had sunk to the floor and was sitting in the doorway. "Tell me how she did it," she asked through tears. "My poor Aisha."

"Poison." Maryam was becoming uncomfortable. They'd find out anyway, she reasoned, if nowhere else than during the trial. It was better they know now, and be prepared, than to be shocked in public. She hesitated. "*Kecubong.*"

Aisha's mother thought for a moment. "From the jungle? She must have brought it here from Kuala Krai then."

Maryam and Rubiah nodded, and Azizah began crying again. Maryam squirmed slightly, not wishing to say what came next. "She put it in her tea, and then more in the box of tea."

Azizah and her son stared open-mouthed at Maryam. "No," Ali finally managed.

Maryam nodded miserably.

"No," he repeated. "So, when I..." he swallowed hard. "When I brought Aisha back from seeing Ghani, and she was crying, and I made her tea to make her feel better..." he couldn't go on. "I killed my own sister!" He looked frantic.

"No!" Maryam surprised herself with the vehemence of her reply. "No, you did not!" She looked towards his mother for help, but she was crouched and no longer paying attention. Rubiah jumped into the breach.

"Ali!" Rubiah cried, shaking his shoulders. "You did nothing! Faouda poisoned her the first night she was here. You had nothing to do with it. You tried your best to save her! You can't think like that! It's wrong, do you hear me?"

The commotion on the porch brought his father to the door. "What's all this?" he asked angrily. "What are you all talking about?" He looked down at his wife next to him and petted her hair with indescribable tenderness. "Well?"

"*Ayah*," Ali answered. "They've found out who killed Aisha!"

"You have?" he demanded.

"Yes," Maryam began nodding again. "Faouda."

He was silent for a moment. "I knew it. Look at the evil Ghani brought into our family," he raged. "He killed Aisha as sure as if he plunged a knife into her heart. Faouda! She should be cursed; she should be plagued by pain and sorrow for the rest of her days."

Maryam and Rubiah gave the full sad account one more time. At the end of it, Aisha's mother slumped over again in deep grief.

Her husband helped her up off the porch and guided her indoors. "Thank you, *Kak*," he added over his shoulder.

Ali stayed seated, shocked into silence again.

"Ali," Maryam begged him, "please try to remember anything else you can about that night at the performance, was there anyone else there? Anyone at all?"

Ali tried to get his emotions under control and ran his hand over his face in a gesture reminiscent of his sister. "Well, after the performance, I waited with Aisha so that she could talk to Ghani. This was after I had the fight with him. So I kept away, you know.

"Aisha was wild. She looked quiet and even—" he thought for a moment, "obedient, but she had a lot of fire, Aisha did. After the performance she talked to Ghani again, and they were really going at it.

"Ghani threatened to divorce her, and Aisha was crying on the ground holding on to his ankles. There weren't many people around anymore." He considered what to say next. "Faouda and her new husband were there, but they'd already left. Aisha wouldn't have a conversation like this in front of her," Ali assured them.

"He finally ended it and said they'd talk about it when he got home Thursday night. He told her to calm down, everything would be all right, but he made her promise not to see a *bomoh* about him. I took her home after that. You know, *Mak Chik*, I was even afraid to take her home on my motorbike: I was afraid she'd fall off, or jump or something. She was still crying when we got home." He rubbed his face again, and Maryam recalled Aisha doing the same thing.

"I took her to her own house; the kids were with my parents, and I thought she needed to rest first. I made her tea." He began crying again. "Oh, Aisha!"

"Then what?" Maryam asked, trying to get him past the memory.

"When she felt better, I took her back to my parents to go to sleep. And then in the morning, the police came for her and told her Ghani was dead." He leaned his forehead on the heel of his hand and wept.

Maryam patted his back as she would a small child. "She loved you, Ali. And you're taking care of her by adopting her children. You've been so loyal to her." Ali did not stop crying. Maryam looked over at Rubiah, her face creased with concern.

"Ali, listen to me. It's important: did you see anyone before you left?"

Ali shook his head.

"Where did Ghani go?"

"Back into the stage."

"And you saw nothing?"

He shrugged. "Maybe someone was awake there; I thought I saw a shadow."

"Who?"

Ali shrugged. "I couldn't see. Just a shadow. And I had to worry about Aisha: I couldn't take the time to go investigate, not that I would have, anyway. I just wanted to get out of there."

"Of course you did," Maryam agreed. "Anyone would have felt the same."

Chapter 28

MARYAM FOUND A TAXI early in the morning while the air was still cool, and watched the now familiar route to Tawang slide by. The winds were changing, and the rains were coming. They couldn't come soon enough for Maryam: she wanted a change of season to seal the end of all this. She banged her head back against the soft seat of the car. She hated going out there again, but if she didn't find out who'd left the *jampi*, she'd be looking over her shoulder for the rest of her life.

And who better to help her than the wives of the musicians she'd met? She'd met the "boys", and believed their coaching would hold up under cross-examination, but their wives...that might be different. She doubted Dollah would have involved the wives in his direction, but they'd hear all the gossip and over-hear conversations their husbands had. If anyone could offer new information, it would be these young women, and Maryam was determined to see them.

She found Awang's house first, since it was closest to the road. Like Ghani's, it was small and unpainted. A broken tricycle lay on its side near the ladder going to a porch, and the sound of pouring water came from the back: the kitchen, where the lady of the house was most likely to be.

And there she was, washing out bowls next to a small charcoal brazier heating a large metal pot. She was a plain girl with a no-nonsense air about her: wearing a simple cotton blouse, old sarong and scuffed plastic flip-flops. She looked up as Maryam peeked around the corner of the house.

"Good morning," Maryam greeted her cheerfully. "You must be Awang's wife."

"Yes."

"I'm *Mak Chik* Maryam, and I'm looking into…"

"Oh!" She rose to greet her, drying her hands on her *sarong*. "Awang told me." She regarded Maryam with interest. "I'm Rashidah." She gave a quick smile. "What can I do for you?"

"You know, we women hear so much that men don't notice," Maryam confided, trying to forge a bond between them. "I thought maybe you would know something about Ghani, maybe have heard something."

The woman looked at her blankly. "Heard about what, *Mak Chik*? I don't know anything about that. Maybe Awang can help you."

"Well, I just wondered if you'd heard anything about *jampi*. You know, someone put one under my house."

"Really?" Rashidah breathed. Maryam realized this news would be all around the village in no time. She nodded at the girl. "Have you heard any gossip about it?"

She shook her head. "No, nothing. I mean, poor Aisha, was that part of it?"

"No," Maryam answered hastily. "No, not that." This girl really didn't seem to know much—or had been told by her husband to say nothing if asked.

As if she knew what Maryam was thinking, she told her, "I don't know anything about *jampi*, *Mak Chik*. But anyone who would put one under your house certainly wouldn't talk about. How would I hear of it?" She shrugged her shoulders and looked Maryam straight in the eye, and Maryam couldn't help but agree. It wasn't going to be widely disseminated. However, the person who did it, and his family, might know and might give themselves away. Maryam gave her thanks, and went to find the next house.

Arifin's house had a tiny, immaculately swept yard. A pretty young woman, with a figure more voluptuous than often found in Kelantan, hung laundry on a line while a little girl held on to her leg. The girl's slightly older brother kicked around a woven palm ball with a friend.

"Hello! It's *Mak Chik* Maryam." Maryam was again cheerful.

The woman looked up at her, warily. "Yes?"

Maryam introduced herself, while the girl's expression did not change. "I'm Zurainah," she said shortly. "Why are you here?"

"I'd like to talk to you." Maryam smiled graciously.

"Why?" Zurainah asked again, making no move to abandon her laundry. "Isn't it all over?" she asked, shifting her eyes back to her wet clothing as she continued to pin it to the line.

"Just a few loose ends," Maryam explained. "I thought you might have heard something…"

"Why me?" Zurainah seemed angry and Maryam retreated.

"Well, not just you," she stammered. "The wives of the musicians here."

"What about us?" Zurainah interrupted. "Why would we know anything?"

Maryam was intrigued by Zurainah's reaction. While Rashidah seemed puzzled, Zurainah seemed furious. "But you see, there was a *jampi* left under my house." She flicked her eyes up to meet Zurainah's.

"Is that what you came here to say?"

Maryam nodded.

Zurainah sighed with irritation. "*Mak Chik*, what do you want me to do about it?"

"I need your help," Maryam entreated in her softest voice. "I cannot live with such fear, all the time." She shuddered to demonstrate the burden under which she toiled.

"Why do you think I could help you? I don't know anything about it."

"You know everyone involved," Maryam said quietly, determined to get Zurainah to talk. Perhaps if Zurainah would offer her some coffee, they could sit down and speak more easily to each other. But Zurainah made no move to offer anything, or even to invite Maryam onto the porch. It was growing hotter, and Maryam would have welcomed some shade, but Zurainah remained intent on her laundry. Maryam began to sweat; it would soon become a torrent.

"Everyone involved?" the younger woman repeated. "*I* know them? No, I don't."

"I thought perhaps you all might have seen things I cannot see." It seemed unlikely Zurainah would volunteer any information, but she might be willing to lecture if Maryam would allow it. She bit her lip to ensure she stayed in character, inviting Zurainah to scold her.

"You're the detective," Zurainah muttered before she stopped herself. She seemed determined to keep her temper in check. "Not me."

Maryam agreed. "Perhaps I shouldn't be. Putting all this together, it's so…complicated. And I'm scared." She lowered her voice and Zurainah leaned over to listen. "The *jampi*…I'm so frightened. I can't think anymore." She squeezed a trickle of tears down her cheeks.

"Just leave it alone," Zurainah suggested bluntly. "Leave it to the police: it's too dangerous for you."

Maryam nodded miserably.

"You can't just blunder into people's lives," Zurainah lectured. "You're in a dangerous place. *Jampi*! To an old *Mak Chik* like you."

Maryam gritted her teeth and kept quiet.

"Come, *Mak Chik*," she admonished. "Your time for playing detective is over. The police can do this: you don't have to."

"But I'm afraid," Maryam whined. "I must find out who's tried to kill me. Otherwise, what if they do it again?" She sniffed (she hoped) pathetically. "I can't leave it: I have children and I must protect them."

"You'd protect them better by leaving this alone," Zurainah told her. "I'm sure if you stay away from this, this murder, there will be no more *jampi*."

"How do you know?" Maryam asked, adjusting her head scarf and wiping her forehead. "I will leave now. If you hear anything…"

"I won't," Zurainah told her sharply. "I don't know anything about this! I don't know why you came to me, but you ought to take my advice. Stay out of it."

Maryam nodded her assent, and walked away along the blacktop road shimmering in the heat. Din lived just across it. Her thoughts returned again to Zurainah's face; there was something there, something threatening. She pulled herself up to full height with a sudden jerk. It was her! She was the woman searching for her in the market. Absorbed in this realization, she never saw the push which threw her into the road.

Chapter 29

"WHAT HAPPENED?" she asked, waking as if from a dream. She could barely focus her eyes, and it hurt to talk. "Mamat?"

"Right here, *sayang*. Don't worry," Mamat soothed.

She sank again under the waves. When she next awoke, she was restless and struggled to sit up. Rubiah was next to her, helping her on to her pillow, and Mamat's anxious face swam into view. She looked around and remembered the dull green walls occasionally revealing their dirty cream undercoat, the Spartan furnishings, and registered the unremitting roar. "Am I hurt?"

"Not so bad," Mamat assured her, stroking her arm. "Bruises and cuts, a broken arm…"

"What?" Maryam looked at her left arm, motionless in a large white cast.

"You're lucky," Rubiah told her. "You could easily have been killed, you know. Lucky that car stopped before they ran right over you. You'll be fine! You just need to rest a little. You're going to be very sore," she warned her, "but fine."

"Who did it? What happened?"

"Osman's been investigating," Mamat assured her. He laughed at her raised eyebrow. "Yes, Osman! He got on it right away when he found out what happened to you."

"It was Zurainah," Rubiah added somberly. "She pushed you."

"Why?" Maryam was having a little trouble remembering.

She'd never forgive Zurainah for sending her to this hospital. The room was noisy, the din from the street outside unimpeded by closed windows. To close them was to invite certain heat stroke. Her shoulder hurt. Why did Zurainah want to kill her? Zurainah needed to take care of her children, not end up in jail for murder. No, Maryam at least was still alive. She closed her eyes for a moment, cursing Zurainah, but was too sore to give this string of expletives voice.

"I'll bet she put the *jampi* under the house, too," Rubiah continued.

Maryam now remembered the *jampi*. She shook her head to clear it, but it hurt.

"Osman's been investigating," Rubiah informed her. "He's found out a lot."

Maryam raised an eyebrow. "But why?"

"It's his job!" Rubiah answered sharply. "Why wouldn't he investigate? You can't keep doing everything, you know. We shouldn't be surprised that he's working!"

"No, not that." Maryam was too tired to argue. "No, why did she push me?"

"Oh," Rubiah said in an almost disappointed tone as she fussed around the pillows. "I thought you meant… Never mind. I don't know much about what he's found out: I think he wants to talk it over with you."

Maryam nodded and closed her eyes. When she opened them, the sun slanted low in the windows and it looked about to set. Osman and Mamat were talking softly in a corner of the room, each watching her surreptitiously.

"Here she is!" called Mamat with exaggerated heartiness. "She's awake!" He came over and sat lightly on the bed next to her. Osman walked over shyly and ducked his head. "*Mak Chik!*" he said. "I'm so glad to see you're better."

She smiled tiredly and nodded again.

"Are you thirsty, *sayang*?" asked Mamat anxiously. "Do you want some tea, or water?"

"Tea," she said, and fixed her eyes on Osman. With an effort she asked, "What happened?" It seemed to her she'd been asking this ceaselessly, and hadn't yet had a satisfying answer.

Mamat slipped away to find tea, and Osman drew up a chair next to her, resting his elbows on his knees and looking at the floor. "*Mak Chik*," he began, "I can't tell you how sorry I am." Maryam gave him a look she hoped he'd interpret as an order to start on his story. Apparently, he did. He cleared his throat.

"So, someone actually saw Zurainah push you. It was the middle of the day, but still there were people around and she didn't do anything to cover up what she was doing. She just walked up behind you and shoved." He looked up at her. "Not very subtle, is it, but I think it was a spur-of-the-moment kind of thing. She won't admit anything, won't talk at all. Her husband Arifin came in to see her, but he said nothing either. She won't even explain why she'd do such a thing.

"I have her in custody, of course: it's attempted murder. I'm trying to put it together myself though, and I think you're getting very close to the truth here and she's threatened by it." He looked at Maryam, but she didn't respond.

"Arifin was there at the murder, though I can't prove he held the knife. But there must be something to it: Zurainah isn't going to push you into a car for no good reason. It isn't just meanness."

"It could be," murmured Maryam. "What about the *jampi*?"

He shook his head regretfully. "No, nothing yet. *Mak Chik* Rubiah thinks it's Zurainah, and it would make sense, but I don't know yet."

Maryam considered him silently. He seemed to have grown up a little, grown into his job. Maybe all he needed was her encouragement and guidance, and then she needed to get out of his way.

As though he heard her thoughts, he said, "I'm trying only to keep things ready for you, *Mak Chik*, when you get back to work. I can't let the case grow cold while I wait for you." He smiled sweetly, and Maryam laughed at his flattery.

"You've really taken this over now, haven't you, *Chik* Osman?" Such a long sentence made her head ache again. "You don't need me at all."

"How can you say that? I'm lost without you!" He stood up. "You need your rest, *Mak Chik*. I'll leave you to sleep for a while."

She was already asleep. He passed Mamat in the hall as he left. Mamat carried a plastic bag with sweet iced tea. "Leaving already, *Chik* Osman?"

"I'll be back," he promised. "She needs her rest now."

Chapter 30

Maryam held Rubiah's arm as they walked into Osman's office. Even the short walk from the car seemed unending, and both Osman and Rahman were assisting her. "Let's sit down. I'm exhausted. So much misery." She sighed.

"How are you?" Rubiah asked anxiously. "Are you too tired to be out here?" Rubiah was already looking toward the nearest chair, planning the shortest route to it.

"I'm fine, I'm fine," Maryam assured her, although she was not so sure herself. She felt increasingly fragile these days.

Osman placed her carefully in her seat, and arranged the room fans around her.

"Sit down," Rubiah ordered. "I'm getting some coffee."

"It's done," Rahman assured her, as Maryam stared moodily around the room. She was depressed by Aisha's death more than she could express.

"What are you thinking about?" Osman softly interrupted her reverie. "Here, drink this."

Maryam took a sip of coffee. "About Aisha. Her husband as good as killed her himself."

"That's a little harsh," Rubiah commented.

"It is," Maryam agreed, "but it's the way I feel. Ghani helped kill her himself." She put down the cup. "But who killed Ghani?" She paused for effect. "It's Arifin," she announced. "I'm really beginning to think it is."

"Of course, it certainly would explain what happened, but," Osman held up a finger, "let's just think first. Did she push you because she put the *jampi* under your house? Or was she protecting her husband?"

Maryam looked at him sharply. "Both," she answered, and looked at her coffee as though the answer was written in it. "Think about the shadows," she instructed. "Only the performing troupe sleeps in the stage, no one else goes in after it's all over. There isn't enough room for anyone else, and they'd be thrown out anyway."

Osman nodded. Rahman listened raptly.

"Only Dollah and Arifin could have been shadows. And if they were up, I think they could have followed Ghani outside."

"Couldn't Johan have been there also? He could have been sitting in the gloom, waiting, like a spider," Rubiah suggested.

"He could have, but I think they'd already left. Aisha would never talk in front of Faouda. How humiliating would it be? It's impossible to imagine."

Rubiah grudgingly agreed. "I guess she wouldn't."

Maryam made a face of disbelief. "You guess? Aisha must have been sure Faouda wasn't around."

"OK, I agree."

"So the only people left are Dollah and Arifin," Maryam's logic was inexorable. "And after what Zurainah's done, it's Arifin. I'd swear to it."

"Haven't you already spoken to Arifin, *Mak Chik*?" Osman asked.

"I spoke to all of them," Maryam answered crisply, "and heard nothing but lies. I wasn't sure he had anything worth hearing, but now I think he's the killer."

"I'd have to agree. Why else would Zurainah try to kill you?" He lit a cigarette and beamed at Maryam. "I'll pick him up right away and we can get his confession."

"One minute, Osman!" She began to waver, "Maybe it isn't him. Maybe Dollah was the one…"

Osman stood behind his desk, clutching his hat to his chest. "Well, at least we have it down to two suspects. Now we have to find out which one is the killer." He waited for a brief moment. "I think we're done."

On his own, not surrounded by friends, Arifin was visibly nervous. Maryam confronted him sitting at the table in the room she took for her own, playing with his tea, lighting a second cigarette before he'd finished the first. He was awed by the police station and officialdom in general, and his portrayal of earlier profound repentance was nowhere in evidence.

She let him feel the strain of silence while Osman sat quietly next to her, watching. She deliberately positioned her tea and her cigarettes, put the curry puffs on a plate, and even unpacked a few of Rubiah's sweet cakes. At last, satisfied with the arrangement, she looked up at Arifin with a smile both regretful and understanding.

"So, here we are again, *Che* Arifin," she began. "I'm sorry this had to happen, but I didn't think we got very far in our last talk." She waited to see if he had anything to say, but there was only silence. "I wish you'd been more honest with me before, but maybe you didn't feel you could with *Pak Chik* Dollah there. Was that a problem? I'm sorry if it was." She paused. Arifin stared at his lap and fidgeted with his cigarette. "Was your wife angry at you for talking to me?"

He looked frightened when she asked a question. "Um, no." He fidgeted for a moment. "She's sorry, you know, *Mak Chik*. She didn't mean to hurt you."

"No? That's good! I'd hate to think she did this on purpose. Can you explain why she might have done it?" She paused, but Arifin sat staring at the floor. "You're really in love with your wife, aren't you?"

He looked puzzled. Maryam laughed at him. "Don't look so confused! It's a wonderful thing for a husband to love his wife. It doesn't happen often enough, I think," she congratulated him. "I just got the feeling, you know, talking to you and talking to her, you two are so close. And so in love." She smiled approvingly.

"I guess," he mumbled.

"A bit jealous, too," she teased him. "I can see that, too."

He nodded. He was wary, unsure of where this was going, but positive she hadn't called him here to tell him how much she admired his marriage.

"Now Ghani, he was a good-looking man. I'm old enough to be his mother, and I could still see how good-looking he was. Just the kind of looks women go for. You grew up in the same town, you must have seen it all your life: the girls going for Ghani. Is that the way it was?"

He shrugged.

"Did he ever court your wife, Zurainah? When they were younger, I mean, before either was married, of course."

He spoke carefully. "Ghani flirted with all the girls. I don't think he courted her, no."

"I think it's something you should know. A man prone to jealousy often forgets what his wife is really like. He's jealous so he thinks she's provoking him. I'm telling you: Zurainah isn't doing that at all. You ought to appreciate it." She swallowed hard to prevent herself saying what she really thought about Zurainah. There would be nothing gained by it.

He nodded.

"Have you?" She asked him, speaking in a near whisper. "Have you appreciated it?"

He twisted his hands together in his lap, afraid to speak, afraid to stay silent. "I, I haven't trusted her as much as maybe I should have." His voice was tense and tight. "I was suspicious of Ghani. That's why we argued a lot. But you didn't know Ghani: he'd never say anything like 'I'm not interested in Ainah,' or 'She isn't interested in me.' He always pushed it. 'Your wife's really pretty, great figure,' he would say. Or, 'I saw her at the market, looking terrific. She's so easy to talk to.' He used to say things like that all the time when we were performing."

She shook her head disapprovingly. "That isn't right for a married man, or any man, to say about a decent married woman. It just isn't right. I doubt Ainah gave him the time of day." Maryam leaned back in her chair and watched Arifin. "Did you fight with her about Ghani?"

He nodded. "Sometimes."

"And you really suspected her with Ghani?'

"Yes and no," he answered, now ready to talk. "If I thought about it, I could see she wasn't unfaithful. You know, she was never gone where I couldn't find her, she never stayed out late, she took good care of the house and our children. I've heard when women are fooling around, these are the signs. My mother talked to me about it: she said if anyone suspected a daughter-in-law, it would be a mother-in-law, and she thought Zurainah was a good wife and good mother."

"Absolutely!" Maryam agreed. "If there was anything wrong going on, your mother would be the first to see it. If your mother didn't even believe it, it's because there was nothing happening."

"I know." He looked close to tears. "I know. But sometimes I just couldn't help myself. I'd suspect something, and when I did, Ghani was always there to make it worse."

"He was just teasing you," Maryam said firmly.

"Maybe."

"The two of you acted like you were still in Standard Two," she said, becoming exasperated with him. "You react, so he teases you. Really, for two grown men..."

Arifin lit another cigarette. "Maybe," he answered morosely.

"Did you have a fight with Zurainah before you started performing at my house?" she asked gently.

He sat smoking for a long moment. Maryam feared he'd forgotten where he was.

"Arifin?"

He didn't answer. He took a long drink of his tea, and continued smoking silently. She sat back to wait it out.

He stood up. "I'd better go home," he said.

"Not yet," Maryam advised him. "You aren't finished here."

"I am."

"No!" Maryam ordered him.

Before Osman could stop him, he'd fled out the door and past the shocked policemen.

"Catch him!" Maryam screamed at them, "Hurry!"

Two police piled into a car, but Rahman and Osman took off after Arifin, running after him on Jalan Ibrahim, threading the busy sidewalk and outrunning the stalled traffic. Arifin ran like a man possessed, but Rahman stayed close behind. The siren blared as the police Land Rover tried to get past afternoon traffic at the circle, and cars tried unsuccessfully to move out of the way. Osman stopped finally, his hands on his knees, gasping for air. His head was pounding, he thought he'd faint on the street. He watched Rahman run with undisguised admiration.

Rahman chased Arifin as he ran toward the market and the thicket of taxis and trishaws around it. The crowd would make it impossible for the police car to get near him in time: it was up to Rahman alone to catch him. He wanted to call out to passersby to stop Arifin, but he didn't have enough wind to do it while running, and if he stopped, he'd lose him. Arifin seemed to fly though the streets. He ran straight toward the market and cut through the fishmonger's area in the middle of the building. It would bring him to the other side of the *pasar*, beyond the ability of the car to make it, and if he could make it to the tangle of alleys on the other side of Kota Bharu, he could hide in the sprawl and get away.

The floor was wet and slippery, and Arifin missed his footing, sailing into a stall head first, scattering fish and ice everywhere. He lay for one paralyzed second on the floor, festooned with silver scales. Rahman made a flying leap at him, landing across his legs, holding on to his ankles. In a moment,

Arifin kicked Rahman off him, hitting him hard in the temple, knocking his head on the concrete floor.

Arifin scrambled frantically to his feet, wiping his shirt as he did, leaping across the street on the other side of the market, onto the hood of a passing car. He tumbled off the other side of the car. Rahman stood up, determined to keep running even after his head had taken such a beating: he couldn't see clearly, but lurched in the direction Arifin had taken. He never saw the car: he hit it shoulder first, head down, bringing the full force of his body as he slammed against it. The pain was excruciating, and he collapsed against the tire, unable to breathe or even remember where he was.

The driver fell out of his seat, staring at two injured men on either side of his car. "I didn't do anything!" he wailed at no one in particular. He ran to Arifin first, who was no longer conscious, lying on his back in the street. A crowd had gathered. "Don't move him!" someone shouted, and the driver backed away, turning now to Rahman. He too lay silent in the street, his head bleeding badly, his breathing rough.

His colleagues arrived soon after, now racing down Jalan Temenggong, sirens bleating, lights flashing. Osman ran to Rahman. "Wake up," he whispered, as though it would lift Rahman out of his faint. Osman was becoming frantic: Rahman was still breathing, but... "Get an ambulance!" he croaked to the police crowded around, but it wasn't necessary. They had already called for one, terrified to see one of their own so still and pale.

Their suspect was out cold, with one leg clearly broken, his head bleeding, his cheek already swelling where it hit the pavement. Osman stood over him, overcome with the desire to pound his head into the street, his fists clenched and neck muscles bulging. No one moved to help Arifin: they either ignored him completely or looked as though they might spit on him.

The ambulance arrived, surprised to find two men in the street, one surrounded by concern, the other left to survive as well he could. The doctor looked unhappily at Rahman as they prepared to lift him, softly touching his head, and trying to open his eyes.

"What is it?" Osman demanded, feeling near tears. The doctor said nothing, but put a sympathetic hand on his arm, and silently climbed into the truck behind Rahman.

Chapter 31

THE KOTA BHARU HOSPITAL was crowded with police, as it had been for several days while Rahman lay still under a tangle of wires and tubes. It was the first time in recent memory an officer had been downed in the line of duty, and Osman felt personally responsible for Rahman's injuries. He replayed the incident constantly, changing it in his mind to another, happier ending.

Rahman's parents, his brothers and sisters and what appeared to be his entire extended family took turns sitting by his bed, willing him to wake up and come back to them. They did not answer the police who spoke to them with more than monosyllables, though his mother would occasionally burst out to describe a pain she could hardly bear. "He hasn't even been married yet," she told one of the older policemen, while looking right through him. "His life is still ahead of him!" The older man nodded quietly, his eyes full of feeling for her. There was no answer necessary, and none he could give anyway.

Maryam dragged Osman away from Rahman to see Arifin, who lay conscious in another room with a police guard who neither spoke to him nor responded to his requests for drinks or help with sitting up.

Osman set a rapid pace down the hallway, anxious to return to his vigil, and Maryam was breathless when they arrived at Arifin's room. Osman pushed the door to the room open wide, revealing a much-bandaged Arifin and a weeping older woman sitting beside him.

Maryam smiled at them, trying to be sympathetic but failing, keeping in mind she may have been smiling at a murderer of two people. Arifin had broken his cheekbone in the fall: his face was puffed and swollen, turning all shades of purple and yellow. His head was covered in white linens; his right arm was in a cast as was his right leg. He looked defeated.

"How are you feeling?" Maryam asked politely, though coldly. He didn't answer, nor did the woman cease crying. Hoping for better luck, she turned to her. "Have you been here long, *Kak*?"

She nodded dully. "Since the police called me," she said, sniffling.

"He'll be all right," Maryam assured her.

"Nothing will be all right," the woman answered, her voice hoarse from crying. "What will happen to the children? Both the parents in jail! Never in my life would I have thought such a thing would happen." She swallowed and leaned her head on the iron bedstead. "I'm his mother," she added unnecessarily. "You're the one my daughter-in-law had…the accident with, aren't you?"

Maryam nodded. It was no accident, she wanted to tell her: Zurainah tried to kill me. She didn't care to argue the point with her, especially with a mother looking into as bleak a future as this one was.

"Can you talk?" Maryam leaned over Arifin. He shook his head and closed his eyes. "Would you like to talk about what you've done?" she pushed. "We know what it is." Arifin glared at her, but refused to speak.

"You killed Ghani, didn't you?" Arifin closed his eyes again. His mother watched Maryam nervously. "After you ran like that, it was obvious, wasn't it? By the way, Rahman, the policeman who chased you, is in the hospital here right down the hall. Only he isn't awake," Maryam informed him tersely.

Arifin mumbled something, but Maryam didn't catch it. "Ghani came back after Aisha left," she continued, baldly laying out the facts as she'd put them together. "He must have been drained; it was such an emotional argument. He still carried the knife to protect himself from Ali, even though Ali had already left. Was he afraid Ali would come back?" She paused, in case Arifin cared to answer. "Well, you must have just lain there quietly, waiting for him to go out. Was it all jealousy, Arifin? Did you really think there was anything between Ghani and your wife?"

"Who knows?" His mother answered for him, "I've seen a side of Zurainah I never thought I would. I would never have believed, never, that she would try to push you in front of a car, *Kak*. And yet..." she paused, thinking. She shook her head almost absently.

"You have a family," she explained to Maryam. "Your kids are married and have their own kids. You think you know them, both your son and your daughter-in-law. But you don't."

She gave Arifin a hard look, but after all, he was her son. Of course, she'd want to blame someone. And Arifin was her own boy.

"Whatever Arifin did—may have done," she corrected herself, "it was because of her." She finished with an air of satisfaction, as though she had set the record right. "This was all in Arifin's mind," she put her hand on Maryam's arm to ensure her attention. "You should believe me when I tell you."

"Maybe," Maryam tightened her lips. "But no matter what may have pushed you, *Che* Arifin, you still killed a man who had done nothing to you."

Arifin's mother jumped in immediately as counsel for the defense. "Nothing? First, *Kak*," she held up her finger. "I'm not saying my son has actually done anything. We don't know, do we?" Maryam gave her a rather cynical look, but stayed quiet. "But even if he did, and again, I'm not saying he did, it certainly wouldn't be considered nothing if Ghani interfered with Zurainah. That's a serious crime, even a religious crime.

You can't just wish that away." There was a battle light in her eyes as she rode to her son's defense. Maryam knew she would object to almost anything she said, but she plowed on.

"That's what made you kill him, wasn't it? He was teasing you and you let yourself get that jealous. It's hard to believe you killed someone for something so meaningless."

She let her words hang in the air, listening to the muted noise from outside.

"You're being charged," Osman added from his corner, "for Ghani's murder."

His mother gasped and put her hand over her mouth, her tears starting again. "You can't," she cried. "You don't know what happened, and besides," she looked around frantically, "there are children to consider here. Children without a mother!"

"I guess it's over," Arifin lisped through his swollen lips. His mother let out a long, low moan and buried her head in her hands.

"Never mind," he said vaguely. "He always made me think it could've happened with Zurainah. That night was awful. Poor Aisha! She was there with her brother, and there's Ghani threatening to divorce her." He paused to recover his energy. He could barely be understood through his broken face, but they all listened intently. "I thought he said that because he wanted to marry Ainah. That's what I really thought." His mother continued her keening.

"He came back after Aisha left, crying so, and lay down with his knife. 'I can't take any more,' he said. Mahmud, the *serunai* player, told him to shut up. 'You've put her through hell,' Mahmud told him. 'It wouldn't hurt you to go through a little yourself.' Ghani tried to answer him, but then everyone told him to shut up, so he went to sleep."

He stopped and panted. He was clearly tired. "I lay there thinking about all those things he'd say about Ainah, getting madder and madder. Then Ghani got up to go outside. Everyone was asleep, I thought, and I followed him out. He put the knife on the ground and I grabbed it and killed him. It was so quick," he marveled. "So quiet. I couldn't believe I'd done it. I stuck the knife back in the ground and wiped my hands with his towel.

"When I turned around, I bumped right into Dollah. 'What the hell have you done?' Dollah asked me. I didn't need to explain."

He panted again and gestured toward a glass of water on the bed table. Osman held the straw for him to take a drink. He nodded and breathed with his mouth open, deep gasping breaths. "Dollah smacked me across the face and told me to get back into the stage and keep my mouth shut. He came in and we both lay down. You saw us in the morning."

"Why would Dollah protect you?" Maryam was shocked to hear this.

"Don't know." Arifin was falling asleep. "Doesn't matter. What can you do?"

"What will we do?" his mother plucked at Maryam's sleeve. "What will happen to him?"

"Jail, I guess," Maryam shrugged. She looked at Osman, who nodded.

"But, can't you... I mean, look how ill he is," she babbled. "Don't you think it would be better just to let him go home?"

"You mean to just forget about it?"

She nodded eagerly. "Exactly. Of course, he'd never do anything like this again!"

"No," Osman shook his head slowly. "I can't do that. There's also the police officer in a coma, damage your son caused."

"But the children!" she reminded him, clearly not listening to anything he said. "I think it may have been Zurainah at the bottom of it all," she continued, speaking faster with each succeeding word, "I don't think Arifin really knew what was happening, you know. I think..."

"*Mak Chik*," Osman said calmly, implacably, "murder is murder."

Chapter 32

"I DIDN'T THINK it would be Arifin," Maryam confided to Osman over a large iced tea at Rubiah's stall. The upper floor of the market was empty now, in the quiet between the high tides of morning and afternoon shoppers. "I really thought he was killed because he took a second wife. I didn't dream it wouldn't have anything to do with that at all. It was just a schoolyard fight, if you ask me."

Rubiah leaned her elbows on the counter, flicking a dish of cakes towards Osman with a meaningful look. "He killed Ghani because Ghani teased him. They're just boys! Never grew up."

Maryam lit a cigarette and passed them around. "How can you explain something like that? A young man losing his life for really no reason at all. At least if there was something beneath it all. But no! Nothing at all, not even something going on with Zurainah. And now he's dead, and Arifin, well, I suppose he's as good as." She looked over at Osman who had a mouthful of cake.

He swallowed guiltily, as though he'd been caught stealing. "He'll be in prison for his whole life, unless he's hanged." He stopped. Perhaps that wasn't the right thing to say in front of ladies. These ladies, however, took it well; they had suspected such an outcome all along. "You're right," he hurried to agree. "He hasn't got much of a life in front of him."

"The poor children," Maryam sighed. "I feel so sorry for them. And they're so young. They'll never remember their parents."

"I guess they'll grow up in their grandparents' family," Rubiah said briskly. "And do the best they can. What else is there to do?"

They nodded as Osman chose another cake. "At least now I know why Zurainah pushed me. It made no sense if it wasn't to protect her husband. But, *Che* Osman, what about the *jampi* at my house?" Maryam asked. "It wasn't Arifin. Someone tried to kill me," she reminded him. "Whoever it is, he's still out there. It's dangerous!"

Osman nodded. "And there's one more piece to be fitted into this puzzle."

Maryam feared her calmness misled him into thinking it wasn't terribly serious. "This has to be solved. It isn't funny, and it isn't a small thing." She paused, thinking. "Who do you think did it?" she asked Rubiah.

"One of the *dalang*," Rubiah answered evenly, her eyes on the counter. "It makes the most sense. Besides, I'm concerned about what Arifin said about Dollah."

"Me, too," Maryam nodded. "He saw Ghani was dead and went back to sleep? And then pretended the next day he knew nothing about it? What do you think about that?"

Osman could think of nothing to say. "You know, *Mak Chik*," he began, "I just can't think clearly about Arifin just now. I'm so worried about Rahman, still unconscious. I mean," he continued, struggling to describe exactly what he felt, "It just seems to matter less to me. I don't care what happens to this guy."

"I know," Maryam sympathized. "But we can't just stop. We've got to finish this up." She put her hand on Osman's arm, pulling his attention back to the matter at hand. "Could it have been he wanted him dead?" Maryam continued. "We've got to bring him in." She turned to Osman. "Or should we go to his house and see him there? He's always turning up at my house to hand out misinformation. Maybe we should do the same."

"Lie to him?" Rubiah asked.

"No such thing," Maryam affected to be offended. "No, just talk to him when he hasn't had time to prepare some flowery explanations."

She wanted to tug on Osman's sleeve and force him to bring the case to a close. She, too, was deeply worried about Rahman, but there was still Dollah's role in the murder, which couldn't be ignored. "Come on," she ordered Osman. "Let's go!"

They pulled up to Dollah's home, a small plywood house nestled among fruit trees. It was an idyllic setting: the perfect Malay village as described in poem and song. Quiet and green, shaded by short banana trees as well as towering coconut palms, the road winding through rice paddies and rubber groves. Maryam admired it as she stepped from the car. It was lovely, but too far from the market for Maryam's taste. Her foray into Ulu Kelantan had forever cured her of believing she wanted to live in a small house surrounded by nature. She wanted to live where it was busy—and not too far from work.

She called from the bottom of the steps, and Dollah's wife came to the door, dragging three toddlers clinging to her sarong behind her. She was a pretty girl with a long, thin face and a chipped front tooth and she immediately invited them up. "Don't stay down there with the sun beating on you, *Mak Chik*; come up here where it's cooler." She smiled, inviting them into the house, away, thankfully, from the burning sunlight.

In one corner of the room was a sofa with matching armchairs, all made of rattan, and a small coffee table. This was clearly for entertaining. The children retreated with their mother to the kitchen below this room. Dollah himself was sitting in the corner, leaning against the wall reading the newspaper and drinking coffee. He rose immediately: "What a surprise! Please come and sit down. We'll have something right away for you." He guided them over to the sofa and sat down across from them in a chair.

"How are you all?" he gave his widest smile.

Maryam nudged Osman in the ribs, signalling him to speak. "We're here to talk to you, *Pak Chik*," he began, avoiding small talk and getting right to the point. "We've found Ghani's killer."

"No! Really?" Dollah put on the appearance of fascination. "Who was it?"

"Don't you already know, *Abang*?" Maryam asked quietly.

Dollah made a face and shrugged his shoulders, signifying complete ignorance.

"Are you sure?" she gently prodded. "He said you saw."

Dollah sat very still, but didn't reply.

Maryam shook her head slightly. "I hoped you'd make it easy for us all, *Pak Chik*. Well, never mind. He told us you saw him when he killed Ghani. He also said the two of you went back and pretended not to know what happened in the morning."

"Who said that?" Dollah tried to laugh. Maryam and Osman sat quietly, watching Dollah, who swallowed hard.

"He did. He's in the hospital you know. Badly hurt." Osman added. Dollah looked surprised.

"I know, it's shocking, isn't it?" Maryam took over. "But we were talking with him at the police station, and he suddenly jumped up and bolted out. You should have seen him take off, *Pak Chik*! One of the younger guys chased him down, but Arifin was running so hard he ran straight into a car. And so did the policeman chasing him. Right in the middle of Jalan Temenggong, too." She sighed. "That young policeman is still in the hospital," she said severely, "neither dead nor alive."

Dollah was staring: this was clearly news to him. "I thought you knew," Maryam informed him. She looked at him keenly, trying to decide whether his surprise was mimed or real. "Arifin's in the hospital now. Broken bones, bruises, cuts," she waved her hand as if dismissing his injuries. "He can hardly talk. But he did talk, *Abang*. He knew it was the end for him and he talked."

Dollah's wife came in with tea and cookies. She was clearly alarmed when she looked at his face, but he didn't acknowledge her. They sat in silence waiting for Dollah to say something. He opened and closed his mouth as though getting ready to speak, but no sound came out.

Maryam had never seen Dollah so disconcerted. He was the epitome of self-possession, never at a loss for words, always knowing the right thing to say. He finally cleared his throat.

"Really?" he managed.

Maryam nodded, and waited again.

"Well." He seemed incapable of continuing, but a look at his audience told him he must. His wife leaned over, but he abruptly waved her away, and she retreated to the kitchen with her children. They all sat on the steps, leaning into the room, listening.

"He told you want happened?" Dollah's voice was hoarse.

"Yes he did, and I believe he told the truth because he's afraid of dying. He's pretty badly hurt."

"No!" Dollah lit a cigarette to give himself something to do. "My God, what next?"

"What next indeed, *Abang*? Perhaps you would tell us your version of what happened that night."

"Not much to tell." Dollah was beginning to recover and attempted to dance around the facts. "Ghani was killed in the middle of the night."

"By whom?" Maryam prompted.

Dollah looked at her, clearly calculating what exactly Arifin had said. He sputtered, "You already know, so why do you…"

"*Pak Chik* Dollah," Osman sputtered. "If you won't talk here, we can talk at the station. This has already gone too far." He looked at Maryam and inclined his head.

Dollah slumped in the chair, putting his head back against the brightly flowered cushion. "I didn't kill Ghani. Why would I? I've known him since he was a child. He was more like my son. But he got himself into a world of trouble with his second marriage. I couldn't believe he did it, and I told him so.

"I think he regretted it as soon as he left Kuala Krai: he was hoping once he got home it would all go away and she'd disappear into the jungle. When she showed up here, he was furious. He loved Aisha, you know. He'd flirt with every woman he met, but he loved Aisha, and I believe until this thing, he never considered marrying anyone else." Dollah shook his head. "He was more talk than action, really. I don't think he even fooled around. Ghani always wanted everyone to think he was a ladies' man, and had girls all over Kelantan, but I don't think he did. He talked big, that's all. *Memakai kulit harimau*: he wore a tiger's pelt but he was no tiger.

"Anyway, that night, what a mess. Aisha shows up with Ali, and you've already heard, haven't you, about the huge fight? Ghani took the knife and sat with it right next to him. Then that second wife shows up with her new husband. Ghani didn't care. She didn't care either: she just wanted to show him she'd married again. So that's OK, no fights there; I just worried she'd meet Aisha, and I didn't want Aisha to be more upset than she already was."

He sighed again, this time filled with real regret, and told the story about the confrontation. "Aisha was heartbroken. I felt so bad for her.

"I gave him a good talking to before he came back. 'Haven't you done enough?' I asked him. 'How can you tell that poor girl you'll divorce her after what you've done?' I smacked him on the top of his head. 'For God's sake, Ghani! I'm ashamed of you.'

"He looked a little embarrassed, and said he told Aisha they'd talk it over when he got home. He told me he didn't really want a divorce, he just lost his temper when Ali asked him to see a *bomoh* to make sure he stayed faithful. I told him he was wrong to get angry; he should be doing everything he could to make it up to his wife. I think he agreed.

"We were all going to sleep, and Ghani kept teasing Arifin. They always fought like little boys. You know, Ghani would tease Arifin and tell him how much he liked Zurainah, and

Arifin always fell for it. Ghani was really relentless that night; I guess he was blowing off steam from his fight with Aisha. I finally told them both to shut up."

Maryam listened in something close to bewilderment. It was hard for her to consider all this was going on so close to her house, and she was completely unaware of it.

"I heard Ghani go out while it was still dark, and then I heard someone go out after him. I got up to see what was going on, and when I reached the fence, Ghani was already dead. So quick. Arifin was standing over him, holding the bloody knife. It looked black in the darkness," he remembered dreamily. "It didn't look real.

"I was completely shocked, *Kak*," he appealed to Maryam. "I couldn't believe it. Arifin just stood there, staring at Ghani. He took Ghani's towel, and wiped off the knife, then stuck it into the ground, up to the hilt. 'What are you doing?' I asked him. I mean, it's a stupid question, but you can't even think in a situation like that. Your brain is completely frozen. 'I've done it,' he says to me. 'I've killed him.' I smacked him right across the face. Idiot! It was unbelievable."

"And then?" Maryam prompted.

"And then I told him to go back. I did too, and just lay there thinking about it. What was there for me to do? *Sudah terantok, bharu tengada*: you look up only after you've bumped your head. Ghani, poor thing, was already dead. I didn't want to lose another musician."

"What?" Osman asked. He couldn't credit what he thought he'd just heard.

"I didn't want to lose another musician," Dollah repeated. "Well, what could be done for Ghani now?"

"But you knew who killed him. Why couldn't you have told me, instead of making me run around and taking some real chances?" Maryam demanded.

Dollah shrugged again. "I didn't think it would make much difference," he explained. It was dawning on him that Maryam didn't share his perspective. Neither did the police.

"Not make a difference! What are you talking about? I wouldn't have nearly died because of the *jampi* under my stairs, I wouldn't have been pushed off Hassan's porch, I wouldn't have gone to Kuala Krai; twice! Aisha might have been saved, I don't know for sure," she added honestly. "But maybe Arifin and Rahman wouldn't have been hurt. What do you mean, not make a difference? You've almost killed me, saying nothing. And you may still have killed that poor policeman: still a boy, really."

Dollah sat silent. Finally, he eased out a few words. "What's done is done."

"Not exactly." Osman looked uncharacteristically stern. "You've misled the police. You've tried to cover up a crime. You know that's a crime in itself." Osman was magisterial. "We'll see about this."

Dollah stared at him, his mouth hanging open.

"And you, *Abang* Dollah, what have you done?" Maryam regained the lead.

"What?" He appeared confused.

"Why were so you anxious to stop me looking? Was it losing another musician?"

"What do you mean, *Kak*?"

"You tried to kill me."

"No, I never did anything like that."

"You put the *jampi* under my porch."

"Not me."

"Who else would do it?" she badgered him. "Why would anyone else do it?"

Dollah narrowed his eyes. "You're wrong, *Kak*. You were right about everything else, but you're wrong about this. I wouldn't do that. I've worked for you! You paid us for the performance! Why would I want to kill you, or maybe your children?" He shook his head deliberately from side to side. "That's something I would not do." He glared at Osman, daring him to contradict this statement.

"There's no one else, *Abang*," Maryam said quietly. "It has to be you, and I'm tired of lies."

Osman stood up to go. "We've heard enough, *Pak Chik*. You'll be coming with us now."

Dollah leapt to his feet. "Wait a minute," he ordered them. They all stood looking at him. "It was Hassan," he said desperately, "It was him. I didn't want to say anything because, well, I didn't want to get him in trouble. But he did it. I wouldn't!" He looked from one face to another, begging them to believe him. "I'll go with you to Hassan. We can have it all out there."

Maryam was not happy about this plan. She'd promised herself never to set foot in Kampong Laut again. She pulled Osman's sleeve lightly. "I don't know, *Che* Osman," she began, but Osman interrupted her.

"No," he said firmly, and then repeated that "No," this time more softly. Osman nodded and rose from his seat. "Come with us now, *Pak Chik*. We'll have to talk at the station."

Dollah looked around his house. "I don't think…"

"Come now," Osman said gently, and he took his arm to guide him down the stairs to the waiting car.

Chapter 33

"I DON'T CARE WHAT you think anymore. You've ruined my life." Zurainah picked viciously at her thumb, keeping her gaze well away from Maryam. The visiting room at the Kota Bharu's Women's Jail was utterly depressing: its drab and dirty gray walls exuded untold hours of hopelessness, anger and despair.

"I have?" Maryam was amazed. "How did I ruin *your* life?"

"You found Arifin. Now I'll be all alone with my children. Everything was going fine till you had to come snooping around."

"It's my fault your husband killed Ghani?"

"Why couldn't you just leave it alone? What would have been so terrible if he wasn't found? We'd live here quietly; no one would ever have any trouble from us again."

"It's nice of you to say," Maryam offered sarcastically, "but you've both done quite of bit of damage already. Arifin's killed someone, maybe two people, and you've tried to. Doesn't that deserve some punishment?"

Zurainah dismissed it. "Ghani teased him. Ghani knew what he was like. He pushed him. Ghani should have known to leave him alone."

"I can't believe I'm hearing this," Maryam declared.

"You can't keep baiting someone like Arifin. He has a temper. It was Ghani's fault to keep teasing him. You know, I'm not saying Ghani deserved to die, but honestly, he knew he was playing with fire. But that was Ghani all over: he never learned."

"Are you telling me that murder is justified because of a schoolyard fight?"

"Maybe not to you," Zurainah retorted.

"And that's why you tried to kill me?"

"I didn't try to kill you; stop whining, *Mak Chik*," Zurainah said nastily, and very rudely. "I just wanted you to leave us alone. *Pak Chik* Dollah was trying his best, but you just won't listen."

"Did you put the *jampi* under my stairs?"

Zurainah shrugged. "What does it matter who put the *jampi* there? I'm not in here for that, you know." She began to gather intensity. "I'm here because I tried to push you into the road…"

"Under a car," Maryam corrected her.

She shrugged again. "I don't know what the big deal is. You seem OK to me."

Maryam was outraged. "I seem OK to you? You could have killed me! Haven't you any shame at all?"

"I could have killed you. But I didn't. They can't keep me here for not killing you, *Mak Chik*."

Maryam sighed and rose. "I don't have anything to do with what's going to happen to you, thank God. I've had enough trouble to last me my whole life," she said fervently. "I'm just asking you: did you put the *jampi* under my house? Did Dollah help you?"

She shook her head. "Dollah wouldn't have done it. He's very straight that way. He wasn't happy with Arifin, I can tell you."

"I can imagine."

Zurainah brushed her comment away. "Can you help me get out of here? I've got to get back to take care of my kids." She looked straight at Maryam as though willing her to reply.

"I have nothing to do with this, I told you. I can't do anything."

"The police listen to you, *Mak Chik*. I've seen it," she wheedled. "I know you can help if you want to."

Maryam sat very still, not reacting. She didn't think she could help, even if she wanted to, which she didn't. Zurainah would always be a menace to anyone she considered in her way. Maryam reviewed all the new scars to her body and her sense of well-being. Her face, her arm, her bruised hip; and this didn't include her belief in the world as a safe and ordered place, which was completely in shreds. It had been a brutal investigation, and Maryam wondered whether all investigations were like that and all murderers so completely uninterested in the people around them. She waited another moment and then stood to leave.

"I went to a *bomoh* in Bacok," Zurainah finally admitted, examining her thumb with great interest. "He gave me the *jampi*."

"Did Arifin know you were doing it?"

"Of course; I told him. He came with me to put it under your stairs. He knew where you lived." She sniffed. "Too bad, right, *Mak Chik*? I guess you'll be careful whenever you reach under the house now, won't you."

"I will," Maryam nodded.

"You'd better watch yourself," Zurainah hinted darkly. She stood up, and smirked at Maryam. "Go ahead, tell the police," Zurainah mocked her. "See if I care anymore. You're a nosy old woman and you'd be better off staying out of other people's lives." With that, she walked to the door and signalled to the guard. The interview was over.

Chapter 34

OSMAN WAS AWAKENED from what seemed like his first decent sleep in weeks. He fumbled at the phone, hoping it would not bring him another crime so hard on the heels of the one he had just solved. Or someone, anyway, had just solved. "Hello," he mumbled sleepily.

"Wake up!" His mother's voice crisply commanded him over the phone. "Are you asleep?"

"What?" He sat bolt upright in his bed, welcoming the familiar sounds of Perak Malay. He tried to gather his wits about him, feeling he might need them for the upcoming conversation. "What is it, *Mak*?"

"I've found her!" she announced proudly. "You're getting married!"

"I am?" he mumbled, unable to get his bearings. "Someone from Perak?" he asked hopefully.

"What do you think?" his mother demanded. "Wake up!"

He arrived at Kampong Penambang in the evening, when he calculated supper would have long been over and the dishes put away and Maryam wouldn't feel obligated to feed him. He suspected she'd feed him anyway, and the thought did not distress him.

"Come in, come in," Mamat invited him from the porch, where he sat with his birds, feeding mashed bananas to one in his lap. "I can't get up," he apologized, "but you can go inside. Yam!" he bellowed without moving, "We have a guest!"

"I'm getting married," Osman blurted, even before he reached the top of the stairs, "My mother called last night."

"Well, well," Maryam smiled. "*Anak baik, menantu molek*: a good child and a pretty daughter-in-law. Your mother now has it all."

Osman blushed and smiled sheepishly; maybe even fatuously. "It's about time," Maryam congratulated him, ushering him into the living room and giving Aliza the sign to prepare a tray. "I think you'll be much happier married. Have you heard, Mat?" She turned as he came in the door. "*Che* Osman here is getting married."

"Well done!" Mamat congratulated him.

"I didn't really do much of anything," Osman explained to his widely grinning audience. "I mean, it was all my mother..."

"It always is," Mamat assured him gravely. "A Perak girl?"

Osman nodded. "My mother knows her parents. I think we might be cousins somehow, I'm not sure. I don't know her, I mean..."

Maryam beamed. "Well, I'm so proud! Your first big case, and now you're getting married!"

"Well," he explained, "I know. I guess."

"No, really," Maryam assured him. "You know, you're getting used to your job, now you'll be married, it's all growing up! After all, who doesn't get married?" she declared firmly.

"You'll still help me, won't you?"

"As though you might need it," she scoffed. "You're a professional..."

"The Chief of Police," Mamat interrupted. "An important man."

"Right," Maryam agreed. "Besides, I'm not sure I like this kind of thing. It's very hard on me. Falling down stairs," she shuddered and the men looked pained, "being run over. Honestly, I'm thankful I wasn't killed. And Rahman..."

They stood silently for a moment. "It seems wrong to be happy about getting married when he's still in the hospital," Osman said mournfully. "I don't know when he'll wake up."

"But he's still with us," Maryam countered. "He's a young man and strong." She paused briefly. "We must believe God will help him. Bring him back to his family."

She shook her head as though to clear it of these thoughts and concentrate on more practical matters. "I've never had people trying to kill me before. I don't like it," she said firmly. "I'm staying with my *songket*. You never get attacked in the market." She turned briskly to Osman as Aliza set down a tray with dinner, "Come, sit and eat. You look hungry."

Osman demurred, more from politeness than conviction, and Mamat put friendly though forceful hands on his shoulders and put him in his seat. "I'm glad to be out of it," Maryam continued, "I don't think it's for me."

"You're very good at it, *Mak Chik*," Osman assured her. "You should think about it. You have a gift for finding things out, you know."

"You mean give up my stall? Never. I like to be where I know just what I'm doing. Besides, I like the market. You don't meet a very nice group of people investigating a murder. I never suspected our own people could be so vicious. And rude! It's another world," she said philosophically. "But to think what goes on right here without us even knowing about it! People doing things I just can't believe. You haven't been here very long, *Che* Osman, and maybe you think it's like that here all the time, like the Wild West. But it isn't: it's very calm and peaceful.

"And people care about each other. Kelantan is such a good place," she explained to him, fearing he might not believe her. "We have manners, you know, and people help one another." She looked over at Mamat, who nodded in agreement. "Of course,

I knew there were people like Faouda and Zurainah, I'm not naïve, but I never met them! I never wanted to meet them either, and to deal with them? I don't think so."

Osman nodded, his mouth full of rice and curry. He widened his eyes in an attempt to look interested and alert, a man fully engaged in the conversation. Maryam, however, was not even paying much attention to him.

"I would never have believed women would act this way. Not that I'm saying it's OK for men, you understand. But women are supposed to be more, I don't know, thoughtful. Sensible. This has been quite an education, and I'm glad you've caught the murderer," she said graciously. "But maybe from now on, your wife can help you."

"But she won't speak Kelantanese either," Osman said quickly, nearly choking on his rice in his hurry to convince Maryam otherwise. "It will be impossible, you see…"

"Oh, don't worry so," Maryam waved a dismissing hand at him, "How do you even know anything else will happen? You could spend the next five years here with nothing more serious than someone accusing their neighbor of stealing a chicken, and then finding the chicken wandering around down the street. Murder doesn't happen here all that often."

"It might start," Osman answered somewhat glumly. "I might have just gotten here at the start of a new crime wave."

"I hope not, for your sake," Maryam answered quickly. "I can't imagine what this place would become with so many killers around. We'd all be dead in the road! No," she moved the cigarette between her lips to free up both hands to pour more coffee. "I don't see a lot of trouble here anymore, not with these murderers put away. We'll all be safe in our houses now."

Osman swallowed hard and ducked his head. "But you'll help me if there's trouble, won't you?"

Maryam didn't answer him, but gave Mamat a proud and satisfied grin. "We'll have to see, *Che* Osman. Now, why don't you concentrate on what you're eating?"

Acknowledgements

Hassan and Dollah Baju Hijau are based upon real *dalang* in Kelantan, quite famous and active from the '60s to fairly recently. The characters presented in this novel bear little resemblance to the real Hamzah and Dollah Baju Merah, who were extremely professional, generous with their time and knowledge, and very polite and kind. Neither would have considered any of the nefarious deeds ascribed to their characters in this book, and these fictional characters should be considered just that.

I did my anthropological field work in Kelantan in 1977-81, studying *Wayang Siam*, the Malay shadow play (puppet theater). At the time, I worked closely with Hamzah and Dollah Baju Merah, as well as other *dalang* and musicians, and I thank them all for their consideration towards me. Wan Hamidah Wan Nawang and Abdul Malek Jusoh invited me into their homes and treated me like family: I will always be grateful to them and their many relatives in Sungei Pinang. Ashikin Mohd. Ali, and her younger brother, Yi, were the best neighbors anyone could have.